PRAISE FOR EMILY LISTFIELD

"Listfield unspools a delicious web of family secrets and lies that pulls you in and doesn't let go until the very last page."

—Tamara L. Miller, author of *Into the Fall*

"A tragic death on a junior class overnight trip is the catalyst for Emily Listfield's latest propulsive thriller. Was it an accident? A suicide? Or murder? It seems impossible to untangle the truth when the administration, students, and parents all seem to be hiding something. Told from the perspective of three disparate mothers, Reasons to Lie pulls you in on the first page and doesn't let you go."

—Greer Hendricks, *New York Times* bestselling coauthor of *The Wife Between Us*

"I loved this smart, intriguing, captivating mystery! How did Emily Listfield make every character—the good, the imperfect, the suspicious—so true to life and relatable? Who died by whose hand is an absorbing enough question, but for added and delicious tension, Reasons to Lie is set at the kind of snobby Manhattan school I love to hate. Highly enjoyable, flawlessly written, and highly recommended!"

—Elinor Lipman, author of *Every Tom, Dick & Harry* and *Ms. Demeanor*

REASONS TO LIE

OTHER TITLES BY EMILY LISTFIELD

It Was Gonna Be Like Paris

Variations in the Night

Slightly Like Strangers

Acts of Love

Waiting to Surface

Best Intentions

The Last Good Night

Reasons to LIE

EMILY LISTFIELD

THOMAS & MERCER

This is a work of fiction. Names, characters, organizations, places, events, and incidents are either products of the author's imagination or are used fictitiously. Otherwise, any resemblance to actual persons, living or dead, is purely coincidental.

Published by Thomas & Mercer, Seattle

www.apub.com

EU product safety contact:
Amazon Media EU S. à r.l.
38, avenue John F. Kennedy, L-1855 Luxembourg
amazonpublishing-gpsr@amazon.com

ISBN-13: 9781662534379 (paperback)
ISBN-13: 9781662534362 (digital)

Cover design by Olga Grlic
Cover image: © peterspiro / Getty

Interior logo image: © Gstudio / Adobe Stock

Printed in the United States of America

For Sasha

A lie that is half-truth is the darkest of all lies.

—Alfred Lord Tennyson

From: Jerome Nederlander, Headmaster

To: Dearborn Parents

Date: Saturday, October 11

Subject: A tragic loss on class trip

Dear Parents,

It is with profound sadness that I must inform you of a tragic incident that occurred on the junior class trip to the Forest Valley Camp in Clearview, New York last night. Despite our commitment to ensuring the safety of all students, we have experienced the loss of one of our own.

At this moment, we are not at liberty to disclose the identity of the student out of respect for the family's privacy.

The safety of your children has always been our highest priority, and we are taking every measure to support these efforts. We are working closely with Forest Valley and local authorities to investigate the circumstances surrounding the death.

We understand this news will be distressing. A crisis team will be in place Monday morning to help any students who may need it.

We look forward to sharing more information in a fully transparent manner as details become available.

Sincerely,
Jerome Nederlander
Headmaster
Dearborn Academy

Part One

Chapter 1

Abby

Twenty-two days before the murder
Thursday, September 18

The first morning I walked through the double-height red doors of Dearborn Academy and saw the brass plaque inscribed "Established 1857," I realized what a vastly different world it was from the one I grew up in. I thought, in time, I would come to feel at home here. Accepted, even. I hoped, at least, it would tip the scales for my daughter, Rachel.

The opposite has proved true.

I shift my legs under the desk as Mrs. Rafferty scribbles computations on the whiteboard, a sexual flush brought on by the wonders of Precalculus 2 rinsing her pale Irish face. All around me, parents are taking notes in pebbled leather journals and snapping pictures of the whiteboard. Curriculum Night at Dearborn is taken very seriously indeed.

I dig my fingernails into the soft flesh of my palms.

I'm lucky to be here.

I tell myself that every time I walk into the twelve-story building with its NASA-worthy labs and sun-drenched studios.

How lucky I am.

How lucky Rachel is.

And yet.

*

The minute the bell rings, there's a mad dash for the door, the mothers' laughter ricocheting down the broad hallway as they catch up on who let the summer's rosé go to their hips, locked in the best SAT tutor, or found the genius new Pilates instructor, while their husbands nod smugly to each other. All the fathers have to do to win is show up.

I slip through the scrum, looking for Kara, who rescues me again and again on nights like this. When I can't find her, I make my way to the white-linen-covered table groaning with platters of gluten-free cookies and grab one, not stopping to deliberate between oatmeal and chocolate chip. It's generally agreed on by Dearborn mothers that the act of eating is a sign of moral and physical weakness. Food is, on the other hand, of utmost concern when it comes to their children. Last year, a committee was organized to ensure that lunches not only are organic and locally sourced but also reflect ethnic diversity.

I'm hurrying down the hallway with my contraband when Bill and Marci Carter sidle up beside me.

"Crazy that the girls are in junior year, isn't it?" Bill says. "Before you know it, they'll be leaving for college." He oozes slippery charm, his curling chestnut hair long enough to signal he doesn't work on Wall Street but has some creative-adjacent job—media, tech, something Hollywood-on-the-Hudson-ish.

A piece of dry cookie lodges in my throat. It does, in fact, seem crazy. All the clichés are proving true—how quickly your children change without you noticing until suddenly they're teenagers hungry for separation, practicing it in ways small and large. Some safe, some definitely not.

I turn to Marci. "How was your summer?"

As a single woman, it's best to make myself as unthreatening as possible. Smile at the other mothers. Avoid eye contact with their husbands. It infuriates me that the default assumption is that I'm the one on the make. Especially here. With Bill and Marci Carter.

Marci, all cheekbones and moneyed hauteur, sized me up on the first day of kindergarten, ascertaining my address, vacation spots, and school affiliations, and silently dismissed me. The CIA could learn a thing or two about the art of soft interrogation from Marci Carter. "Too short," she deigns to reply.

"Amanda said Rachel worked as a camp counselor?" Bill remarks.

I'm surprised Amanda has mentioned Rachel; they exist on such different social planes. Amanda is not the prettiest or smartest girl in the class, but her sheer confidence allows her to wield a lacerating power. I used to think the Amandas of the world got their comeuppance in the end, but Dearborn is filled with former Amandas.

"Rachel was a CIT at Forest Valley."

"Isn't that the godforsaken place they're going to in three weeks?" Marci asks, alarmed. "I can't believe the school is going ahead after what happened there last year. Are they waiting for someone to die there?"

"I'm sure they'll put extra safety measures in place," Bill assures her offhandedly.

"Let's hope so, because next time, they may not be so lucky," Marci retorts, annoyed by her husband's dismissive tone.

She shakes her head and walks off in search of more fertile ground, leaving me alone with Bill. Who I absolutely do not want to be alone with.

I spot Kara and tear off after her.

"Help."

She glances back at Bill Carter. "You can't be serious? Still?"

"Bathroom. Now," I hiss. Then in a more public voice, "What class are you coming from?"

"Ceramics."

"I didn't know Olivia is interested in ceramics."

"Olivia is interested in anything that doesn't involve homework." Kara groans. "My only goal is to have her survive this year."

The disparities between our daughters are something we tread lightly on. Olivia, sparks shooting out in every direction, constantly daring the world. Rachel, a straight A student who never misses curfew and isn't invited to parties, at least not the ones that matter.

I push open the bathroom door and peer under the stall doors to make sure no one is there while Kara checks herself in the mirror, grimacing as she wipes a smudge of mascara.

"I keep thinking I'm tired, and then I realize this is the new normal. It's like your face plateaus for a few years, then you wake up one morning to find everything dropped and you've landed on the next level down."

"You look fine," I assure her. As we do.

"That's easy for you to say."

At thirty-nine, I'm seven years younger than Kara, a flaw she only grudgingly forgives me for. Not everyone here does.

"What was that in the hallway?" she asks, her voice tinged with revulsion. "I thought Bill stopped baiting you."

Kara, ensconced in a happy marriage, Midwestern probity embedded in her veins, is continually shocked by men's bad behavior in a way that I'm not.

"He did," I assure her. "I'd like to keep it that way."

*

It started last fall.

The first text showed up a day after I sat between Bill and Marci at a volleyball game, making small talk while Dearborn lost.

The text was short. Almost innocuous. Are you free to play hooky? Would love to continue our conversation.

I couldn't remember any conversation that warranted continuation. Nevertheless, even as I told Bill that I was on deadline for a design project, I second-guessed myself. Surely, I misunderstood. No one could be that stupid. Or that brazen. The following week he texted again. Leaving the gym. Hot and sweaty. Thinking of you. Free?

He was that stupid, that brazen.

Ghosting him was an easy call.

*

The bathroom door swings open, and a woman I don't recognize walks in. She has perfectly highlighted hair the exact honey shade that replaced last year's butter blond across the Upper East Side, and porcelain skin, but her eyes are red and drippy.

"Are you all right?" I ask.

"Yes, it's allergies," the woman answers. She finds a tissue in her YSL bag and blots her lashes, her large square-cut diamond ring glinting in the fluorescent light. "We haven't met. I'm Hollis Chapman," she says, looking up.

Dearborn is a small school. It's odd we've never seen her.

"Do you have children here?" Kara asks.

"My son, Daniel. He transferred in for junior year."

"Our daughters, Rachel and Olivia, are in the same grade."

"Is it a good class?"

"Good is one word for it," I mutter.

The junior class is known for its preponderance of rowdier-than-usual boys, the number of kids on various ADD medications (the collective amount of extra time granted for tests is legendary), and the volatile cliquishness of the girls. Meetings have been held. A psychologist has given talks.

"Don't listen to her," Kara says. "I'm sure Daniel will be happy here. Did you just move to New York?"

Kids rarely transfer into Dearborn for junior year unless there are special circumstances. On the contrary, kids are "counseled out" if they aren't cutting it. It's Kara's biggest fear.

Hollis shakes her head, avoiding the question, and stashes the tissue in her bag.

"Do you have other children here?" she asks.

"A younger daughter, Maya."

Hollis turns to me.

"Only one."

When the bell rings, indicating it's time to head to the auditorium, Hollis's eyes flit to the door. There's something fragile about her, like a china teacup with spidery hairline cracks so fine you're not sure if they're part of the pattern or a sign of long-ago breakage.

"Why don't you come with us?" I offer.

We make our way down the crowded staircase to the two-story auditorium with crimson velvet curtains where the scent of furniture polish lingers in the air. Kara spots her husband, Peter, motioning that he's saved her a seat.

Hollis turns to me. "Are you alone?"

I nod, surprised. My situation has long since been dissected—*Does Rachel even have a father? Why have we never seen him?*—and dismissed.

"Why don't we sit together?" I suggest.

As we settle into the second row from the back, Headmaster Nederlander walks onto the stage, followed by a group of school officials who slide into chairs behind him. He clears his throat loudly before beginning. "Welcome to the start of an exciting new year at Dearborn."

There's a sprinkling of applause, though whether it's for him or our own providence for being here is unclear.

Nederlander's voice is more stentorian than ever as he pontificates about Dearborn's commitment to excellence in progressive education, skating over some rather inconvenient details.

Last year was epically bad. Six sophomores were suspended for cheating on a biology final, and three seniors ended up in the ER for alcohol poisoning after homecoming. There was the sext that went viral that caused a deep rift between parents advocating for expulsion and those pleading for leniency, the divide less along moral lines than based on whether their child had received/sent/seen the sext. And then there was Mrs. Epstein, who hallucinated in the middle of World Lit and had to be led from the room. She later claimed she'd accidentally taken

NyQuil instead of DayQuil. Nevertheless, Mrs. Epstein was quietly dismissed. Teachers, too, can be counseled out.

I glance at Hollis, wondering how much of this she knows. Her hands are folded in her lap, her diamond ring turned to hide the stone from view, as she looks expectantly at the stage. Dearborn is a certain station of a certain cross.

We are all lucky to be here.

*

"I'd like to introduce two new teachers joining the Dearborn family," Nederlander continues. "Miss Calhoun will be leading classes in civic engagement." A bright-faced young woman in beaded dreadlocks and a boldly striped sweaterdress rises from her seat and waves. "And I am particularly pleased to welcome the newest addition to our English department, Eliot Handley, who comes to us from Saint Stephen's Preparatory School in Massachusetts." Nederlander radiates pride as a forty-something man in khakis and a tweed blazer rises, smiling self-consciously as he runs his hands through his sandy-brown hair.

"I will now turn the stage over to Miss Cleary to talk about the upcoming junior class trip to Forest Valley."

At somewhere under five foot four, Miss Cleary fusses clumsily with the microphone. When she finally looks up, she pauses to savor the attention, her plump face glowing with missionary zeal.

The room collectively crosses their arms. Miss Clearly Not, the kids call her. Parents privately do the same. All that panic she caused last year with her email warning against any touching on Dearborn's premises turned out to be about—what? A little hand-holding on the staircase? Nederlander was forced to reassure parents that nothing more nefarious had taken place, though doubts remain. Nevertheless, Miss Clearly Not's starchy puritanism combined with her desperate need for redemption have been deemed precisely what are needed to oversee a horde of feral teenagers away from home.

"The two-night visit to Forest Valley has been a Dearborn tradition for over fifteen years," Miss Cleary begins, a tiny droplet of spittle forming in the corner of her mouth. "We've found it's the perfect time to strengthen bonds of trust before the pressure of college applications begins.

"Permission slips must be returned one week ahead of time, and your children will be asked to sign an honor code governing their behavior. Any transgressions including alcohol, drugs, bullying, hazing rituals, or inappropriate relationships will be met with swift discipline. To ensure rules are enforced, we are adding extra chaperones." Her face softens into a broad smile as she beams at Nederlander's latest prized possession. "I'm happy to announce that Mr. Handley will be joining us as part of his integration into the Dearborn community."

A look of surprise flashes across the new teacher's face.

*

"Thank you for being my guide tonight," Hollis says as we stand on the tree-lined street.

"It can be a tough crowd," I reply, instantly regretting it. Maybe Hollis is exactly the kind of woman and her son exactly the kind of boy Dearborn is made for.

"I'd love to stay in touch," she says hesitantly, as if we're cruise ship passengers disembarking on shore.

She's looking for a backdoor source of information, someone to ask if this party is safe, if that group is too risky. Unfortunately, I'm not that mother, and my daughter is not that girl. Nevertheless, we exchange phone numbers before I head to the subway to go downtown.

*

Pounding house music greets me when I step out of my elevator on the seventh floor. The building has become a way station for NYU students who smoke weed at nine in the morning and leave crumpled beer cans in the hall. There's a sprinkling of young families in their starter homes, but they get out as soon as they can. I've long since given up that plan. The apartment is rent stabilized. I'll surely die here.

I open the front door and call out to Rachel.

"Hey, sweetie, I'm home."

Nothing.

There was a time when Rachel would run to greet me, nestling her head into my waist. I sometimes feared we were too close—a single mother, an only child. When I was growing up there were fewer only children, and they tended to be weird, grown-ups masquerading as kids. Determined to avoid that, I plied her with sleepover parties and playdates. If other children served as temporary stand-ins for siblings, there was no solution when it came to fathers. I often caught Rachel studying them with cool detachment. She never gave voice to longing but displayed instead an almost clinical curiosity about what a father is, how a father behaves.

Lately, though, something has changed in Rachel. A pulling away, a secretiveness. Trying to get anything out of her is like peering through closed venetian blinds. Every now and then there are shafts of light, but I have no idea what's going on inside.

I call out again, a flicker of panic rising. Since the day Rachel was born, I've worried something will happen to her. If she's even fifteen minutes late, I slide to every worst-case scenario. Rapists, subway tracks, roofies. At times, it veers into conviction. Something *will* happen. Years ago, I went to a therapist who tried to convince me it was OCD-related compulsion, but how could she be sure it wasn't a premonition?

*

Rachel slams her dresser drawer shut before letting me in. Her room is immaculate, the bookshelves arranged by color. The only evidence of a swirl beneath the surface is her habit of ripping her cuticles into bloody slivers whenever she's stressed. I glance furtively at her fingers before sitting on her bed, pretending not to notice her cringe at the intrusion.

"I met your teachers tonight. I didn't understand a word the math teacher said. What was her name, Mrs. Reardon?" My cheeriness rings false, as if I'm trying to court my own daughter. Which, of course, I am.

Rachel's mouth turns down. Her lips are a deep ruby against her wan skin, and her shoulder blades jut out beneath her gray waffle shirt. When she was little, she was so underweight that her rib cage was painfully delineated beneath all but the thickest sweaters. The skeletal outline is gone, but the visual remains lodged in my brain.

"Her name is Mrs. Rafferty," she says disdainfully.

I change my approach. "You didn't tell me there's a new boy in your homeroom."

"Daniel?" Her knobby spine straightens ever so slightly.

"I met his mother tonight. What's he like?"

"He's okay."

For all of Rachel's keen powers of observation, she no longer has the slightest inclination to share her findings with me.

"Is he cute?" Is that the right word? Is there some term only girls under seventeen know, part of the impenetrable code of deep state adolescence designed to lock adults out?

She plays with the drawstring of her plaid pajama bottoms. "I guess. Look, I still have homework."

I'm summarily dismissed.

I'm halfway through the doorway when Rachel calls after me. "Hey, thanks for leaving me the red velvet cupcake."

I smile, the ever-teetering seesaw of teenage resentment and the lingering need for attachment momentarily tipping in my favor.

*

School nights seem specifically designed to throw a klieg light on the one thing I'll never have, someone to glance across the room at who cares about my daughter as much as I do.

I settle cross-legged on my bed and open Bumble. I recently rejoined after a spate of particularly loathsome dates—the Wall Street broker who referred to both of his ex-wives as cunts, the not-quite-divorced New Jersey dad who asked if I was a "sub." There are times—tonight—when I wonder why I can't simply choose someone and stay. Always, though, I've had Rachel to come home to and spoon with, warm flesh against warm flesh.

But for how long?

Chapter 2

Hollis

I watch from the shadows as Miss Cleary scurries through the school doors to catch up with the new English teacher, heedlessly bumping into two parents blocking her way.

"We made it!" she exclaims when she reaches him.

Mr. Handley turns, surprised to find her by his side.

"It was something of a crush," he agrees.

She meant something else—we made it through the night, we are comrades in arms—but she nods eagerly. "It's wonderful that you'll be joining us at Forest Valley."

"I was a bit surprised," he admits. "I don't know anything about the trip."

"Why don't we meet for lunch tomorrow, and I'll tell you all about it? I wouldn't want you to be scared off by any of the rumors."

He looks at her, baffled, but before he can reply, the headmaster saunters over and pats him firmly on the back. "Good job tonight, Eliot."

"Thank you. I enjoyed the evening."

"It was great, wasn't it?" Miss Cleary pipes up.

The headmaster notices her for the first time, nods, and abruptly turns back to Mr. Handley.

"Come, I want you to meet Jim McFarland, one of our trustees." He motions to a tweedy gray-hair a few feet away.

Miss Cleary watches, her lower lip trembling, as the two men walk away.

I've made a study of power since I was a child, the physics of it, the way it travels. I know that the very act of appearing to want something too badly—to be taken seriously, to be accepted—reduces the chance of attaining it. Miss Cleary doesn't seem to have learned that lesson.

It almost makes me sad for her.

It also convinces me that she's the right one.

*

I follow from a few feet behind until she's half a block from the school before tapping her on the shoulder.

She swivels, a look of annoyance on her pallid face that she rearranges when she realizes I'm a parent.

I smile to put her at ease. "I didn't mean to startle you. I'm Hollis Chapman, Daniel's mother. He's in your homeroom. I wonder if I can have a word?"

"Of course. How can I help you?"

"As you know, Daniel is new at Dearborn, and we want to make sure he gets off on the right foot. I was wondering if you could recommend a tutor."

She checks to be certain no one is within earshot. "I tutor a select group of children from other schools," she says quietly. "But"—she pauses—"we're not supposed to engage in extracurricular work with our own students."

"We would make it worth your while."

Tutoring is part of the underground economy that keeps private school teachers afloat. Barring a trust fund, there's no other way they can afford New York City rents. Miss Cleary, in her bright-pink cardigan of indeterminate fabric and paisley skirt stretched across her ample hips, doesn't look like she has a trust fund.

"I might be willing to make an exception," she relents. "I have your email from the parent list. I'll send you some potential times, but it must stay between us."

She barrels across the street as soon as the light changes, and I go in search of my Uber.

*

The driver floors the gas, and the sedan jerks forward. I want to tell him to slow down. I would drive all night if I could, past my building, past the bridges and tunnels, out into the open air.

We've gone five blocks when I lean forward. "I've changed my mind. I'll get out here."

I wrap my deep-blue pashmina around my neck and walk slowly down Park Avenue. With every block that I get closer to home, my lungs constrict.

I say hello to Michael, the night doorman, and walk through the marble lobby into the waiting elevator, where a uniformed operator takes me to the tenth floor. When I first married Jordan, I was surprised by all the small beneficences performed for the sole purpose of making my life easier. Jordan, naturally, takes them for granted. It's all he has ever known.

Hopefully, he'll still be at whatever meeting he used as an excuse not to come tonight. If I'm lucky, it will be late enough when he comes home that I can pretend to be asleep.

My shoulders sink when he calls out as soon as I open the front door. I take my time folding my scarf before going into the living room, where he's sitting on the taupe velvet couch. When we bought the apartment—or I should say, when *he* bought the apartment—I had no experience with a home this scale and was happy to use the decorator he chose. I wanted to acquire taste, to understand the signifiers. As each richly neutral piece appeared, the camel suede chairs, the cream curtains that puddle on the floor, I found it more and more stultifying, but by then it was too late. It was a small price to pay.

Jordan is waiting in his bespoke suit and shirtsleeves, an iPad balanced on his knees. His hair, beginning to speckle with gray, is neatly trimmed, and his face still chiseled, his innate discipline precluding any laxity. There are times when I catch a glimpse of him across the room at a cocktail party and a ripple of the attraction I once felt wafts through me. There was love once. At least I like to think so.

"How was your meeting?" I ask.

"It was client entertaining. The Dutch." Jordan never goes into details about his business, and I've stopped asking. There is, at any given moment, a good chance he's lying. He takes off his reading glasses and looks at me intently.

"How did it go tonight? Did you meet people?"

He means people who can be woven into the safety net that girds our world. "Just in case" people. The wife of a tech cofounder. The partner who sits on Dearborn's financial steering committee. He doesn't mean people like Abby and Kara. "What about the tutor I suggested?" he adds.

"Yes, but I'm still not convinced that's necessary."

"Daniel's past history would suggest otherwise."

Somewhere in our marriage, a division of labor was decided. I'm responsible for Daniel's behavior, his acts and his misdeeds, while Jordan's job is to provide the opportunities and rescue operations his money makes possible. Dearborn, one of the supposedly more artistic entries in the stratified world of New York private schools, would not have been his first choice, but our options were severely limited. He paid the right amount, talked to the right people, to get Daniel in despite his transgressions. Whatever happens now is on my watch.

I never wanted to send him away to begin with. It's incomprehensible to me, untethering your child at twelve, away from parental oversight. I lost that battle, helpless against the weight of Chapman tradition.

Three generations have gone to the right boarding schools and managed not to get kicked out. Yes, of course, one or two drunken nights ended in the infirmary. But these things are to be expected. A good sign, if you will.

It would be a gift if that was Daniel's only crime.

*

I walk down the hallway and knock on Daniel's door. "Can I come in, honey?"

I redecorated his bedroom in a navy-and-white nautical theme before he came home but realized instantly it was wrong, a mother's idea of a teenage boy's room. He removed the trophies from the shelf above his bed and hid them out of sight the first day he was back.

He shuts his laptop and turns reluctantly to face me, shifting his long legs under the desk. His sinewy arms have grown new muscles over the summer; his tousled hair is sun-streaked from weeks spent sailing. He'll break hearts, I'm sure of it. There's more than enough evidence of that already.

On good days, in the right light, I catch glimpses of the innate sweetness lying like still water beneath his choppy surface. The cheerful toddler who other children were drawn to and teachers praised. The sensitive child who slept too long with a security blanket, worn thin with drool. But that's becoming harder. I worry he's turning into one of those callous boys too aware of their magnetism and too heedless of the pain they leave behind.

I want to kiss him but am unsure what level of physical affection is acceptable. For the past five years, he's only been home on school vacations, essentially a guest. We have yet to conquer the rhythm of living together.

"Did you have dinner?"

"I got takeout."

"Good." I nod, despite my disappointment. I left him macaroni with extra cheese. It used to be his favorite. I have no idea if it still is. I keep trying to make up for lost time with special dishes, outings to places we used to go, but teenagers don't want to make up for lost time. They want to propel it forward, faster and faster.

"Can we talk for a minute?" I ask.

"What's up?"

"I spoke to your homeroom teacher, Miss Cleary, tonight. I thought it might be a good idea to have her tutor you while you adjust to the new environment."

His eyes narrow. "I don't need a tutor."

"Your grades fell off a cliff last year, Daniel. We can't afford for that to happen again. You're too smart for that."

"If I'm so smart, why do I need a tutor?"

"Just try it."

"Why did you choose her of all people?"

"What's wrong with Miss Cleary?"

"She's a total joke, Mom. She starts every morning with a ridiculous quote from some self-help book, like Helen Keller or some shit like that, and wants us to share what it *means* to us. It's pathetic."

"I don't see what's so terrible about that. She's trying to get to know you." It does, in fact, seem misguided. An inability to read the room is never as fatal as it is with teenagers.

"I'd also like you to reconsider joining the track team," I tell him.

Daniel's record in the 400-yard dash was one of the accoutrements Jordan dangled before Dearborn, but it's not his records I care about. Daniel once told me he ran to get the crazies out. Without that, what?

"I already told Dad no."

I sigh, exasperated. The antipathy between the two of them is knotted too tightly to untangle. When Daniel was little, Jordan would balance him on his shoulders in the park, a tall boy atop a tall man. He would bring him to his office, swiveling him in his leather chair until Daniel grew dizzy. But that connection snapped years ago, and something poisonous took root. If there was a specific cause or incident, I'm not privy to it. The determination to keep it secret is the only thing they agree on.

"Daniel, you need to make it work this time. Dearborn is your last shot."

"You do realize there's such a thing as public schools? Don't they have to take me?"

"That's not what I mean. I can't stand seeing you throw away every opportunity I never had." The cliché sounds hollow. Nonetheless, it's true.

"It's going to be okay, Mom," he says softly.

"I hope so."

I lean down and kiss the top of his head. I can see the scalloped edge where his hair meets his neck, the same pattern I used to trace with my fingertips when he was a baby and I still thought I could keep him safe.

*

The apartment is quiet, each of us locked in our worlds. I settle on the gray chaise in my bedroom and stare out at the trees stippling Park Avenue. I'd hoped Daniel coming home would fill the holes that punctuate my days, but loneliness evades every defense, creeps into every cell. For so long, Jordan's friends were my friends. His goals, mine.

I have little experience bonding with other mothers. Building new friendships as an adult is a tenuous proposition. Other people's lives are so busy, their relationships already formed. I have friend-like acquaintances, the women I see at the barre studio, a few fraying connections from Daniel's elementary school, but those ties have grown increasingly awkward. I can see the judgment in their eyes when the subject of our children comes up, and I suspect they only speak to me because of Jordan. I'm not confessional by nature. I can't afford to be. But I long for some sense of shared experience. Dearborn can be a fresh start for both of us.

I take my phone from my bag and find Abby's number.

Thank you for showing me around tonight. Are you and Kara available for lunch next week? Hope so, Hollis

I press send and take a two-milligram Xanax.

Chapter 3

Kara

I am forty-six years old, sitting in a cubicle two yards from a pod of prattling girls hired for their sixth sense about which micro-influencer is about to break big. Forty-six years old. In a cubicle. My retinas burn from staring at a screen all day. My spine aches. I used to think people who complained about their backs were whiners. I was wrong. I brush aside crumbs from the lunch I ate at my desk and, in case anyone is watching, pull up the marketing campaign for a company that sells tequila in easy-to-stash test tubes. Glancing around to be sure no one can see, I begin to type into my phone.

> Q. My husband is texting with his high school girlfriend. He says they're only catching up but he has a picture of her in a bikini.

I pause. Begin again.

> Q. We haven't had sex in seven months. Is this normal?

It started when Abby forwarded Bill Carter's egregious texts to me. Then others—men she was dating, men she was thinking of breaking up with. I haven't been on a date in over twenty years. I'm not sure if the old rules apply. I'm not sure what the new rules are. But no one else appears to know either. Finding a fresh way to address the rampant confusion seemed like a business opportunity waiting to be filled, one that the tech bros never deigned to consider.

Abby and I sketched the idea for Jyst four months ago. An app where women can anonymously post relationship questions they're too embarrassed to ask their friends, a safe zone where they can admit their desires and their sins. When Abby couldn't come up with her half of the money for the beta version, we agreed she'd put more time into the design, and I withdrew funds from my 401(k), which I neglected to tell Peter.

I'm well aware that less than 11 percent of start-up funding goes to women, but I've spent my entire life opting for safety. All it's gotten me is a windowless cubicle and a thirty-four-year-old boss who takes sadistic pleasure in reminding me how tenuous my job is. I need out. From this cubicle. From the mounting bills and increasing spate of panic attacks at three in the morning. Out, before it's too late.

For testing purposes, we need at least fifty questions. I join dating apps, making up fake identities. I never wanted that life. It's one of the reasons I got married right out of college to a stable man who's waiting for me thirty blocks away. Only sometimes I wonder what it would be like to have all that choice still spread out before me.

*

The meter clicks inexorably on as the cab crawls through Midtown traffic. The city presses in, squeezing me with its demands, its pace, all the things that first lured me. I wish I could go home, or better yet, check in to a hotel room. Alone. And sleep.

Friday nights have always been fraught for me and Peter, especially when the girls were younger and our nerves were ragged. The "Friday night fight," we used to call it, as if naming it would keep it contained. The two of us worn out from long days at our jobs, the chaos of school mornings, the endless bedtime bargaining. By Friday night, we were squabbling over how to stack the dishwasher as if our lives depended on it. I look back now and wonder, were they the inconsequential spats all couples have? Or should I have paid more attention? Were they precursors?

*

Peter is sitting in Dr. Mendelsohn's waiting room when I walk in. He glances at his watch, frowning.

"I'm sorry, the subway got stuck at Seventy-Second Street," I lie, unwilling to deal with his annoyance at the expense of a cab.

He doesn't answer. Marriage therapy wasn't his idea, but while I never gave him an ultimatum, he sensed the wedge worming between us. His only prerequisite was that I don't tell anyone about these Friday nights, not even Abby. "Can't anything stay between us?" he asked. Demanded, really. I owe him that much.

I follow him into Dr. Mendelsohn's office. One month into the process, Peter has found a freedom in the sessions I hadn't counted on, disinterring long-buried gripes and filling the room with them, while my apprehension grows.

"How was your week?" Dr. Mendelsohn begins. He's a short man with a halo of curly gray hair and the pug nose of an aging child actor who was never able to find another role.

I look at Peter, trying to gauge whether I'll be met with a list of stored-up grievances or a tired shrug so we can limp through the next fifty-five minutes convinced we don't really need to be here.

"Not one of our better ones," he answers, pushing the bridge of his tortoiseshell glasses up his nose.

"Can you be more specific?"

I jump in before Peter can make his case. "Olivia was an hour late for dinner and wasn't answering texts. When she finally got home, she said she'd left her phone at Starbucks."

Dr. Mendelsohn waits. Surely there must be a greater crime than this.

"She was lying," I continue. "Her friend, Hannah, texted Maya that she had Olivia's phone. Hannah's house is one of *those* houses. Her parents are divorced, and her mother is never home. Kids from all over the city go to get high there. It's only a matter of time before someone ODs."

Dr. Mendelsohn stares at me impassively. I have a sudden urge to punch him, though I realize this is not a therapeutically desirable response.

"Olivia was lying. And she was high. On a school night," I add.

"What did she have to say about this?"

"She denied it."

"I gather you don't believe her?"

"No."

"Do you have anything you'd like to add, Peter?"

"Obviously, I'm not going to defend Olivia's behavior. But," he says, turning to me, "did you really think screaming that she was headed for certain disaster was going to be helpful?"

"I'm sorry, but maybe if you didn't always cast me as the bad cop . . ." I stop. There are rules here. Things that are not "constructive" to say. *You never, I always.* We're supposed to begin every sentence with "I feel."

"Is everything my fault?" I ask Peter. *Fault*, another verboten word.

His face relaxes. "Of course not. This is tough."

Tears rim my eyes. "I know I overreacted. I was scared."

I'm suddenly so tired. Raising teenagers is as exhausting as having a toddler. Back come the temper tantrums, the inability to interpret their moods, the boundary-testing as they hurtle heedlessly into a world filled with deadly hazards.

"Do you think Olivia has a drug problem?" Dr. Mendelsohn asks.

"Isn't any use of drugs a problem?" Peter, ever the lawyer, interjects.

"There are matters of degree. Motivation can tell us a lot. Does Olivia seem unhappy?"

"Is any teenager happy?" I ask. It seems a rather high bar.

"I don't think she's in the right place," Peter says.

"Are you speaking metaphorically?"

"No. I don't think Olivia should be at a place like Dearborn, hanging out with kids with town houses and parents who are never home."

"We made the decision to send Olivia there together," I remind him.

"You wanted the girls to go to some fancy private school we can't afford because you thought it would guarantee some warped version of success."

"I wanted them to go there because her public school was so overcrowded, she was getting lost. Half the time they didn't even tell us when she cut classes or got detention."

There was something growing in Olivia, a seedling I hoped would wither but appears, instead, to be thriving, that Peter cannot or will not see. There was a time when we viewed our family through the same lens. It's one of the things I miss most.

"You were the one who was so impressed by Dearborn's so-called progressive values," I remind him. "We both agreed the girls would have more opportunities there."

"They're not proving to be the opportunities I had in mind."

"What do you mean, Peter?" Dr. Mendelsohn asks.

"I mean this girl, Hannah, and her parent-free home, for starters."

"Lack of supervision is not specific to any one school or socioeconomic bracket," Dr. Mendelsohn points out. "Has anything changed to make you regret your decision?"

"It's what hasn't changed," I mutter.

"Go on."

"The tuition keeps going up, and our incomes don't."

"Did you think I was going to wake up one day and suddenly decide to become a corporate lawyer?" Peter retorts.

"Of course not." I sag against the scratchy tweed couch.

I fell in love with Peter at twenty-one in part because of his commitment to fighting the good fight at nonprofits, most recently litigating for global access to clean water. I never thought how that might limit my options. It's unfair to blame him for staying true to the principles I was first drawn to. And yes, I'm equally responsible for our finances. None of that helps.

"How is Maya handling these disruptions?" Dr. Mendelsohn asks.

"She's fine," I reply.

Maya, thirteen, is the polar opposite of Olivia, a bookish girl who long ago calculated that she couldn't compete on the same territory as her sister and withdrew from the race.

"She's *too* fine," Peter amends.

"What do you mean?" Dr. Mendelsohn asks.

"She carries around a little notebook and lists everything, Olivia's misdeeds, new rules to follow. Everything."

"We all find ways to maintain a sense of control." Dr. Mendelsohn looks at his watch. "I'm going to give you the name of a child psychologist for Olivia. There are so many kids getting high, it's almost the new normal. It's the manner in which it happens we must keep an eye on. There's a difference between doing it for fun and doing it to escape a deeper, more dangerous issue."

"What deeper, more dangerous issue?"

"That's what we're here to discover," he says. "Before it's too late."

*

"Do you want to walk home?" Peter asks when we get outside.

It's a gentle, almost warm night. Soon, the season will drift into the brisk heart of fall.

"Sure."

We match each other's pace without speaking until we stop for a light. I look at Peter, the edges worn off his face. "I don't know how to do this," I tell him.

"Do what?"

"The kids, parenting. Did we set too few boundaries? Too many?"

"We'll get through it."

"Are you sure?"

"Would you settle for fifty-fifty odds?"

I try to smile at Peter's attempts to leaven the mood, but Mendelsohn's last words, *before it's too late*, lodge between every breath. I shake my head, trying to forget them, but they tug at my deepest fear.

The lush green-gray air draping over Central Park fades from view as we veer away from the turreted buildings to the side street that leads to our less majestic neighborhood.

"Do you want to pick up a roast chicken?" I ask. "Maya is sleeping at Zinia's, and Olivia is going out with Todd."

"See, that proves my point. Why are they at a school with girls named Zinia?"

I can't help but laugh.

"It's something to consider," he says. "Yes, a chicken sounds good."

While I pick up the chicken and a side of Peter's favorite garlic mashed potatoes, he goes to the wine store and chooses a bottle of the Chablis I like. Small offerings of atonement as we step away from the precipice and make our way back to each other.

*

With both girls out, the apartment has an eerie stillness. I get out plates and silverware while Peter opens the wine. We move easily, the muscle memory of a long marriage. I watch his earnest face beginning to weather and see beneath the creases all the versions of him. Peter at twenty-five, bent over his law books. Peter, balancing Maya on his hip, holding Olivia's hand as they jump through puddles. Peter kissing my neck in the night. Peter, resentful, turning his back to me. It's too much to unwind—how we got here, how to get out.

The wine is gone when we collapse onto the faded navy couch. On the left arm, there are traces of white paw prints from the time Nomi, our mute rescue cat, leapt from the freshly painted windowsill. Our legs intermingle, his, mine, tangled in familiarity.

"Has it occurred to you that Mendelsohn isn't the brightest bulb?" Peter asks. "I'm not convinced it's legal to tell us not to worry about our daughter's drug use. Doesn't he realize how many kids are dying from fentanyl?"

He's right, but it took so much to get him to get therapy, I'm loath to admit it.

"Maybe he's building up to something?"

"Yes, a stupendous bill."

He shifts his weight, and we resettle.

"Beneath this, we're basically okay, right?" I ask quietly.

"Yes." He presses his mouth to my temple. His place, he used to call it back when we were claiming parts of each other's body.

"Was there a question mark in that? Did I hear a nanosecond of hesitation?"

"None at all. Come," he says, and leads me into the bedroom.

We're used to muffling our sounds when we make love, waiting until the girls are asleep or rushing before they wake up, but even that has become infrequent. A subject that has gone unremarked on in Mendelsohn's office. Tonight, I only want to lose myself. I feel him enter me, and it still, after all these years, surprises me with pleasure. I cling to him tightly, longing for something I can no longer name.

Peter drifts off to sleep easily, a skill that never ceases to annoy me. I roll over, check the time. Eleven o'clock. No need to worry. Olivia's curfew isn't until midnight, and she's out with Todd, the track star not known for excessive partying.

Midnight comes and goes.

At quarter past twelve, I text Olivia. Where are you?

No reply comes.

At one o'clock, I wake Peter up.

"Olivia's still not home."

"Did you text her?"

"Three times."

"Call?"

"Her phone is off, but yes, I left two messages."

"Who did you say she went out with?"

"Todd. You remember, her boyfriend?"

"I know the name of her boyfriend," Peter snaps. "Did you try him?"

Olivia fought tooth and nail, but I insisted she give me the number of whoever she goes out with at night.

"He's not answering either."

At quarter to two, anxiety overcomes pride, and I call Todd's mother, Gina Hanson. She answers on the third ring in a voice soaked in sleep.

"I have no idea where your daughter is. I assumed you knew; Todd and Olivia broke up last week," she says, with an infuriating blend of sympathy and superiority. "There was a party at Hannah Streitfeld's house. You might check there."

There's no answer at Hannah's house.

I climb out of bed and begin pacing the living room, clutching my phone, anger and anxiety swirling until I can't tell one from the other.

At two in the morning, I contemplate calling the police but doubt a teenage girl out two hours past curfew will be enough to mobilize them.

At four thirty, I begin scrubbing the bathroom walls, waiting for the sun to rise.

Chapter 4

Abby

Rachel's humid exhalations seep from her bedroom to fill our small apartment.

When she was younger, I would rise at the first light on weekend mornings, relishing the time alone before I had to fill long hours with activities: on good days, playdates, on days when everyone else was tied up with their own families, outings that went on too long before ending with an early dinner at the thin crust pizza place on the corner that serves wine in water glasses. Then we would dance down the street on the way home.

"You're always so much fun when we eat out," Rachel said, giggling as we locked arms. It was, of course, because of the second glass of wine, though there was no reason to explain that to a seven-year-old.

I pace anxiously, desperate to wake her to find out if she knows what happened to Olivia last night. Unfortunately, purposefully rousing her would result in surly resentment rather than any useful intelligence.

I walk more loudly than necessary to the kitchen and make a smoothie with frozen acai, almond milk, flax, and collagen powder, my latest foray into the promised land of anti-aging miracles that I scorned as voodoo until I found myself facing forty with far less aplomb than I care to admit.

The motor of the industrial blender is a perfect replica of a propeller plane gearing for takeoff. It does the trick, and I finally hear stirrings come from Rachel's room.

"Do you want some breakfast, sweetie?" I ask after knocking on her door.

She stares at me, dumbfounded at the idiocy of the question. "I just woke up."

This is not a good beginning. "Can we talk for a minute?"

She squinches away when I sit on the edge of her bed.

"How was last night? Did you have fun at Hannah's?"

"It was okay."

Despite the disturbing rumors of what goes on at Hannah's, I was relieved when Rachel got invited. Even a risky connection seems preferable to none at all. It worries me that she lacks the gluey friendships with secret codes and private jokes that girded my teenage years.

The first time Rachel went on a playdate with a girl from Dearborn, she came home and told me that their kitchen was bigger than our living room. *Bigger than our entire apartment,* she exclaimed, outraged, though whether at them or me was unclear. At six, she knew instinctively she may be granted temporary visitation rights to that world, but she would never truly belong. I've asked numerous times since if the reason she doesn't invite Dearborn kids over is that she's embarrassed by how we live. Which, I remind her, there is absolutely nothing wrong with. She denies it but offers no other explanation.

"I thought you were looking forward to the party?" I prod.

"Because I'm such a loser no one asks me to anything?"

"I didn't mean that."

"Not that it's any of your business, but Hannah and I are friends now."

Hannah, with her anarchic parties, seems like a curious choice for my loner daughter. Except for one thing. She's an outsider too. A large, pale puff of a girl who blushes too frequently and says yes too eagerly, Hannah orbits the inner circle, admitted only when she serves a purpose. Her hunger to belong is as palpable as Rachel's refusal to admit she cares.

"Did you see Olivia there last night?" I ask carefully.

Rachel's brows furrow in suspicion. "Why?"

"She didn't get home till past six this morning. Kara was terrified something happened to her." It's a warning and a plea. *Please don't ever do this to me.*

"What does that have to do with me?"

"Olivia said she fell asleep at Hannah's while they were watching a movie."

"Seriously, that's what she said?" Rachel's eyes flash with indignation. "She left with Daniel," she spits out, disgusted with the brazenness of Olivia's lie or something else entirely.

"Do you know where they went?" I keep my voice casual. The trick to getting information out of a teenager is to betray as little shock or dismay as possible until the entire story is out. Then all bets are off. Needless to say, that amount of emotional rigor is not always feasible. Then again, it's not my child's disappearance or lies we're talking about.

"How should I know? What Olivia does is so not my problem."

"Honey, if you ever need me to come get you or feel threatened in any way, all you have to do is text. No questions asked."

"You've told me that, like, a million times. Besides, there's such a thing as Uber."

"This may come as a complete surprise, but there are some situations Uber can't get you out of," I snap.

Rachel rolls her eyes, picks up her phone, and begins scrolling.

*

The smoothie has turned an unappealing shade of blue that might boost my immune system, but it will surely stain my teeth. I dump it into the sink and stare at the gelatinous lumps, wondering what, if anything, to do. If I tell Kara that Olivia is lying, it will be evident that Rachel, already an outlier, is the source. No one likes a snitch. Besides, Olivia is home now, safe.

The problem is I'm having lunch with Kara and Hollis, and I have no idea what Daniel's version was. Or whether he is someone we need to worry about.

Kara has been my shadow coparent since the Stricklands transferred to Dearborn four years ago and we were assigned to be their welcome buddies. When I first heard her carefully modulated voice, I assumed she existed on the other side of the velvet rope that cuts through the school, the city itself. I didn't foresee the harried woman who greeted me at the ramshackle apartment on the fifth floor of the scuffed Upper West Side building. The girls, deep in middle school tweeniness, disappeared into Olivia's bedroom while we sat in the living room, tiptoeing around each other until Kara asked if I'd like a glass of wine. Somewhere into the second glass, she looked at me and asked, "Is it true that someone once brought a tin of caviar to a food drive? Because that's definitely not our MO."

"It's not beyond the realm of possibility," I admitted.

Olivia dismissed Rachel within a week, racing off in search of higher ground, but Kara and I began to seek each other out at school events, and then outside of them. For the first time since Rachel was born, I no longer felt adrift in the maternal seas without a guide.

I'm still clutching my phone, trying to decide what to do, when it begins to vibrate.

I don't recognize the number.

"Hello?" I answer hesitantly.

There is only breathing on the other end.

Then the line goes dead.

Chapter 5

Hollis

Eighteen days before the murder
Monday, September 22

Scent from French lavender sachets hovers in the air. The calming aroma and meticulous row of silk blouses in the walk-in closet usually soothe me. When I was a teenager forced to scour the musty offerings of secondhand shops in a futile attempt to replicate what my classmates wore, I fantasized about what it would be like to walk into a store without a constantly clicking calculator in my head. Now it's become one more thing I have to do to maintain who I've become.

I realized as soon as I moved to New York that dress codes change not with zip codes but block by block. My goal was never to impress but to blend in. Today, though, the clues conflict. Abby, with her tangle of long, dark-blond, bedhead hair and white leather moto jacket. Kara in her office-appropriate charcoal wool pants; a sartorial odd couple with few inflection points.

After trying on three outfits, I settle on dark jeans, strappy heels, and a single-breasted navy blazer. Despite all my wardrobe peregrinations, I arrive fifteen minutes early and walk around Madison Square Park three times.

*

Kara and Abby are already seated, bent over a laptop, in the back of the barnlike restaurant.

Kara notices me first and stashes the computer in her bag.

A hectic buzz fills the air as I settle into the empty chair while Abby moves a mason jar of iced tea out of the way.

"This seems to be what we are doing now," she remarks sardonically. "Virtue signaling via glassware."

I spent over an hour researching restaurants after sussing out where Kara worked from her LinkedIn profile, hoping convenience would increase the likelihood of acceptance. "I'm sorry, I've never been here before."

"Don't be silly. I've been dying to see what all the hype is about," Kara says.

"Do you work near here too, Abby?"

"I work from home. I'm a graphic designer, strictly freelance."

"I admire people who are artistic. I have zero talent."

"I create logos for taco trucks and organic dog food companies. I'm not sure that qualifies as artistic."

"She's very talented," Kara says. "Insecure and not great with deadlines but talented."

"Thanks for that." Abby swivels to face me. "How's Daniel adjusting to Dearborn?"

"He seems to like it, but it's hard to get anything more than grunts out of him. I guess most teenage boys are like that."

"I believe the refusal to communicate is nonbinary," Kara remarks.

"Remind me where Daniel was before Dearborn?" Abby presses, leaning forward. She wants something. I just don't know what. Or why.

"Thomasville Academy up in Rhode Island."

"It must have been hard to take him out in the middle of high school."

"It was the lesser of two evils. Thomasville is my husband, Jordan's, alma mater. He loved the tight-knit community, but Daniel was miserable. It seemed pointless to sentence him to two more years of unhappiness."

"Is it too late to send my kids?" Kara asks. "A few hundred miles of distance sounds ideal."

"I couldn't wait to have Daniel back home," I admit. "When he was gone, I had no idea what he was up to, so I didn't know enough to worry, but I have no idea what the rules are here. When he went out the other night, he tried to convince me that no one on the entire East Coast over the age of sixteen has a curfew. I told him one o'clock. Is that what you do?"

"Theoretically," Kara says. "My daughter and curfews are not on the best terms."

"Did it work?" Abby asks. The intensity of her green eyes is discomfiting. I assumed she would be the easy one.

"He said he was home by then, but honestly, I fell asleep," I tell them.

They seem to believe me, though I'm not sure how any mother can fall asleep while their child is loose in the city. I had lain awake until I heard Daniel sneak in right before dawn. Jordan slept through it, or pretended to, even when Daniel's cell phone crashed to the floor. It's our unspoken pact—to act as if nothing happened before. That nothing will happen again.

"Dearborn seems like such a social school," I say, changing the subject. "Marci Carter asked me to be on the Spring Benefit Committee. Are you involved with that?"

Kara shakes her head. "We're not Spring Benefit Committee material."

"I did try once," Abby says. "I volunteered to design the invitations. They acted like I was going to spray-paint their penthouses with graffiti. Then again, everyone else was offering up villas on Lake Como and cameos in Hollywood movies."

"What about the safety walk?"

"That one is mandatory," Abby answers. "One afternoon a year, you go to the school, pick up walkie-talkies, put on orange safety guard vests, and patrol a three-block perimeter. It's crazy that they still think the sight of us in those ridiculous getups will act as a deterrent to anything, but it's yet another tradition they refuse to give up. Last year, Gina Hanson kept telling me to speed up to get her heart rate into peak zone."

In a world of mass shootings and terrorist threats, safety is the most elusive promise of all. Like so many rituals, this one seems to be perpetuated because doing something is almost always better than doing nothing.

"Speaking of safety, that email from Miss Cleary this morning about the class trip wasn't exactly reassuring," I remark.

"The part about prohibiting weapons may have been a little over the top," Abby says, "but no one has ever accused Miss Cleary of subtlety."

"She mentioned hazing. Has that been an issue?"

"I'm sure there have been lots of issues we don't know about," Kara says. "Leaving out the standard drugs and alcohol," she adds wryly.

"But you're going to let your kids go?"

"I don't think we have a choice."

"I wish my husband agreed," I say.

The line stating that anyone caught leaving the lodge after curfew would risk expulsion did nothing to reassure Jordan. He only relented when I convinced him that the risk of Daniel acting out in some unforeseen way would be greater if he was the only one not going.

"I hope I'm not getting too personal, but are you divorced?" I ask Abby.

"I'm a single parent." The statement leaves little room for follow-up.

"That must be hard."

"Having to be good cop and bad cop can be exhausting," Abby admits. "There's no one to talk you off the ledge when you're obsessing over which battles are worth fighting."

"There's no one you want to push off the ledge either," Kara remarks. She turns to me. "Do you know any men for Abby?"

Abby groans.

"What? Maybe Hollis's husband has some friends for you."

"I can ask."

I seriously doubt Jordan's friends would be Abby's type.

"How did you and your husband meet?" she asks.

"We worked at the same investment banking firm."

"That sounds complicated."

"I left before it could get messy."

"Is that what you do now?"

I dread the "Do you work?" question. Everyone trying so hard not to judge, everyone judging.

"I stopped after I had Daniel. Jordan travels a lot for business, and it made sense at the time."

Both women nod politely.

*

Every marriage has a deal. People assume they know mine. An older, extremely successful man. A junior analyst who came from nowhere. With nothing. It's not that they're wrong, but they aren't totally right. I'd been working since I was a teenager and was far more tired than anyone in their twenties has a right to be.

Jordan offered me relief. Security, stability. Most of all, a sense of protection. He opened up a world I'd been looking at through the wrong end of a telescope. Art, music, travel. In return, I made his life easy. After a brutal divorce, it was what he wanted most.

I'm careful to make his life easy still.

*

"I'm thinking of going back to work," I add.

"It's highly overrated," Kara says. "At least working for other people. Abby and I are starting a business."

"You're kidding. What is it?"

"An app where women can post relationship questions they're too embarrassed to ask in public. It's proving a little harder than we thought, though. If you think being a forty-something woman makes you invisible to the outside world, try the tech community."

"They're probably threatened by you."

"How can they be threatened by us? They don't even see us. We have one last shot. We were accepted into an accelerator program next weekend. If we don't win the $50,000, I'm not sure we can make it."

"I'd be happy to speak to Jordan about it. His company has a mandate to invest in more women-owned businesses."

"If you're serious, we can send you a link to the beta version. Feel free to go in and make up questions and answers."

"Are questions about marriage off the table?"

"Not unless you have the only marriage in history without issues."

"We can save that for lunch number two, though it might require drinks."

When the check comes, I insist on paying.

*

We air-kiss goodbye, and I head west with no particular goal. I have too many empty hours to fill, something I'm embarrassed to admit in this least idle of cities. Especially to women who work, much less start businesses on the side.

By the time I realize it, I've walked all the way to Chelsea Piers. I settle on a bench, staring out at the boats bobbing in the Hudson River. I haven't been to the sprawling complex since Daniel was little and there was an endless rotation of birthday parties at the tumbling gym, the ice-skating rink, the bowling alley, all of them ending in sugar-induced pandemonium. I dreaded them then. I would give anything for them now.

I pull out my phone to answer Marci Carter's email. I'm sorry I won't be able to join the benefit committee, but Jordan and I plan to contribute substantially to the auction.

Kara has already sent me an invite to do the safety walk with her and a link to their app. I realize instantly that Jordan would never be interested in it. Women comparing notes on men is his worst nightmare. I put it away and reach for the burner phone in the bottom of my bag.

Adam answers on the third ring.

"Did you get the money?" I whisper, though no one is close enough to hear.

"I've got things under control." His voice is strafed with anger.

"What about our deal?"

He hangs up without answering.

I bury the phone in my bag and stand up. Miss Cleary will be arriving in thirty minutes, and I can't risk Daniel sending her away.

*

Miss Cleary, shoulders squared, is standing in front of the concierge, Patrick, resplendent in his military-grade uniform, when I walk into the lobby.

"Is Mrs. Chapman expecting you?" he asks skeptically.

Doormen are the true social arbiters of New York. The woman in front of him is obviously here to provide a service, but there are numerous substrata within that class—the people who provide music lessons and test prep, the personal trainers and professional organizers, the dog walkers and domestic help.

"It's fine, Patrick," I assure him. "I'll take Miss Cleary up."

I lead her through the double-height lobby, past the porcelain vase of fresh daylilies and gilded mirrors.

"I'm so glad you could come," I tell her as she catches a glimpse of herself and smooths her chin-length hair.

"I've been looking forward to it, Mrs. Chapman."

"Please, call me Hollis."

We both know this will never happen.

Upstairs, I hang up her nubby maroon coat and lead her inside where the cream walls are stippled with late afternoon light. Miss Cleary's eyes dart about the beige-on-beige living room as if nervous she might break something, despite the fact that she's standing still.

"Can I get you anything to drink? Coffee? Water?" I ask, to put her at ease.

"I'm fine, thanks." She pauses. "Do you want to tell me what would be most helpful?"

This is the thorniest part, when expectations are communicated—grade thresholds with bonuses written in, essays to be composed with enough flaws not to be caught while still earning an A. How many parents hire Miss Cleary as a preemptive strike long before any problems occur? How many email her at all hours, demanding exoneration for whatever transgressions their child has been accused of but could never—*must* never—be their fault?

Miss Cleary has the power to wipe the slate clean. Or not.

"Daniel has always been a good student," I tell her. "He simply needs help adapting to the Dearborn Approach."

The famous Dearborn Approach consists of great expanses of free time in each student's schedule designed to allow them to work on projects independently. Some parents buy into the program wholeheartedly; others complain about spending tens of thousands of dollars for their kids to do nothing. For many, the only Dearborn Approach that matters is the one that gets their kids into the Ivy League, and only the top three Ivies at that.

"Why don't I have Daniel give me more details about his past work, and we can fill in any gaps?" she suggests.

Daniel is hovering in the doorway, his hands deep in his pockets.

"Oh, Daniel, good. I'm so glad you're here," I tell him.

"That's kind of the point, isn't it?"

Miss Cleary follows him down the hall, taking in the carefully curated family photographs lining the walls. Daniel building sandcastles on the beach; Daniel and his father in Venice's Saint Mark's Square surrounded by birds.

"You look so much like your father," she remarks.

His shoulders tense beneath his gray T-shirt. "I don't. At all," Daniel mutters.

The best thing about Dearborn has been his anonymity. Daniel is good at letting people—especially girls—think they know him, the *real* him. None of them do. I'm not sure he knows himself.

Miss Cleary doesn't stand a chance.

Chapter 6

Abby

By the time I'm two blocks from the cocktail party for Dearborn's downtown contingent, a torrential rain is slamming into my drugstore umbrella. I'd give anything to turn around, climb into bed, and binge-watch TV. When Rachel first started at Dearborn, I was grateful for the annual tradition at Debra and Mark Seymour's loft at the start of every school year. Fewer families lived downtown, and it helped to band together. I went in hopes of meeting people who could take Rachel to school when I was lying on the bathroom floor felled by a stomach bug, families I could arrange playdates with when the uptowners protested it was too far to travel. The geographical divide has grown irrelevant, but I remain thankful for the help when I needed it most.

I hang my coat on the rack in the entryway, musky with the scent of wet wool, and jam my dripping umbrella into the overflowing stand. My hair is splaying out, and I run my fingers through the knots, trying to tame them. A staccato thrum fills the open loft as I make my way past the massive ceramic sculpture of a centaur rendered in crackled glaze, the excited chatter of old friends reuniting, parents new to Dearborn angling for position. The contingent has grown, now largely composed of financiers and their wives who work in film or fundraise for nonprofits, tech mavens, and celebrated artists with waiting lists for their work. The more illustrious parents—the indie director with the breakout hit, the hedge funder whose recent scandal does nothing to dim his magnetism—form tight groups, making navigation difficult logistically and politically.

I head to the granite island counter, dense with silver buckets of wine, small-batch tequila, and herb-infused sparkling waters. The help-yourself aesthetic is a purposeful juxtaposition to the uptown soirees where caterers pass flutes of champagne and everyone is forced to act like grown-ups. Tonight, parents freed from the tyranny of domestic responsibilities can indulge in nostalgia for the loft parties of their youth. Dearborn remains the connective tissue though, and while conversations wander to art shows, divorces, and diet drugs, they always loop back to the school, complaints about the amount of homework, who will take Nederlander's place when he retires, sly gaming over college applications.

The party is crowded with people drawn on this rainy night out of curiosity as much as obligation. Over the summer, Mark Seymour left Debra after nineteen years of marriage for a man half her age. Whether it's the paramour's youth or his gender that's most disturbing is hotly debated. Debra, flamboyant in an iridescent orange silk scarf, tight black leather pants, and a sharp-edged bob, laughs loudly as she makes her way from group to group. I'm not sure if her good cheer is a defensive veneer or if she truly feels liberated. Regardless, Debra Seymour is, in some elemental way, unleashed.

I pour myself a glass of red wine and take a large sip before turning to find Gina Hanson standing next to me. The Hansons have done a reverse migration, trading their Upper East Side classic eight for a duplex overlooking the High Line, and are reveling in the purported boldness of their move.

"How's Rachel's year going?" Gina asks. "Has she started her list?"

Junior year kicks off the blood sport of ferreting out the competition's safety schools, reaches, and legacies, and the "development" kids whose families can be counted on for large donations. Recent efforts to abolish these advantages are mere inconveniences. There are always work-arounds.

"We haven't talked about it," I admit. The few times I've tried to ask Rachel what type of college she might want to go to—city or rural, large or small—she shuts me down. More than school rankings, my biggest hope is that she finds a place where she can shed her loner status.

"Is Todd being recruited?" I ask Gina.

Since he set the citywide record for the 400-yard dash, D1 schools have been circling. "Yes, but I wish they'd ease up on the practices," Gina complains. "Three hours a day is too much."

I nod in commiseration. Rachel is on the volleyball team, but the only time the coach puts her in is if the team is winning or losing by such a wide margin that her presence is in no danger of affecting the outcome. Despite forceful hints, she refuses to quit. Stubbornness may serve her well later in life but is gaining her no currency among teammates. I no longer go to her games, which suits us both.

"I heard the new boy, Daniel, holds a state record in the 400-yard dash," Allison Gardner interjects. A petite brunette with a pointed nose and too much bronzer, she's been trying to slip into Gina's social circle with little success.

"Yes, but in Rhode Island. Does that even count? Besides, Todd told me he's not joining the team," Gina replies dismissively.

"Why else would Dearborn let him in?" Allison replies, puzzled.

"You do know his last name is Chapman?" Gina retorts, rubbing her forefinger and thumb together.

I hover, curious to hear more, when someone bumps into me from behind. Wine splashes over the rim of my glass onto my white embroidered blouse.

I turn to find a man who looks vaguely familiar looking at me with panic.

"I'm so sorry. Can I get you some water?"

"I'm fine." Crimson splotches seep across my chest.

"You're nice to say so." He smiles sheepishly. "I'm Eliot, by the way."

"Oh, yes. Aren't you the new teacher?"

"Guilty."

"I didn't know they allowed your type in here."

He laughs. "I didn't realize this was supposed to be parents only."

Debra slithers up from behind, putting her hand on his shoulder. "I made an exception, and he does live downtown."

People will always make an exception for an attractive single man over forty, especially if you're a recently divorced woman with a generous settlement and something to prove.

"I thought character was destiny, but it appears in New York, geography is destiny," Eliot remarks.

"Do you believe in destiny?" Debra asks flirtatiously.

Her smile reveals newly plumped lips and startlingly white teeth. It's a given that while Dearborn divorcées may assume a haggard look in the first weeks post-break-up, within six months they will appear younger, slimmer, and chicer than they have in years. It's paid for more than one plastic surgeon's summer home.

"Only when it's convenient," he answers lightly.

I've begun to feel like an intruder and wander off to join Renata Sawyer, her husband, Phil, and their group. "We were talking about the Forest Valley trip," Renata says, drawing me into the conversation. "I think we should petition Dearborn to rent out a hotel for younger siblings and watch over the little monsters so parents can have some we-time."

She stops short, remembering that I have no partner, no other children. She makes a valiant effort to backtrack, diving into the comparative merits of leaf-peeping in Woodstock, Vermont, versus Woodstock, New York. They barely notice when I slip away.

"I should get going," I tell Debra. "Thank you for having me."

"You just got here," she protests unconvincingly. She has zero interest in having another single woman on the premises.

"Unfortunately, I have a dinner to get to."

"I should get going too," Eliot, who has not budged from Debra's clutches, says.

"Don't be silly," she replies, her upper lip quivering as much as her latest round of injectables will allow.

"I'm afraid I have papers to grade and miles to go before I sleep."

I'm rifling through various permutations of black coats when I find Eliot by my side.

"You don't really have a dinner to go to, do you?" he asks with a conspiratorial flicker.

"And you don't really have papers to grade, do you?"

"Actually, I do, but the truth is, I felt like a chaperone at a prom."

When the elevator opens, dispensing more guests, we get in together.

"I'm sorry about your shirt," he says. "I hope it isn't ruined."

"Don't worry about it." It's definitely ruined.

Downstairs, he holds the front door while I open my flimsy umbrella, showering him with fat droplets. "Oh God, I'm sorry."

He smiles. "We're even now, though at least water doesn't stain." We hover on the street. "Which way are you going?"

"South. I only live a few minutes away."

"Do you mind if I walk with you? I'm going in the same direction."

We begin to make our way down the sodden street, our eyes focused on the ground to avoid pools of water, when Eliot comes to an abrupt halt.

"Rita?" he exclaims.

I look up to find Miss Cleary huddled under a purple floral umbrella, her skirt falling six inches below her rain jacket. She glances from Eliot to me with decidedly less pleasure, then back to him.

"What a surprise. Do you live nearby?" he asks.

Her eyes brim with confusion. "You asked me to join you at the Seymours' party when we were meeting about the trip yesterday. You said we'd have more time to talk then."

"Ah." His fingers tighten around his umbrella. "I'm so sorry. It turns out the event was meant for parents. My mistake."

She remains rooted, her gaze fixed on him, as the rain continues to fall around us.

"I'm being rude," Eliot adds hastily, nodding in my direction. "This is—"

"Rachel's mother," she interrupts. "I know."

"We were leaving at the same time," Eliot explains.

It may be true, but it doesn't *feel* true, at least not completely. Certainly not to Rita Cleary.

"I'm sure you'd be welcome at the party, since you came all this way," he tells her.

The proffered salve is ignored.

"I'll see you tomorrow," she tells him before mumbling good night.

"I feel terrible," Eliot says, as we begin walking again. "I don't remember mentioning the party." He shakes his head, eager to leave the interlude behind. "So, you're Rachel's mother?" he asks, assessing me anew.

I smile. "You're not sure who she is, are you?"

He laughs. "How long can I play the new card for?"

"You can relax. She's not in any of your classes. You're under no obligation to tell me how brilliant she is."

"I'm sure she's a natural-born leader." He smiles. "How long have you been a Dearborn parent?"

"Forever. Rachel started in kindergarten."

"I'm not used to schools that go all the way through. It must be a very close-knit group."

"You'd think so."

"That might require further explanation."

Despite dogged efforts, no one at Dearborn has been able to determine which faction to park me in. I'm not exactly young, but younger than them. Not married, but not divorced. Not poor, but poorer than most of them. The inability to quantify me initially caused bafflement, then discomfort, and eventually disinterest.

"Another time," I tell him.

"Did you go to Dearborn?"

"God, no. I went to public schools."

"Do you mind if I ask why you didn't choose that for your daughter?"

"Academically, Dearborn made sense, but socially it can be a tough place. You want to teach your kid that success isn't defined by money, but it's difficult when they're constantly confronted with evidence to the contrary. There are kids in Rachel's class who've never been on the subway."

"That explains the email asking parents to avoid blocking the street with town cars. Do you regret your decision?"

"It depends on the day."

The emotional math is too much to explain to a near-stranger on a rainy night. My mother left a small inheritance that helped me set up my design business and covered tuition in the early years. I was too busy putting out fires to realize the funds would run out by the time Rachel was in middle school. When I told Dearborn we had to leave, they offered a full ride, worried that losing a straight A student due to a sudden loss of funds would run counter to their progressive narrative. The psychic debt that left is never explicitly mentioned but never completely forgotten.

The wind picks up as we wait at a red light, splattering rain onto our legs. Across the street, the windows of a bistro glimmer in tones of amber and white.

"Please, don't take this the wrong way," Eliot says, "I'm happy to pay your dry-cleaning bill, but can I buy you a glass of wine instead? If nothing else, we can wait out the downpour."

"You've done nothing to make me believe you're safe with a glass of wine."

"Life is full of risks."

It's been so long since I bantered with an attractive man, my synapses snap to attention like a long-lost friend waving hello.

"A glass of wine does sound like the better option."

The small bistro is filled with people dodging the elements. We find seats in the back at a red leather banquette near the kitchen.

With none of the distractions of walking, an awkwardness descends. I look across the table at Eliot in all his shaggy post-preppiness, his warm brown eyes flecked with gold, his face the right side of seasoned, enough to reveal experience, not enough to show decline. Maybe it's the fact that we both lied to get out of the party or got caught by Miss Cleary, but being with him has a slightly illicit feeling.

We start talking at the same time, stop, start again.

"You go," Eliot says.

"I was going to ask how you like living in New York."

All you have to do is pepper men with questions about themselves for them to think they're on the best date of their lives. Of course, this isn't a date. It's merely a, well, something.

"I'm still settling in, but after so much of my life taking place within a five-mile radius, I enjoy exploring. What about you?"

"I grew up in the suburbs. My parents distrusted the city and its 'loose values,' so naturally it was the only place I wanted to be. I used to sneak in on weekends when I was a teenager and wander the streets, picturing my life here."

"Did it turn out as you imagined?"

"Does anything?"

We stop talking when the waiter approaches. I order a glass of pinot noir.

"Club soda with lime please," Eliot says.

His abstinence feels like a bait and switch, but he did mention he has work to do.

"Dearborn must be a big change from Saint Stephen's. What made you decide to come here?"

"Honestly?"

"Preferably, yes. As a matter of policy."

"I was going through a divorce, and my wife got Saint Stephen's."

"I didn't know you can get entire schools in a divorce."

"I've learned you can get pretty much anything. Let's just say she was staying with her soon-to-be new husband, who happens to be the vice provost."

"Ouch. I'm sorry."

"It was bad enough that she cheated, but it turns out everyone knew except me. I felt like a fool. We don't have children, so when Dearborn came courting, it seemed like a godsend. Don't get me wrong, it wasn't only a way out of that mess. I was intrigued by Dearborn's less stodgy approach to education." He smiles. "If anyone asks, that's the official reason for the move. What about you?"

"I've never had an affair with a vice provost."

"A definite point in your favor. How long have you been divorced?"

"I'm not."

Confusion creases his forehead. "Separated?"

"I've never been married."

"I'm sorry. I didn't mean to pry."

"No apology necessary." I recross my legs, anxious to redirect the conversation. "Isn't Saint Stephen's the school that had a sex scandal a couple of years ago?"

Was it the one with the girls' soccer coach giving "massages," the senior boys cornering freshman girls in the chapel's steeple, the dean with a proclivity for holding young boys for "detention"?

"Name me a school that hasn't. Some just manage to do a better job of covering it up."

"Now you're really depressing me."

"I didn't mean to sound so cynical."

"It comes naturally then?"

He laughs. "I hope not."

"What made you decide to go into teaching?"

"Like every English major with delusions of grandeur, I wanted to be a writer. Teaching was supposed to be a way to support myself while I worked on the great American novel."

"What happened?"

"I wasn't a very good writer, but once I got over my smashed ego, I realized I love teaching."

Vulnerability is not a trait men usually display so early on. The world would be a much different place if they realized its appeal.

"I get it. I started out wanting to be an artist."

"Why did you stop?"

"I had a baby. It got complicated."

"Do you want to go back to it now that your daughter is older?"

I curl the edges of my cocktail napkin. "Not really. I worked in a gallery when I was starting out and met too many people who had ambition but not enough talent or talent but not enough ambition. It was a relief to give it up."

It took me years to admit this to myself, and I almost never admit it to others. Being labeled "artistic," especially at Dearborn, suits me. It makes the way we live seem like a conscious choice rather than a failure of ambition. The problem is that it wasn't Rachel's choice.

The closest she came to admitting envy was last spring when every girl in her class started showing up in the same $250 jeans. To the naked eye, there was no discernible difference between those and the ones that cost half as much. Pointing that out did not go over well.

"You have no idea of the things I *don't* ask you for," Rachel told me, her cheeks burning.

I bought her a pair the next day.

"Do you regret sending your daughter to Dearborn?" Eliot asks.

"I don't know. I do wish I'd been better at selling out instead of becoming a freelance designer. At the time, freedom seemed more important than financial security." I question that trade-off on a regular basis, especially when I'm adding up bills in the middle of the night. "What about you?"

"I still try to write every day to keep that muscle from atrophying, but they're only notes for myself."

"At least you're influencing young minds. I'm creating logos for dog food companies."

"It sounds corny, but it's true. Every now and then, something you say connects with a kid, and it's like watching a light switch on."

"How did they wrangle you into chaperoning the Forest Valley trip?"

"I'm not sure. Rita Cleary sprung it on me in front of everyone on Curriculum Night, which seemed rather odd."

"*She's* rather odd."

"I gather she's not a student favorite, but kids often single out one teacher the same way they choose one kid to bully. They can smell weakness a mile away. She seems harmless enough. Maybe a little overly enthusiastic," he concedes.

"She's such a stickler. Most of the parents think she's totally batshit, too, though I'll deny having said that."

"I assume we're going to deny everything about tonight." That smile, again. "Anyway, she seems to think that because I come from a boarding school, I have experience corralling teenagers in captivity."

"Good luck with that. After last year's trip, a highlight reel of every parent's nightmare made the rounds. Hot takes included three kids throwing up outside the lodge, a naked boy and girl jumping into the lake at night, and two people having extremely loud sex under a camp blanket. If Miss Cleary sold this to you as a relaxing weekend in the country, you're in for a shock."

"I began to get that feeling when she mentioned the forest extraction team. Aside from staying away from kids making blackmail videos, what else do I need to know?"

"Don't do anything you can be blackmailed about."

"Duly noted."

"I'm sure it'll be fine. Rachel spends every summer at Forest Valley and loves it."

I've often wondered if she's an outsider there, too, or if she has a separate identity far from home.

We spend the next hour talking about the Whitney Museum, gentrification in the farther reaches of Brooklyn, and the myriad changes the city has gone through since the last time Eliot visited, until we run out of locations and events.

"I should get going," I say to forestall a looming silence.

When the check comes, I reach for my bag to pay my share.

"Don't be silly. It's the least I can do."

I look down at my blouse where the wine has dried into crimson puckers. "True."

The rain has stopped when we step out into the night and start walking south.

"This is where I turn," I tell him when we reach Bleecker Street.

He glances down the narrow block speckled with puddles, then back to me. "I had a good time tonight."

"Me too."

"I don't want to make you uncomfortable, but would you have dinner with me?"

I smile. "I'd like that."

"Great," he says, nodding. "Is Friday too soon?"

"It's perfect."

Unsure how to separate, we settle on an awkward approximation of a hug.

I hurry the rest of the way home, twitchy with something that feels an awful lot like hope.

*

It takes two attempts to get my key into the door as the wine reasserts itself. I kick off my shoes and tiptoe in, hoping Rachel is asleep so I can sink into my bed undetected and replay the evening, but her light is on.

I find her bent over her lilac leather journal, absorbed in scribbling. I was surprised when she expressed an interest in "journaling" over the summer, but it seems to soothe her to write the things she can't say. To anyone.

As soon as she notices me, she stashes the diary in her desk drawer. "What happened to your shirt?" she asks, eyeing me skeptically.

"Someone bumped into me at the Seymours' party. Lovely, isn't it?"

She nods, thoroughly uninterested in my life outside the home, and opens her laptop.

After assessing the damage the night has done in the bathroom mirror, I crawl into bed, going over every word of my conversation with Eliot, looking for loopholes. It's too late to call Kara and dissect the evening. Instead, I reach for my phone, open Jyst, and begin to type.

Q. I'm thinking of dating a teacher. Not my teacher. My daughter's. Is that cool? Not? Help!

I hit enter and listen to a true crime podcast until I fall asleep.

*

Kara calls early the next morning. "I see you've been busy."

"What do you mean?"

"The question about the teacher?"

"Oh God." I open the app to find two replies.

A. Proceed with caution. Unless he's hot. Then go for it.

A. NOOO. If it doesn't work out, he'll find ways to make both your lives miserable, and your daughter will never forgive you.

"Why did you answer twice?"

"I didn't. We gave Hollis the password, remember? What happened last night?"

"I like him."

"Who?"

"Eliot Handley. The new English teacher. I ran into him at the Seymours'."

"Wow. You never like anyone. What's his story?"

"He recently got divorced and moved to New York to get away from his ex. I know you think I only date unavailable men, but I really don't think that's the case this time." I hesitate. "Do you think it's weird that he asked me out for a glass of wine and then only ordered club soda?"

"Would you rather he got shit-faced? How about looking for green flags instead of red for a change?"

"You're right. Can you do me a favor and delete the question? The last thing I need is for this to get around."

"Sure, but you do know nothing is ever really deleted, right?"

Chapter 7

Kara

Sixteen days before the murder
Wednesday, September 24

Kids are clustered outside Dearborn by the time I get there. I weave around the soccer team lining up for the bus to Randall's Island, the track team getting ready to walk to Central Park, the volleyball team heading to the gym three blocks away, all part of the sprawling land grab of the better-endowed schools. Neither of my girls plays team sports, and I wonder now if I should have insisted on it. Maybe it would have instilled the sense of discipline I've failed at so miserably.

My kids are nowhere in sight. Olivia is still grounded from the disappearing act she pulled after Hannah's party and is under strict orders to go home straight after school. Maya has after-school debate club where she is undoubtedly honing skills to be weaponized at the dinner table. As much as I'm curious to see them in their natural habitat, they'd be equally relieved not to find me on their territory. In a perfect world, parents wouldn't be seen or heard.

Inside, Harvey Johnson, a barrel-chested man in a bright-red blazer emblazoned with the Dearborn crest, is tapping his fingers against the security desk. A veteran of twenty years, he's never been known for his patience. The latest wave of students, subjected to sensitivity training about class, racial, and gender inequities, treat him with an exaggerated courtesy that does nothing to improve his mood.

I wait by his desk, eavesdropping as a posse of girls debate whether to take up residence on the steps of the Metropolitan Museum or, hopefully, find an apartment where no adults will be home. Boys with hungry eyes linger on their outskirts, waiting for intel.

Hollis walks in before they reach a decision.

"Are you ladies ready?" Harvey asks impatiently.

He lays out two plastic orange vests crackled with spidery gray fault lines from years of wear and enormous walkie-talkies, showing us which buttons to press should there be an incident.

"Do you understand?" he asks apprehensively as if we are not particularly bright children.

We're struggling into the neon vests when Amanda Carter sidles up, all fiery-red hair, swaying hips, and insouciance, an amoeba-like cluster of girls inching up with her.

"Are you Mrs. Chapman? I'm Amanda, a good friend of Daniel's."

Hollis nods tentatively.

Amanda is undeterred. "Do you know where Daniel is? We were supposed to meet up after school."

"I'm sorry, he didn't mention anything to me."

Amanda considers Hollis with preternatural self-possession. "Please tell him I said he can come over again anytime." She flicks a lock of hair over her narrow shoulder.

Hollis turns to me, baffled. "How does that girl know who I am?"

"Dearborn's a small school. Everyone has known each other forever. You're new blood. Or more to the point, your son is."

"Is she a friend of Olivia's?"

"Frenemy is more like it."

The two girls have been rivals since the day they set eyes on each other. The prize varies—allegiance of other girls, mastery over boys. The competition matters more than the reward.

"Ladies," Harvey interrupts, nodding in the direction of the door.

*

We head to Lexington Avenue, passing a tiny lingerie store with expensive fishnets in the window, a holdover from the time before big box stores took over, and turn the corner to the block that houses Dearborn's five-story gym. I glance at Hollis as we walk. With her cashmere blazer, fresh blowout, and lithe grace, the orange vest has never looked more disconsonant on another human being. Everything I'm wearing feels suddenly wrong, every movement I make oafish.

She catches me studying her, and I look away, embarrassed.

"Has anyone ever used one of these?" she asks, holding up the walkie-talkie.

"No, but there are rumors someone left it on by mistake, and Harvey overheard enough gossip to arm him with ammunition for years. There's a good chance money changed hands."

"It's kind of terrifying that the school thinks that the sight of us is all that's standing between our kids and bodily harm."

"No one actually believes it. Least of all them. They're throwing us a bone under the guise of 'parental involvement,'" I tell Hollis.

As we approach the gym, a group of lanky boys in the red-and-white shirts of Dearborn's basketball team hurry by, late for practice. Snippets of their conversation filter out, something about what a girl did or what they did to a girl at a party last Saturday night. A picture is making the rounds, though the angle is blurry enough that precisely what happened is open to interpretation.

"I've told Olivia and Maya a million times that just because they see a video or picture doesn't mean it's true," I say, shaking my head. It's hopeless, really.

"What about that video from last year's class trip? Was it a prank, or were kids actually caught having sex?"

"Unclear. The school made a lot of threats about expelling whoever shot it, but they never figured it out."

Olivia, along with most of the kids, changes her social media handles on a regular basis. They're all masters of deception.

"At least with boys you don't have to worry as much about their physical safety," I add.

"There are always things to worry about. After Daniel was born, I used to stare at him for so long when I fed him that I would see his face like a ghost in front of me everywhere I went. I've never totally relaxed again."

"I know Peter loves the girls as much as I do, but I don't think he feels that way."

"Men are better at compartmentalizing. Maybe our kids' generation will be different."

"I thought ours would be."

"Did you?" she looks at me, surprised.

"At least we gave lip service to fifty-fifty parenting. I've only seen one father volunteer for a safety walk, and his wife was in the hospital. Apparently, the whole evolved father thing only goes so far."

"Jordan doesn't pretend to be evolved."

"At least you know what you're getting into."

"I don't think anyone ever really knows what they're getting into."

For all our closeness, I seldom discuss the vicissitudes of marriage with Abby. I'm not sure she would understand how your children can bind you as a couple and then become a thorn in the fabric of your relationship. How you can desire someone you don't actually want or want someone you don't actually desire because desire itself has been worn down by endless proximity. How you can sense the presence of love but can't always grasp it. All Abby has to do is swipe left.

"This whole thing is ridiculous," I say. "Do you want to hide out someplace and get a cup of coffee?"

Hollis exhales in relief. "Absolutely."

We slip out of the orange vests like naughty schoolchildren and stash them in our bags.

*

The café six blocks from Dearborn is filled with people working away on laptops. It's a quarter of four in the afternoon, that in-between hour when the acceptable beverage is unclear and every option risks revealing more about your state of mind than it would at, say, six in the evening.

"Would it be awful to have a glass of wine?" I ask.

Hollis smiles. "It's imperative."

We're midway through our first glass when I broach the subject of Jyst.

"Did you have a chance to look at the app?" I ask casually, though I rehearsed the opening salvo five times this morning.

"Yes, I love it. It's impossible not to relate to the questions, even if they're made up."

"Some of them are real." The table wobbles as I lean forward. "You mentioned you might show it to your husband?" If we don't win the $50,000 at the accelerator this weekend, Jordan Chapman is our only hope of staying afloat.

Hollis is about to answer when an insistent ringing comes from deep inside her bag.

"Do you need to take that?" I ask.

"No, I'm sure it's nothing."

She wraps her arms around the bag, muffling the ringing until it stops. Her eyes are skittish, though, her attention fractured.

When the ringing starts up again, it's clear I've lost her.

"I must have forgotten about an appointment," she says nervously.

"Go," I tell her. "I'll take everything back to Harvey."

She rises quickly, bumping into a chair as she hurries out.

Chapter 8

Hollis

I round the corner and find a recessed entryway two blocks away before pulling out the burner phone to call Adam back.

"They took her away," he barks.

"What do you mean?"

"The police fucking took her. They have her on a seventy-two-hour involuntary hold."

"They can't take her for no reason. What happened?"

"She was out for a goddamned walk, that's it."

It's never that simple. We both know that.

"Where were the aides I'm paying for?"

"I let them go. I don't want strangers in the house."

"We had a deal."

"Your money doesn't give you the right to tell us how to live. If you don't get that Dr. Akoris bitch at Harkendale to release her, I'll call that asshole husband of yours and have him apply a little pressure. Oh right, he doesn't know the truth about her, does he? I wonder how he'd like to learn you've been lying to him all this time."

*

I lean against the building, running through options—pleas, reasoning, money, threats.

I was nine when my mother became convinced that Mrs. Catton, our neighbor, was trying to kidnap us and barricade us beneath the jumble of broken furniture in the basement. Eleven when my father bolted from the tiny upstate town where everyone knew about the woman who attacked a storekeeper with a fire extinguisher.

We moved three times to ever-tinier tract homes in ever-more-desolate towns, but there was a scent about us. Everyone has heard the stories. The patient who was fine until they killed their children. The one who stabbed their neighbors. The one who saw flames where there were none and jumped from a ten-story roof. People kept their distance.

Adam went to the local junior college while my mother cycled in and out of institutions. He quit before graduating. "My mother is my mission," he announced. Not "ours," *his*. It made it easier for me to leave. I got a scholarship to NYU and packed within weeks of finishing high school. I wanted obscurity. I wanted the city. I wanted to start over where no one knew who I was.

I put the phone away and head home, lost in a past I can't change and a future I can't control.

*

I drop my keys on the marble table in the foyer, still trying to figure out my next move, when a faint rustling comes from the back of the apartment. The musky scent of weed slithers down the hall.

Everything sinks even further.

I take a breath to steady myself before knocking on Daniel's door.

"One minute," he answers, his voice rushed, husky.

"Now."

Daniel, his hair disheveled and an alarmed look on his face, opens the door three inches. Peering out behind him, a girl, bosomy and flushed, is zipping her jeans with barely contained laughter.

Part of me wants to run as far and as fast as I can. The other part wants to kill them both.

"What's going on here?" I demand, though it's all too clear what's going on.

"You told me you wouldn't be home until five," Daniel protests.

"So this is my fault?"

Behind him, the girl/woman looks at me with glassy, defiant eyes behind a curtain of auburn hair.

"This is Olivia," Daniel says. "From school. We're working on an English project together."

I stare at Olivia. Kara's Olivia. Brazen and unapologetic. "I'd like you to leave."

Rather than being mortified and scurrying away, which wouldn't salvage the situation but would at least not make it worse, she turns to Daniel.

"Call me later?"

She leans over to kiss him and then squeezes past me.

I wait until the front door closes before speaking. "How long has this been going on?"

"What?"

"Your room stinks of marijuana. There was a girl in here half-dressed."

"She was fully dressed."

"Barely."

"I told you, we're working on a project together."

"What part of your project involves taking your clothes off?" I exhale loudly, exasperated. "You can't do this again."

"What do you mean, again? She was here of her own free will."

"You were getting high."

"Weed is legal."

"Not at your age. Drugs are more dangerous for you than other people."

"I know you think so. That doesn't make it true."

"Past evidence would suggest otherwise. Is Olivia the only girl you're seeing?"

Daniel eyes me suspiciously. "What do you mean?"

"I met one of your other 'friends' today, Amanda Carter. She thought you two had plans for this afternoon."

"Are you spying on me?"

"Of course not. I had to be at Dearborn."

"Amanda is crazy. I never promised her anything."

Promises are open to interpretation when you are a seventeen-year-old boy testing out his charms. "Does Olivia know you're seeing someone else?"

"I'm not 'seeing' anyone. Besides, Olivia's cool."

"Girls may pretend they're cool with things, but that doesn't mean it's true. I don't want you to grow into the kind of man who's careless with women."

"I'm not like that, Mom," he says quietly.

*

My hands are shaking as I pour myself a glass of water, anger spiraling through me. At Daniel. At Olivia, with her extravagant cleavage and insolent gaze. At Kara, for not controlling her daughter, though I know that's not fair. And something deeper than anger. Fear. Daniel isn't pushing boundaries; he's smashing them in my face.

He has no idea what waits for him on the other side. Neither of us does.

I won't tell Kara about this afternoon. Whatever happened, it was in my house. With my son's drugs and my son's history and my son's genetic predispositions. I won't tell Jordan. The ice between them is already too thin.

I'll handle it alone.

*

"Do you remember the app I showed you?" I ask Jordan, handing him a whiskey when he gets home. "The one two Dearborn mothers are working on?"

"I remember being singularly unimpressed by it."

"I think it would be a good idea to invest in it."

"Why? Anonymous apps are notoriously difficult to monitor and even harder to monetize."

"You told me we should strengthen our ties to Dearborn in case of trouble."

"Does this have anything to do with Daniel?"

"It might."

Jordan is used to paying to make problems disappear.

"All right, I'll take care of it," he says. Irritated, he takes the whiskey into his study.

*

I call Dr. Akoris, Harkendale's clinical director, as soon as Daniel and Jordan leave the next morning. It's been two years since we last spoke, but she quickly dispenses with pleasantries.

"I understand your brother wants us to release your mother to his care, but we're not able to do that," she states matter-of-factly. "The police found her wandering barefoot and nearly naked on Route 5b at two in the morning. She was exhibiting clear signs of paranoia and repeatedly hit the officers. Despite what your brother may want, we have no choice but to keep her on a mandatory seventy-two-hour hold."

I wish it was harder to visualize. My mother, hallucinating, thrashing out violently. I wish it was harder to imagine Adam exposing my carefully constructed world if I don't somehow get her released.

"What if we guarantee round-the-clock care?" I beseech Dr. Akoris.

"You've tried that in the past," she replies. "Schizophrenia can only be managed with consistent use of antipsychotic medication and clinical oversight. There is no evidence that your brother can provide that. In fact, his behavior is increasingly troubling."

This, too, is not hard to imagine.

"He's worried about my mother," I explain. "Surely you can understand him being excitable under the circumstances."

Dr. Akoris's voice softens. "Of course, but his conduct is in danger of edging past what we consider safe for our staff. You and I have talked about early warning signs of schizophrenia in the past, I believe due to your concern about other family members. As we've discussed, symptoms, including irrational outbursts, tend to begin in the late teens in men. It's rare for them to show up at Adam's age, but we can't rule it out. In the meantime, after mandatory hold is up, we plan on having a meeting to review the next steps on Saturday, October 11. You're welcome to attend."

Daniel will be at Forest Valley that weekend, completely cut off from civilization. Jordan's attention is so rarely focused on me. It will be easy to slip away.

"I'll be there," I assure her.

Chapter 9

Abby

Fourteen days before the murder
Friday, September 26

Despite the fact that I'm thirty-nine years old and readily proclaim myself a feminist, I find myself standing in the middle of my bedroom watching a sixteen-year-old influencer with a lip flip expound on the "Three Style Mistakes to Avoid on a First Date." It's fatal to look like you're trying too hard. Disastrous to wear anything too fussy. Imperative to blur concealer with an egg-shaped sponge. I briefly consider the sponge sitting on the bathtub coated with soap scum but, in a moment of great clarity, decide it might be wiser not to risk permanent vision loss.

The last time I went on a blind date was four months ago. Midway through our first drink, the guy looked into my eyes and asked where our relationship was headed.

"I'm still on my first glass of wine. I'm not quite ready to answer that," I replied, trying to keep it light. Unfortunately, he was dead serious.

"I want to fall in love. I want to wake up with someone by my side on Sunday mornings. I think that person could be you."

"You do realize we've only known each other for fifteen minutes?"

"Yes, but where do you see this going?"

Cornered, I answered as tactfully as possible. "I can see us being friends, but I don't see a romantic relationship."

He stared, then suddenly lurched across the table, grabbed the back of my head and kissed me on the lips. Hard.

I pushed him away with both hands. "Did you not hear what I said?"

"Pretend you're in Paris," he replied.

It's the only time I walked out in the middle of a date. I called Kara as soon as I got outside and stayed on the phone until I was safely in a taxi.

"I thought his face was red from the cold, but he must have pregamed. I've reached a new low," I groaned.

Kara laughed. "You've managed to be courted, asked to go to Paris, and broken up with all within fifteen minutes. Even for you, that's a record."

It's hard not to get discouraged, but Eliot isn't a rando from Bumble where men exist without context or accountability. He's someone I've already met and is preapproved by the Dearborn community. Rather than reassuring me, this heightens my nerves. The chances are more palpable, the stakes higher.

I dab on a neutral berry lipstick, realize it is more berry than neutral, worry this might fall into the category of trying too hard, and wipe it off.

*

Eliot is seated at a rear table in Quanterro, a narrow wood-beamed restaurant in the West Village with a turquoise bar, baroque chandeliers, and Northern Italian cuisine.

He smiles when he sees me walk in. I try to hold his gaze but barely last three seconds. I have no problem looking men in the eye unless I am attracted to them, in which case I find it impossible. You'd think I would've outgrown this by now.

I slide into the banquette beside him, unsure whether we're supposed to kiss hello. We make a clumsy move toward each other that results in our cheeks grazing. His broad open face is freshly shaved, and a pleasant scent of sandalwood clings to him.

"It's good to see you." When he smiles, his cheeks crease in vertical parentheses.

"You too."

"How've you been?"

"Fine. Good."

Second dates are harder out of the gate than first ones. You've already offered up the rough sketches of your biography, but there's no rhythm yet, few reference points to hang a conversation on. You're starting fresh, but your best lines have already been used.

We're both relieved when the waiter approaches. "Can I start you off with drinks?"

Eliot waits for me to answer.

I glance from the wine list to him, hoping for a clue.

"I'll have a club soda," he tells the waiter, "and I believe the lady might like a glass of wine. Abby?"

I choose the first white on the list, barely noticing what it is.

"I don't need the wine," I tell him as soon as the waiter leaves.

"Abby, I don't care if other people drink. I've never had a problem with alcohol. There was no cataclysmic event or stint in rehab." He pauses. "My father was an alcoholic. I had a sister who drowned when we were teenagers, and after that, his drinking got out of hand. It destroyed what was left of my family. I decided it wasn't something I want in my life."

"I'm so sorry about your sister."

"It wasn't an easy thing to survive, for any of us. Speaking of family, can I ask you a question?"

"Of course."

"Did you tell your daughter where you were going tonight? It's none of my business, but I assume she'll be going to Forest Valley. There's no reason it should come up, but I want to be prepared."

"No. I'm not a proponent of total transparency when it comes to parenting."

"Good to know." A gentle ripple curves his lips. "Where did you tell her you were going?"

"Meeting my friend, Kara, to prep for an event tomorrow. We're thinking of launching a business."

I explain the premise of Jyst, leaving out my drunken post from the other night.

"For the record, I don't generally lie to Rachel, but I'm careful who I introduce her to."

"Is there a test for potential suitors?"

"That would imply more logic than I possess."

"I've found logic has very little to do with dating."

I'm usually guarded about my romantic history, but I've come to wonder—or rather, Kara has caused me to wonder—if that precludes the intimacy I profess to want. There's something about Eliot, his directness, his confession about being cuckolded, that makes me want to open up, not completely but enough to let a shaft of light in.

"I learned the hard way. When Rachel was eight, I dated a man who also had an eight-year-old, and we tried to integrate our lives. We sat the kids down and told them we were in a committed relationship. He lived on the Upper West Side. On weekends Rachel and I would go there for 'sleepover' dates."

Eliot laughs. "Did you take your sleeping bags?"

"Pathetic, I know." So much of romance is ridiculous in retrospect.

"What happened?"

"A month after we sat them down for that talk, he dumped me. By email. After that, I vowed not to go out more than two nights a week and never involve my daughter."

Guilt leached into every minute I was away even though Rachel loved Joanna, the teenage babysitter who left a trail of potato chip crumbs across the living room and painted her nails purple.

"Does your two-night rule still apply?"

"I'm not sure. I thought dating would get easier as Rachel got older. I thought it would get easier as *I* got older, but it's more confusing than ever."

"I was married for so long, I have no idea how to do this either. Stop me if I'm being too personal, but is Rachel's father in the picture?"

Over the years, I've developed a multiple-choice shorthand to explain my marital status on dates. The options, depending on whether or not I want to see the person again, include: *"I was never married. Full stop. Next question." "Rachel's father and I separated soon after she was born, and they have no relationship." "I got pregnant from a vacation fling my first year out of college, and he left in the middle of the night. It turns out I never even knew his real name."*

The last version is the one I've told Rachel, told everyone at Dearborn. It's the one I tell Eliot now. I scan for judgment in his eyes but find none.

"That must have been tough."

"The pregnancy was an accident, but I thought having a baby would ground me, give me a sense of purpose. I realize that sounds selfish."

"Did it?"

"Yes. Absolutely."

"But?"

"I love my daughter more than anything in the universe, but sometimes I can't help wondering what I missed."

"Like what?"

"Whatever it is people do in their twenties."

The only chance I've had to experience duty-free days and reckless nights was when Rachel was at Forest Valley. Even then, I only enjoyed the freedom because it was temporary. I knew she would come home, and we would be together again.

"Raising a child is a lot more important than anything you might be imagining. I admire single mothers." He grimaces. "I'm sorry. That sounds incredibly condescending."

"Not at all," I assure him, though it absolutely sounds condescending. "It wouldn't matter anyway. You can't go back. I'm turning forty in a couple of weeks, and it's hitting me harder than I realized."

"You make it sound like you are turning ninety. You're still young. You have all the time in the world."

"Do you really believe that?"

"I have to. I'm forty-three and suddenly have a blank slate. Moving to a new city. Starting over. Not knowing anyone here yet except the people I work with. And you."

"What about your dating history?"

"I haven't done much of it," he admits. "I was married for fifteen years, and Saint Stephen's is a small community, which made it difficult. When I weighed the pros or cons of moving to New York, it was one of the reasons that tipped the balance."

"So your big career move was really designed to improve your dating life?"

"It seems to be working."

I laugh, pleased. Of course, pleased.

"Seriously," he continues, "if I was ever going to have a chance at rebuilding my life, I had to leave what happened there behind."

"You're an English teacher. You must know 'The past is never dead. It's never even past.'"

"True, but at least here if I have dinner with a beautiful woman the whole town isn't gossiping about it the next morning."

I flush. Another thing I thought I'd outgrown.

"You're better at this dating thing than you think."

"I'm working on it." He plays with his spoon, moving it slightly to the left, then back, before looking at me nervously. "Is it all right if I kiss you?"

I nod and he leans over, pressing his lips, soft and pillowy, to mine.

"I've wanted to do that since you walked in," he says.

Heat squirrels down my chest, wraps around my abdomen. We're on different footing now, tipsily off-balance. There's a brief reprieve when the waiter brings our food. We busy ourselves with making sure each is happy with our choices (yes), and comment about the amount of salt in the sauces (a bit too much). The kiss and its promise hover between us.

"You know what the real problem with the Forest Valley trip is?" he asks, smiling.

"There are too many to count. Which one did you mean?"

"You'll have a totally child-free weekend, and I'll be an hour away. Do you have any moms-gone-wild plans?"

"Are you asking me if I'm dating anyone?"

"Yes, I guess I am."

"I'm not seeing anyone."

"Good. Me neither." He regards me closely. "Okay, then."

"Okay," I agree, wriggling in my seat.

I wasn't sure I could feel this way again. I'm not even sure I want to. Where has it ever gotten me? Rachel, of course. It got me Rachel.

When the waiter comes to clear our plates, we skip dessert. I make a feeble attempt to reach for my bag, and he shakes his head before paying the check.

We step out onto Carmine Street and pass under metal scaffolding, the omnipresent ceiling of a city in constant revision. Eliot stops and pulls me to him, kissing me more deeply this time, his mouth open, searching. His arms, surprisingly strong beneath his coat, enfold me.

This is what you forget: the feeling of fitting.

This is what you never forget.

We walk another block before stopping at the corner, uncertain which direction to go in.

"Can I walk you home?" he asks.

I am slightly disappointed that he hasn't asked me back to his place. I would have said no. Not yet, not tonight. But still.

Chapter 10

Kara

Thirteen days before the murder
Saturday, September 27

The diamond-faceted steeple of the Freedom Tower pierces the early morning sky over the financial district. The dealmakers have fled for the weekend, and it's too early for the hordes of tourists who cluster around the bronze parapet engraved with the names of those who died on 9/11, taking selfies on hallowed ground. I repeat the pitch over and over as I walk, surrounded by ghosts.

Abby is waiting under the canopy of the Millennium hotel, so absorbed in texting she doesn't notice me approach.

"You're early." It comes out more surprised than I intended.

She pushes her aviator Ray-Bans to the top of her head, her face too glowy to ascribe to excitement about the accelerator. "Good morning to you too."

"Judging by your look, I gather your date went well?"

"He's great, Kara. Smart, interested in my life, a good kisser."

She holds up a text from Eliot, watching me read it like a child spilling a secret.

Good luck today! I know you'll kill it. I can't wait to celebrate tonight. E

"Two nights in a row? That constitutes a major commitment for you."

She snatches the phone back. "What did Olivia say about him?"

"All the girls have a crush on him. To quote her, 'He's hot. Not hot-hot, but teacher-hot.'"

"I'll take it."

*

The hotel's vast dining room has the generic feel of every convention center in every city; the same chandeliers of cascading glass, the same beige geometric carpeting and windowless air that turns time into a rumor. We find seats at a white-clothed table with four men wearing sustainable sneakers and expressions of cocky self-assurance.

"I would say we have imposter syndrome, but we *are* imposters," Abby whispers as she picks a croissant from the pastry basket.

"We're entrepreneurs, not imposters. Do you think men tell the truth about their experience when they pitch projects? It's not lying; it's getting shit done."

Kevin Ratskin, the artfully stubbled CEO of Start4NY, takes to the podium in a tight, short-sleeved T-shirt that flaunts his biohacked biceps. "Welcome, founders," he begins in an incongruous high-pitched voice. "We couldn't be more excited to have you here. Today will be filled with opportunities for you to learn from each other, find mentors, and get advice." He beams with satisfaction. "Looking around the room, I see people with ideas that have potential to change how we shop, how we interact with each other, how we eat. And I see something else. I see a room with 37 percent women and 26 percent people of color!"

I see a room where 99 percent of the people are younger than me. None of the math is working in our favor.

After explaining that we've been divided into groups that will travel together until the final pitch competition at the end of the day, Kevin Ratskin encourages us to "Go forth and scale!"

*

We find seats in room 411 for our first seminar, "Market Fit and Customer Acquisition."

Renata Goodwin, a lawyer from the sponsoring firm of Harrington, Dorsey, and Bond, struts in, her high heels clacking against the floor. Everything about her is razor sharp, her precision-cut chin-length bob, her knife-tailored navy pantsuit, her delivery.

"We're here to make sure you don't just meet the bar but surpass it in the final $50,000 round," she begins. "The judges you're about to meet have been hand-selected after reviewing the videos you submitted. These people are invested in helping you succeed."

The room hushes as the judges are introduced. Gloria Prospero, a seminal leader in design thinking at the MIT Media Lab; Ira Gersten, VC soothsayer from Silicon Valley; Scott Amberson, professor of entrepreneurship at Dartmouth.

"Let's begin," Goodwin says once everyone has settled. "I'd like each group to give us four sentences. What your product is. Who your target is. Why you. Why now. Not one word more."

Two teams go before us: Unfilled, an app that connects companies dedicated to eradicating toxic landfills, and Bean There, a vegan coffee subscription service. Both are so polished it seems impossible they didn't know the prompts ahead of time.

I glance over at Abby for reassurance, but all the color has drained from her face. Her left leg is tapping uncontrollably, and her breathing is shallow. I know she's uncomfortable with public speaking. For God's sake, she sits alone sketching all day. But we can't afford to blow this.

"We've got this," I whisper.

She makes no show of hearing me.

When our names are called, I squeeze by the person next to me and am halfway to the aisle when I realize Abby is still glued to her seat.

"They're waiting," I hiss.

Abby finally pushes herself off her chair and trips over the feet of the Bean There cofounder, nearly losing her balance. Her eyes glaze over as she looks frantically around the room, a trapped animal desperate for escape.

"I can't do this," she says, her voice cracking. "I'm sorry, I can't do this."

Before I can say a word, she tears out of the room.

Chapter 11

Abby

Blackness creeps across my peripheral vision until all that's left is a pinprick of pavement. I somehow make it around the corner before crouching against a building façade, rivulets of sweat trickling down my back. I try to inhale and exhale to the count of four but can't get past two. Finally, the darkness recedes enough for me to rise warily and start walking. I don't know where I am or where to go. All I know is that I have to get away. Fast.

A trio of tourists is walking three abreast, oblivious to my attempts to skirt past them, when a hand grabs my shoulder.

"Abby. Stop."

The rich baritone echoes through every chamber.

His fingers dig deeper, refusing to let me go.

After all the years imagining what it would be like to see Scott Amberson again, praying for it, dreading it. After all the days and nights telling myself it will never happen, it's here. On his terms, his timing. Not mine.

I break free and turn to look at him. His face is coated with time, changed and unchanged. His angular cheekbones, the slope of his full upper lip, the three freckles in his gray eyes, so familiar and so jolting.

"I'm sorry, I didn't mean to scare you."

He releases his grip. His hand hovers as if to stroke my face, then drops.

"Why are you here?" I manage to get out.

"I've been a judge at Start4NY events since they began." He looks down the street, then back to me. "When I watched the video you sent in, I knew I had to see you."

I cyberstalked Scott for years. I saw his son holding up a handmade sign on his first day of kindergarten. I saw his daughter's christening. I knew when a white paper he coauthored was quoted in *The Washington Post*. I knew when he got tenure. Every picture ripped the scab off the wound anew until I forced myself to stop looking. It took far longer than it should have, but it was the only way to heal.

"You could have found me anytime," I tell him.

It's a question, really. *Why didn't you find me? Why didn't you want me?*

"I didn't think you'd want to see me." He cocks his head to the side, his voice hesitant. "Would you have?"

"What happened is ancient history, Scott."

It's been seventeen years. I was someone else then. Young, trusting. I can never be that person again.

"I thought it was ancient history, but now I'm not so sure."

"What do you mean?"

"You mentioned you have a daughter in your bio."

The blackness seeps back, millimeter by millimeter, narrowing my vision.

"What about her?"

"You tell me." His hesitancy is gone, replaced by a cold steeliness.

The ground beneath me begins to melt.

Scott grasps me before my knees buckle and guides me to a bench in the tiny pocket park a few yards away.

*

We sit staring out at the cobblestone street, a relic from long ago when the narrow tip of Manhattan was a busy port. A pigeon skitters up looking for breadcrumbs, then scampers away.

I study him more closely. His face has softened, his dark-chocolate-brown hair is shorter but still mussed, as if each strand is an offshoot of a mind that holds too much to be contained.

"What do you want, Scott?" I ask when my pulse begins to slow.

"I've been doing the math. Maybe I'm wrong about your daughter, but is that what you wanted to tell me when you came up to Hanover?"

I've relived that day so many times. The nausea that rocked through me during the five hours on the coach bus to New Hampshire. All around me students lost in textbooks, not much younger than me. Carrying those early weeks of pregnancy like a gift. Rehearsing the words over and over. Changing them, amending them. Here, this is yours, ours. This is the future.

"You mean that time I came up and found you with your wife and kids?" The fury as fresh now as on that day.

Stepping off the bus on that early spring afternoon in front of the arched façade of Dartmouth's Hopkins Arts Center, his address in hand. Walking a quarter mile past the verdant New England lawns until I came to a white clapboard house and stopped a few feet from the front yard to find Scott pushing a baby in a yellow swing set, a toddler by his side. His wife, kissing him. Both of them laughing.

"You knew I was married," he reminds me, his tone lost in the no-man's-land between defensive and offense.

"You told me you were leaving her."

"I never said that," he insists.

"Didn't you?" Maybe not precisely, but close enough.

"I'd broken it off between the two of us, Abby," he says flatly. As if it was that simple, that clean.

"You told me you needed to think things through. You didn't tell me you were going back to your wife."

He sinks back. "I didn't know what I was going to do. I'm sorry you found out that way. If I could change what happened, I would."

"Which part would you change, Scott? Being with me in New York? Telling me you loved me?" The pain, after all this time, is still tinged with outrage.

"All of it." There is something shattered in his voice.

He runs his fingers through his hair. How many times did I watch him do exactly that when he was thinking through a problem, when we were lying in bed after making love? Once, I separated his fingers and kissed each fingertip. I was twenty-two, new to love, every moment a revelation.

"That's not very convincing."

"You knew I was a visiting professor and had to go back to Hanover."

"You left out some important details. Like the fact you weren't only going back to your teaching position, you were going back to your family."

"You weren't exactly innocent in the situation," he reminds me.

I weighed the degrees of guilt for years, the scales forever teetering. "Were you ever going to leave her, or was everything a lie?"

"Not everything. I did love you," he says quietly.

I shouldn't feel such relief at hearing that now. It shouldn't change anything.

"I thought your time in New York was a trial separation. I thought you would choose me, but that was never really an option, was it?"

"I loved you, *and* I had responsibilities. Both things were true. What about my question?" he asks. "Is she my daughter?"

"Would it matter?"

"Of course it would matter." His anger is palpable now, every word pointed. "If I have a child, a part of me, wandering the earth, I have a right to know."

"You forfeited that right."

"There's no excuse for what I did. That doesn't mean I forfeited the right to something I didn't know existed."

"*Someone*, not something."

"Were you pregnant that day you came up to Hanover?"

I will myself not to cry in front of him.

Scott, his abject terror evident from across the street, saying something to his wife I couldn't hear. Running over to me, hurrying me into his car, and driving up into the lush mountains that ring Hanover. A child's car seat in the back, its blue plaid covering beginning to pill. The scent of spilled apple juice and another woman's vanilla perfume making me sick.

"You literally drove me away."

"I'd ended our relationship, and you showed up with no warning. What did you expect?" he asks, frustration burning.

"I didn't expect to find myself in your car listening to you beg me not to ruin your life."

Sitting next to him in that stifling Subaru, the windows closed, as he drove me back to town, until I thought I would explode, pieces of me splattering the seat, the dashboard, him. Insisting he pull over, walking the rest of the way, sitting on the rough stone bench in front of the arts center, waiting for the only bus that afternoon to take me back to the city.

"I could have ruined everything for you, and I didn't," I tell him.

"I know." He looks down, shaking his head, and then slowly turns to me. "Maybe things would have been different if I'd known the truth. Were you ever going to tell me?"

I thought about it, a million times, a million ways. How I might do it, when. Each day, each year that passed made it less possible.

"You've been lying to me this entire time," he says angrily. "Maybe it's a lie of omission, but it's still a goddamned lie. Who does your daughter think her father is?"

"I told Rachel I never really knew him, that he was some random guy from a vacation fling. Which turned out to be true."

He flinches. I'm gratified that I have the ability to hurt him.

"What do you mean?"

"I was your New York fling. It was always going to be temporary for you, outside of your actual life. You were playing by vacation rules, but it was real for me. I loved you." I turn to look at him fully. "Did you think of me at all, or was I just a bullet you dodged?"

The question has woven through the years when I see pieces of Scott in Rachel, the arch of her eyebrows, the way her feet turn out slightly when she walks, her reserved temperament so different from my own. He was never really gone.

"You were more than a fling to me, Abby."

"What was I?"

"The right person at the wrong time."

"How long have you been rehearsing that line?"

"Years, but that doesn't mean it isn't true. I'm not sure I'd ever really been in love before I met you. I messed up. That doesn't make what you did right. When did you decide to have the baby without telling me?"

All those days and nights alone in my apartment back in New York, making an appointment, not showing up, wanting him, hating him, finally wanting only the baby.

"I never really decided."

"At some point you made a decision to have the baby, and at some point you decided not to tell me."

"When I found out you were still with your wife, it destroyed something in me. I kept waiting to figure out what to do, and then it was too late. Maybe I didn't tell you because I didn't want to hear what you would say. You didn't want me; you certainly wouldn't want me and a baby." I look at him closely. "What would you have done if I had told you?"

"I don't know," he admits. "Why didn't you tell me later, in the years since then?"

All the pictures I keep in an unmarked file on my computer, Rachel's first birthday, smears of chocolate icing across her chubby cheeks, Rachel at three, laughing in a pile of fall leaves, Rachel graduating from nursery school with a mortar and tassel falling across her face. Rachel with braces, refusing to smile for an entire year, so uncomfortable in her own skin. I never pressed send.

"You told me you couldn't destroy your family."

"I managed to do that all on my own. That life, my marriage, is over. We divorced two years ago."

"Is that what this is about, Scott, some midlife crisis? A tour of what you missed out on?"

"No. Maybe." He pauses. "Every time I've come to New York, part of me was scared of running into you, and part of me was longing to. Once, I looked up your address and walked by your building for two straight days, hoping to see you. I want to meet her," he says firmly. "I want to meet my daughter."

"That's not going to happen." I can't upend everything Rachel believes in. Who she thinks she is, who she thinks *I* am. A life built on quicksand.

"I'm her father."

"She doesn't have a father."

"You never gave me a chance, Abby. You can't blame me for not helping when I didn't know the situation."

"You're asking me to tell her I've been lying to her for her entire life. She'll never forgive me."

"I don't want to hurt her, or you. I only want to know who she is." He reaches into his coat pocket and hands me his card. "I'm here through next week."

He puts the card in my palm, closing his fingers in a grip too tight for comfort.

Chapter 12

Kara

Peter emerges from the kitchen, a dish towel on his shoulder, when he hears me come in. "You're home early. How'd it go?"

"It was a disaster."

"I'm sure you're overreacting."

"We didn't even make it to lunch, much less the final round. Abby bolted from the room before our first chance to pitch. I knew she didn't really believe in the app, but I never thought she would purposefully tank it."

"Maybe she had stage fright."

"I don't care if she had the stomach bug from hell. Who does that?" I turn to glare at him. "Are you happy now?"

"What do you mean?"

"You never believed in Jyst either."

"That's not true. I'm proud of you. You gave it your best shot."

"You're talking like it's over."

"You told me it's over," he replies, baffled. "I don't know what you want me to say."

I don't know what I want him to say either.

*

We spend the rest of the afternoon avoiding each other. After a desultory dinner, more liquid than solid on my end, the girls vanish to their rooms to sulk, Maya because no one asked her to a sleepover posted all over Instagram, Olivia for reasons she refuses to explain.

Peter comes to sit beside me in the living room.

"I do want you to succeed. I'm sorry if it doesn't always feel that way," he says gently.

"I don't want to talk about it right now. I need some time to ruminate on my many failures."

"That sounds like a healthy plan."

He tries without success to get a smile out of me and, failing, beats a hasty retreat, leaving me to dwell in the darkest pit. The one where I'll be fired. Where Peter divorces me for lying to him about the money I've been using for Jyst. Where the girls self-destruct each in her own inexorable way.

When my phone rings, I flip it over to see Abby's name. I'll have to speak to her at some point. This is not that point.

Thirty seconds later, she texts. I'm downstairs. Can we talk?

There were so many ways Abby could have told me she wanted out. To do it in front of people who could have provided a lifeline is unforgivable. Still, when the white ball starts dancing again, I can't bring myself to ignore it.

You have every right to be mad but I can explain. Please.

I force myself up and get my coat.

*

Abby is skulking in the shadows, her eyes rheumy and red.

"I'm sorry," she stammers.

She looks so distraught that my anger begins to dissipate, leaving behind a bone-deep weariness. I lean against the building and watch two impossibly leggy girls climb into an Uber.

"I need your help. You're the only person I can turn to," she pleads, tears streaming down her face. "I can't do what he's asking."

"What are you talking about?"

She looks at me through watery eyes. "Scott Amberson."

"Who?"

"The judge from Dartmouth."

"What about him?"

"I know him. Knew him."

My indignation returns. "You let some ex-boyfriend ruin today?"

"It's more than that."

"I'm exhausted, Abby. I can't deal with your romantic drama tonight."

"Scott Amberson is Rachel's father."

I swivel to face her, scraping my hand on the building's façade. "Are you sure?"

"It wasn't a one-night stand. Scott was someone I loved. Or thought I did."

"I don't understand. You said you didn't know his last name, that you couldn't find him."

"I'm sorry."

I take a deep breath. "Does Rachel know?"

"No."

"Well, the guy is an asshole for deserting his daughter."

"He didn't know about her. Can we go someplace to talk? Please, Kara."

*

We don't speak until we settle on a bench in Riverside Park.

Staring out at the gray ripples of the Hudson River, the patchy skyline of New Jersey in the distance, I turn each puzzle piece over, trying to snap them into place, but they're too slippery.

"All these years you told me you didn't know who Rachel's father was, that he was a random one-night stand. Why would you do that?"

"If it makes any difference, you're the only person I wish I'd told from the beginning."

I'm not sure if it makes a difference or not.

"How did you know him?"

"He was spending a semester in New York as a visiting professor. We met at a party right after I graduated. He was so different from the college boys I knew, smart and confident, a grown-up. Our chemistry was through the roof. We went back to the loft he was subletting that night, and we were together every day after that. We were a real couple, Kara. We rented a convertible and went to the North Fork. He took me to plays I couldn't afford to go to. We dressed up and went to the ballet. He believed in my art when no one else did. My parents had recently died. I didn't know what I was doing with my life. I thought he was the answer to everything I wanted." Abby hunches over, bracing herself against the wind. "He told me he was going to leave his wife."

"Wait, what? He was married?"

"Sort of."

"There is no such thing as 'sort of' married."

"I thought they were going through a trial separation."

"A married man away from home tells you he's going through a trial separation, and you believed him?"

"I was twenty-two. Didn't you ever make a mistake at that age?"

"There's a difference between a single mistake and a lie you tell every day for years."

"I didn't plan that. I was so young when I got pregnant. I was losing my mind, spending every day and night alone with an infant. I signed up for a 'baby and me' group when Rachel was six months old. I was ashamed to explain the situation to a group of married women, so I made up a story. Two of the mothers ended up sending their kids to Dearborn." She shakes her head. "By the time you and I got closer, it was baked in. It's like elevator people. You know, the people you talk to in the elevator in your building? You watch their children grow up, and you talk about your families, and years go by and it's too late to admit you don't remember their names, so you simply go on that way. Even if I wanted to tell anyone, I was scared it would get back to Rachel."

"We're not elevator people, Abby. We were best friends. At least I thought we were."

"We *are* best friends."

All the times I watched Abby curl around herself, not letting others get close—men, me—begin to make sense.

"How did it end?"

"The night before he left for New Hampshire, we went to the Carlyle Hotel. We got drunk on vodka martinis and had the best sex we'd ever had. Two days later, I got an email from him breaking it off. He told me he needed time and space to think. He neglected to mention that included going back to his wife."

"Never trust a man who says he needs space."

She smiles, stops smiling. "I'm pretty sure that's the night I got pregnant. When I went up to Hanover to tell him, I found him in his front yard with his wife and kids, definitely *not* separated."

"You didn't tell him you were pregnant?"

"I was too shell-shocked. He ran after me and tried to explain, but what explanation is there? I never spoke to him again, until today."

"Don't take this the wrong way, but why did you decide to have the baby?"

"I thought about having an abortion, but I couldn't go through with it. Maybe I wanted to hold on to a piece of him. Then after Rachel was born, she became my whole world."

"You realize what you're telling me is every married woman's worst nightmare?"

She sighs. "I know."

"Do you regret it?"

"Having the baby or not telling him?"

"Both."

"How could I regret having Rachel? She's the best thing that ever happened to me. I can't imagine my life without her."

Abby's phone rings. We wait while it goes to voicemail.

"Now he shows up one day, out of the blue? What does he want?"

"To meet Rachel." She turns to me. "What do I do?"

"You have to tell her."

"How? She'll hate me."

"She deserves to know. She must have been imagining who her father is all these years. Were you ever going to tell her?"

"I thought it would be worse for her to know she had a father who rejected her than no father at all."

"He didn't reject her. He didn't know about her. He rejected you."

"True."

"How did it feel to see him again?"

"Strange. In some ways, even after all this time, he's more familiar to me than anyone has ever been. I didn't think I would ever feel that way again." She shakes her head. "This sounds crazy considering how little time it's been, but the only person I've felt even the possibility of that with is Eliot. If I tell him the truth, I'll ruin that too."

"You don't know that."

"His ex-wife cheated on him. I don't think it's a pattern he cares to repeat."

"At least give him a chance."

Abby considers this. "He's divorced now."

"Eliot?"

"No, Scott."

I study her, a stranger disguised as someone I thought I knew. "I thought you were coming here to tell me you wanted out of Jyst."

"I've always believed in it. Maybe if I had a way to ask for advice back then, I would have made better decisions."

Another thing she never told me.

"I'm not sure how much longer we can hang on." I knit my fingers together. "I feel like I'm failing at everything. Work. My kids. My marriage."

"What are you talking about?"

"We've been seeing a therapist," I admit. "Peter and I are off-course, and I can't seem to put my finger on why. Olivia stays up half the night talking in code to some boy who she seems to have a secret meeting place with. Why does she need a secret meeting place? Maya walks around taking notes like some pint-sized detective collecting evidence. It's all spinning out of my control."

"We were idiots to think we could ever control our kids to begin with."

"I thought I'd have at least a modicum of influence."

Abby rests her head on my shoulder. "Can we start fresh? Not fresh, I know that's not possible, but somewhere along the way, I thought we made a deal to go through everything together. Is that over?"

"It's not over. But it's different."

The dank wind picks up, making us both shiver.

"We should go."

She nods but doesn't move. "I'm terrified of losing Rachel forever."

"She'll still love you."

"Will she?"

"Definitely not at first, but eventually. After tens of thousands of dollars of therapy."

Abby laughs. "Thanks. That's very reassuring."

"That's my job."

"I still need you," she says quietly.

"I need you, too, but I also need time. This is a lot to wrap my head around."

"What are we talking, twenty-four hours? Forty-eight?"

I smile. "I'm freezing, and you need to go home to Rachel before Scott finds her and tells her himself."

Chapter 13

Abby

The Uber makes its way through the flashing lights of Times Square, the deserted streets of midtown, the ragtag demonstrations in Union Square. It's over three miles from Kara's apartment to mine. Not far enough.

*

Rachel's questions about her father have changed over the years. When she was five and still piecing together the mechanics of how babies are made, she turned to me in a crowded elevator and asked, "But didn't I need a father?"

The answer—yes and no—tangled us both up in knots.

When she was in elementary school, she wrote *none* on school forms that asked for her father's name. It was only when she was hovering on the brink of adolescence that I told her I got pregnant on a Caribbean island from a one-night stand with a nameless guy who was gone by dawn. Admittedly, not a great example for a girl heading into the storms of puberty, but it seemed preferable to telling her, *I had an affair with a married man who I never told about you.* When she was old enough to ask if I considered an abortion, I assured her, I'm pro-choice, but I chose *you*. I may have made a mistake, but *you* are not a mistake.

Rachel wrapped herself in the strands I gave her, knit her story together.

To unknot it all is inconceivable.

*

It's almost ten o'clock when I get home. I have no idea what I'll say when I knock softly on her door.

There's no answer.

I trace her phone to the Upper West Side in the vicinity of Hannah's house. It's only when I send her a text reminding her of curfew—something I've never had to do before—that I see three messages from Eliot, asking how the accelerator went, asking if I still want to get together tonight, asking if I'm okay.

*

EDM blares from across the hall where three grad students live in a one-bedroom apartment. Someone else's party, someone else's night. Lights from the building across the street flick off one by one.

My foot has fallen asleep from sitting cross-legged for too long when I finally get up, turn on my bedside lamp, and pull the small, tapestried ottoman over to my closet. Balancing on tiptoes, I reach for a cardboard box behind a row of bags and open the lid, carefully sliding out a sheet of creamy sketch paper.

I climb down and sit with it on my lap, running my fingers along the pencil strokes of the sketch I did of Scott while he slept all those years ago in his loft. The feathery lines of his hair against the pillow, his right forearm resting above the blanket. It was right before dawn. Soon, he would wake up and make us coffee in his French press. Soon, he would take the chipped mug from my hand and lead me back to bed. Soon, he would leave.

*

Rachel stumbles into the kitchen in sweatpants and a faded Forest Valley T-shirt to grab a raspberry yogurt for breakfast. She leaves the goopy lid face-down on the counter and walks away.

"Can we talk?" I ask, following her into the living room where she's settled on the couch.

"I'm sorry I didn't tell you I was going to Hannah's. It was a last-minute thing," she answers without looking up from her phone.

"Rachel, can you put that down?"

She looks at me crossly but reluctantly acquiesces. "What?"

"There's something I should have told you years ago, but you were too young," I begin. "I hope you're old enough to understand it now."

"Understand what?" She takes a spoonful of yogurt, wary but not fully engaged. There's a good chance that whatever I have to say will be something only a mother would deem important.

"It's about your father."

"I don't have a father," Rachel replies cooly as she begins to gnaw at a hangnail.

"Actually, you do." I rest my hand on her knee, but she pushes it away. "Your father wasn't a one-night stand. He was someone I had a relationship with."

I know Rachel's face in the deepest part of my soul, the way she squints in the sun to stifle a sneeze, the obstinate expression that masks vulnerability. Her eyes narrow in a look of alarm I've never seen.

"I don't understand. You told me you tried to find him and you couldn't."

"That's not entirely what happened."

"You know his name?"

"Yes. Rachel, I . . ."

I try once more to reach over, connect with her, but she shoves me away.

"Don't touch me!" And then, "Who is he? Who is my father?"

"He was someone I cared about, very much. We were in a relationship. I thought he and his wife had separated. I was wrong. I made a terrible mistake."

"Is that why he never wanted to know me, because he was married?" Rachel's pain pierces us both.

I take a deep breath. "He didn't know about you."

"How could he not know about me?"

"We'd already broken up by the time I found out I was pregnant."

"You didn't tell him about me? Like, ever?"

"Please, try to understand. He was married, and . . ."

She rears back. "What's wrong with you? Maybe he would have wanted to know me."

"You're right."

"What about me? Didn't you think I had a right to know? I could have had a father," she exclaims, furious.

"I love you, Rachel. I thought I was doing what was best."

"Best for you, not me. Do you know how much time I've spent imagining what he looks like and wondering if I'm like him? You told me there were no pictures, but you must have had pictures. You gave me nothing."

"I gave you everything I have."

"I always knew I was a mistake, but I was worse than that. I was a secret. You were ashamed of me."

"Oh, sweetie, I was never ashamed of you. I was ashamed of myself."

"What's his name?"

"Scott."

"Scott what?"

"Scott Amberson."

A new thought dawns on her. "Why are you telling me this now?"

"He knows about you and wants to meet you."

"You told him?"

"He found out."

"Were you going to keep lying to me forever? My entire life?"

I pull his card from my pocket. "Here's his number. He's waiting for you to call him."

Rachel grabs it, her hands shaking as she studies the name and digits, a road map to something she thought was lost forever.

When she looks up, she's teeming with revulsion. "I don't know who you are or why you did this, but you know what? You have no idea who I really am either. You never have."

She runs from the room and slams her door, clicking the lock into place.

Chapter 14

Hollis

Ten days before the murder
Tuesday, September 30

There are so many places to get lost in New York, the zigzag streets of the West Village, the far reaches of Brooklyn, but so few places to be alone. In a city precision engineered to perpetuate loneliness, it can be hard to go unseen.

At exactly one fifteen this past Sunday, I called Adam as per our agreement.

"You broke your word," he told me angrily.

"Dr. Akoris wouldn't budge. She agreed to a family meeting to hear our case next Saturday. That gives us time to come up with a plan."

"I *have* a plan. It's to take her home."

"I'm doing everything I can, Adam."

"I assume your lack of results means you still haven't told your husband," he retorts. "What about your precious son?"

"Leave my family out of this," I warn.

"I'm not sure that's going to be possible."

*

The threat is the riptide beneath every conversation, every check I've sent, every surreptitious visit.

Five weeks before we were due to get married, I took Jordan to meet my mother and Adam.

I told him my mother had early-onset dementia. It seemed less tainted than schizophrenia, less hereditary risk to his bloodline likely to deter him from the one thing I wanted most, a family of my own.

She was fogged by drugs but calm as we sat at the linoleum kitchen table eating oatmeal cookies. I'd gone up ahead to scrub, but no amount of cleaning could get rid of the smell of grease lodged in the walls. My mother smiled vaguely but was largely oblivious to our presence. Adam, suspicious of the outside world and convinced any success can only be achieved through malevolent means, took an instant dislike to Jordan. Sitting in the small kitchen, the evidence of hoarding barely hidden, was the only time I've ever seen Jordan ill at ease. He was relieved when all I asked was that we pay for her care.

I did him a favor, really. I spared him from waking up every morning wondering if this would be the day your world implodes.

When Daniel began banging his head against the wall as a toddler, I went to a child psychologist who told me it was something to keep an eye on, but it was too early to tell if it was a portent of schizophrenia. When he grew moody and withdrawn for no apparent reason, I was assured by experts that all preteens exhibit similar behavior. But the signs have thickened over the past two years into angry outbursts, unpredictable flare-ups. Violence.

I no longer ask questions.

I don't want to hear the answers.

*

Jordan was getting ready to leave when I got home that afternoon.

"How was barre?" he asked as I put my gym bag down. The possessiveness he demonstrated early in our marriage when he needed to know where I was every minute has dwindled into indifference. He's easily satisfied.

"It was great. The studio is holding a retreat next weekend in the Hamptons, and I thought I'd go. Daniel will be on the class retreat to Forest Valley, so you won't have to worry about him."

"We need to talk about that. If you're still so set on him going, you need to get that teacher to come over here first."

"Why?"

"We both know what can happen on these sorts of outings, and we both know what Daniel is capable of. That woman is our insurance policy if anything goes wrong."

*

Jordan comes home early on Tuesday and rises from the couch as soon as Miss Cleary emerges from Daniel's room. She stops abruptly when she sees him, flustered by his unexpected presence.

"You must be Miss Cleary," he says, taking a step forward. "I'm Jordan Chapman, Daniel's father. I hope you know how appreciative we are of the work you're doing here."

"I'm happy to do whatever I can." Miss Cleary shifts her weight nervously from one foot to the other. Jordan has that effect on people. "Daniel is a talented young man."

"As I'm sure my wife made clear, any guidance you can provide to help Daniel successfully navigate Dearborn will not go unnoticed by us. If there are any issues, we'd like to know about them first," he continues.

"Daniel is doing well academically."

"I'm referring to issues outside the classroom. I understand you'll be leading the camping trip the class is going on. We'd like you to keep an eye on Daniel."

Her pale eyebrows furrow. "We take the supervision of all our children seriously."

"Of course," Jordan replies dismissively. "A *special* eye, if you will. We realize you're bending the rules by working with Daniel. I can assure you that you have nothing to worry about on our end. I've been talking with Jerome Nederlander about joining the board of trustees. While I would never mention our little arrangement, I'm sure I can find other ways to let him know how highly we regard you."

Miss Cleary, who didn't look worried before, begins to look extremely worried.

"I appreciate that," she mumbles.

"I'm glad we understand each other. We'll email the permission slip first thing in the morning."

*

"Was that really necessary?" I ask Jordan after locking the door.

"I'm all too aware of Daniel's proclivities even if you prefer to turn a blind eye."

"You realize I can hear everything you're saying?"

We turn to see Daniel scowling at us from the hall.

Jordan is unfazed. "Good. I prefer you don't go on this trip, but your mother feels otherwise. The point is, there can be no incidents. Not even the hint of one. I'm done covering up for you. Do you understand?"

Daniel swallows hard. "That goes both ways," he mutters.

I look from one to the other. "What does that mean?"

Neither answers.

"We have nothing further to discuss." Jordan turns his back on his son. "Send that woman double, whatever her fee, and I'll take care of the matter with those mothers."

Chapter 15

Kara

Eight days before the murder
Thursday, October 2

Olivia and Maya are at the table passing the tortellini while Peter tries valiantly to pry information about their day out of them. The girls mumble half-responses as if they're actors in a family dinner scene and can't quite remember their lines. Trying to make small talk at dinner with teenagers is a uniquely humbling exercise.

"I have some good news to share," I announce, taking a seat.

The girls glance at me with decidedly low expectations.

"We may have found an investor for Jyst."

"That's fantastic," Peter exclaims with far too much enthusiasm. He's been walking on eggshells since his misguided attempt to comfort me Saturday night. "Who is it?"

"Jordan Chapman."

"Daniel's father?" Olivia looks up, alarmed. "How do you know him?"

"I know his mother. She agreed to show it to him. She called to say he's interested."

"Why would he be interested in your app?" she asks skeptically.

"It's not beyond the realm of possibility that he thinks it has potential."

"You know Olivia is hooking up with Daniel Chapman, right?" Maya interjects, thrilled to be the agent of important news.

"Shut up," Olivia snaps.

"Can you define hooking up?" Peter asks.

This is met with universal eye rolls.

"You know he's seeing Amanda too?" Maya taunts. "Like, everyone has seen them together."

"You don't know what you're talking about. Daniel and I are exclusive," Olivia snaps.

"You might want to check with him about that," Maya retorts. Her lower lip quivers despite the show of bravado. Standing up to her older sister is not an easy task.

The girls retreat into stone-faced silence, and Peter turns to me. "Do you really think it's a good idea to take money from the father of someone Olivia is dating?"

"Yes. As a matter of fact, I do."

*

Maya follows me into the kitchen, piling dishes in the sink without bothering to remove the soggy napkins. "Don't forget about the bake sale tomorrow," she reminds me.

"What bake sale?"

"For the service trip to Guatemala. You promised you'd bake cupcakes. I told you about it four days ago."

I scour the recesses of my brain, looking for where that particular tidbit might have gotten lodged, but find no trace of it.

"You didn't you sign up for a trip to Guatemala, did you?" I ask, only half-joking. There are so many permission slips, could I have signed that one by mistake? Like privacy notices on websites, my default mode is to agree without reading the fine print. I make a mental note to make sure I signed the one for Forest Valley.

"Mo-om."

"I'll take that as a no."

"The bake sale is to help kids who can't pay to go on the trip. Not everyone can afford what we can afford," Maya tells me self-righteously.

"Honey, *we* can't afford what we afford."

She stares at me and walks away.

*

The girls are sequestered in their bedrooms, and Peter is in the living room scrolling his phone when I begin to bake with only Nomi for company.

While the cupcakes are in the oven, I log on to Hinge, where I am Ellie234, and scan texts from men I will never meet. It's merely research, but it's gratifying to know that I—or at least my younger, thinner, island-hopping, yoga-loving avatar—can still elicit a shred of male interest. After swiping for a few minutes, I open Jyst and begin to type.

> Q. My bff has been lying to me for years. I love her but how can I ever trust her again?

I read the entry twice before deleting it. I'm not sure I want an answer.

*

By the time the cupcakes are out of the oven, Jordan Chapman has sent Abby and me a partnership agreement that he claims is necessary before he makes an investment. I don't fully understand the fine print, but for the first time since the accelerator, I feel a flicker of hope.

It lasts less than twenty-four hours.

Olivia races to greet me when I get home from work the next day.

"You need to talk to Maya," she informs me.

"About what?" I ask, sinking beneath the gravitational pull of home.

"You'll see." She smirks and follows me down the hall, hovering as I knock on Maya's door. "Hon?"

Maya swings the door open.

"Is everything okay?"

She glares at me with disgust. "There was cat food in the cupcakes."

"What?"

"There were pieces of dried cat food in the icing."

"That's ridiculous."

"It is not ridiculous. It happened."

I lean against the door, thinking back to baking last night. Some of Nomi's food must have gotten on the knife I used for icing when I put it on the counter.

"In all of them?" My concern is more performative than genuine.

"Only three, but that's not the point. One of the kids called Miss Cleary over, and she threw the whole bunch out. In front of *everyone*."

"I'm sorry, but you have to admit, it's a little bit funny."

"What's wrong with you? You poisoned the cupcakes!"

"Feline Delight isn't exactly poison. "

Maya slams the door in my face while Olivia, happier than I've seen her in weeks, smirks.

Chapter 16

Abby

Seven days before the murder
Friday, October 3

Every time I walk into a room, Rachel walks out of it. For the past thirty-six hours, she's refused to eat with me, speak to me, or acknowledge my existence. The only reason I know she's about to meet her father for the first time is that he called to tell me.

"I've never been so nervous about a dinner in my life," Scott said. "Is there anything I should know?"

"Right now, the only salient fact is that she hates me. Please, don't make it worse."

When Rachel emerges from her room after her third outfit change, I get my coat to leave.

"Where do you think you're going?" she asks suspiciously.

"I'll drop you off at the restaurant."

"I don't need an escort."

"You don't know what he looks like."

"There are a gazillion pictures of him online. There's even a video of him giving a lecture. I have a half sister and brother," she spits out. "Do they know about me?"

"I'm not sure," I admit.

Despite her fervent wish that I vanish off the face of the earth, I follow her out the front door.

Rachel maintains a solid three-foot distance as we walk to the Thai restaurant near NYU, pulling anxiously at the edges of her black bandage skirt. Her thin doe legs are stippled with faint blue veins, and the knobs of her knees jut out precariously. When she was younger, she had a tendency to crumble to the ground without warning, her limbs too spindly to support her. Her gym teacher called her a "folder."

Scott is sitting at a table by the window, glancing from his phone to the door.

"That's him," I tell Rachel.

"I know," she snaps, and walks into the restaurant without saying goodbye.

I watch through the glass as she makes her way to Scott's table. Watch him rise to meet her. Watch them sit down and speak words I can't hear. The man who splintered my heart and the child who resurrected it.

*

I head west, past the deli where I bought Rachel raspberry Chupa Chup lollipops when she was little, past the ice cream shop where they remember her aversion to sprinkles, all of our private rituals now rendered to a past suddenly open to reinterpretation.

In a daze, I almost miss the entryway to the café where Eliot agreed to meet me.

It takes a minute to adjust to the dim light as I peer down the hammered copper bar. Eliot is nowhere in sight.

The bartender, a beefy man with Celtic tattoos ringing his neck, motions to a barstool. I hesitate, uncertain of the etiquette of meeting someone who doesn't drink, and find an empty table instead. The lime ginger mocktail I order does nothing to quell the anxiety churning within. About my daughter having dinner five blocks away with a stranger who happens to be her father. About what I have to tell Eliot. About losing him before we've begun.

I'm halfway through the "drink" when Eliot hurries in.

"Sorry I'm late." He pecks me on the cheek. A demotion kiss but better than none at all. "I got hung up at yet another meeting."

"I'm glad you're here."

"Did you think I wouldn't come?"

"It crossed my mind." I wait until he settles across from me. "I'm sorry I went AWOL on you the other day. I'm not usually like that."

"We haven't known each other long enough for there to be a 'usually.' I'll have to take your word for it. I understand you're caught up in starting a business, but we're too old to play games, Abby. At least I am."

"I should have called. It was just a really bad day."

"What happened?"

Whatever the price might be for telling Eliot about Scott, it will only get harder if I wait.

"It didn't exactly go according to plan."

"It couldn't have been that bad."

"It was. *I* was."

"I'm sure you're exaggerating. Did you spill coffee on a judge? Bitch-slap another contestant?"

"That would require some degree of action. I completely froze."

"I'm surprised. You seem so confident."

"Do I?"

"If not, you do a good job of faking it. Was it nerves?"

"Something like that."

"I see some of the smartest kids turn to stone when they have to speak in front of the class. That doesn't mean I flunk them. I've found very few things in life are irreparable."

I wish that were true. "I won't bore you with the details," I tell him.

"Next time I hope you feel you can turn to me if you're upset about something."

"I will. I really am sorry."

"Apology accepted. Let's chalk it up to growing pains." He smiles and leans across the table to kiss me. A real kiss this time.

The dual soundtrack clanging in my head—what's happening five blocks away, what's happening here—fades. There's only this, his lips on mine.

"What was the meeting that kept you away from me?" I ask when we separate.

Eliot shakes head in mock dismay. "Rita Cleary wanted to talk to me for the umpteenth time about the Forest Valley trip. She's trying to deputize me into some kind of 'us against the kids' battalion."

"So much for trust-building, though that does sound totally on brand for her."

"There's a fine line between precaution and paranoia that Rita has a tendency to skirt. But she has a point. Animals taken out of their natural habitat do have a tendency to turn on each other." He smiles. "Not that I'm calling the kids animals."

I laugh. "Of course not, but you are sounding very *Lord of the Flies*."

"Hopefully no one will die in this iteration." He shakes his head. "Some of the parents haven't sent in their permission slips because they have 'concerns about safety' after the video from last year."

"They're worried that there's more the school isn't telling us about what happened."

"There usually is. Rita told me they found drugs stuffed into one kid's teddy bear last year and vodka in mini shampoo bottles. Her latest plan is to confiscate the kids' phones before they board the bus and hold them until we get back. The official line is they want the kids to be fully present, but it's really to avoid any recorded evidence if something goes wrong,"

"I can't imagine that will go over well."

"The parents are even more upset about it than the kids. The idea that they might be out of touch for even an hour sends them into panic mode."

I force myself to laugh, unwilling to admit that I, too, find the idea unsettling.

"Maybe it's because I come from boarding schools where kids and parents are used to being separated, but it seems completely alarmist. You'll have to explain it to me over dinner."

I hesitate, feeling the tug of a different cord.

"I wish I could. Rachel went out, and I want to be there when she gets home."

"Abby, I don't want to overstep, and I realize I'm not a parent, but Rachel is sixteen. She's a young woman, not a toddler. I get that you have a lot going on, and if you don't have time for a relationship I understand, but this would be a good time to tell me."

"It's not that, it's . . ."

I bite my lower lip, unable to find the words.

"I can't figure you out," he says. "Are you playing hard to get, actually hard to get, or impossible to get? I like you. I'd like to get to know you better, but only if that's what you want too."

"I do."

"Good." He nods. "This doesn't count, by the way."

"What do you mean?"

"Your two-night rule. This is only half a night. How about I cook you dinner before the trip?"

"You cook?"

"I have many hidden talents."

"Good to know."

"Can I take that as a yes?"

"Absolutely."

I leave without telling him the one thing I came to say.

*

I hear their voices as soon as I open the front door and hurry back to find Scott sitting on the bed beside Rachel.

"What are you doing here?" I ask.

"Rachel was showing me her yearbooks."

"I wish you'd let me know."

"We don't need your permission," Rachel retorts.

Scott pats her thigh lightly. "Why don't you let me talk to your mother for a minute?" He turns to me. "I could use a cup of coffee."

He follows me into the kitchen.

"I didn't mean to startle you."

"You can't do this."

"Do what?"

"Insert yourself into our lives and then disappear."

"I don't have to be in your life if you don't want me to be, but I am going to be in Rachel's life," he states firmly.

"You can't be in her life and not be in mine."

"I know that."

"What did you say about me?"

"Whatever we did or didn't do, that's on us. It has nothing to do with Rachel."

"You didn't blame me?"

"You and I still have a lot to talk about, but there are no villains here, only idiots."

"Rachel thinks I'm both."

"My kids have thought I was an idiot since they learned to speak." He stops short. "It's weird. When I say 'my kids,' it means something totally different now. At some point, I want to hear what the past years have been like for you and for Rachel. I missed so much."

"Part of me has always blamed you for not being here," I admit.

"That's not fair."

Fair got lost in the equation years ago.

"How do you see this working?" I ask.

"I don't know. We'll figure it out together. I asked someone to take over my classes for the next two weeks. Why don't the two of us have dinner and start trying to sort this out? For now, all I want is to go back and get to know my daughter."

Chapter 17

Kara

Four days before the murder
Monday, October 6

When the receptionist, Gayle, buzzes at two in the afternoon on Monday, my stomach goes into free fall, convinced it's a summons from Ursula, the grim reaper from HR. Every morning, on the jammed C train, I wonder if today is the day I am made "redundant" or whatever word they use to fire me without risking a lawsuit. Every evening, I allow myself a tick of relief before the worry wriggles back.

"It's your daughters' school," Gayle says superciliously. Even she knows it's never good news when a school calls in the middle of the day.

A stern woman's voice comes on the line.

"Mrs. Strickland, this is Adele Stein, the guidance counselor at Dearborn. I was wondering if you could come in this afternoon? There's something we need to discuss."

My shoulders collapse. "I'm sorry about the cupcakes. Nothing like that will happen again."

"Miss Cleary informed me about that unfortunate incident. We've made note of it should there be repercussions, but this regards your daughter Olivia."

*

Adele Stein, with her cropped gray hair, shapeless linen tunic, and chapped lips, looks like one of those women who has given up fighting the inevitable postmenopausal roll across her middle. On root touch-ups and manicures. On the Sisyphean battle with age itself. The chunky silver and turquoise jewelry around her wrists, though, leads me to believe it's not neglect, but a conscious decision that I have grudging admiration for. What if I let myself look like whoever I would be without makeup and colorists and diets? Would I feel liberated or merely become even more invisible, lose my job, my husband? The price, either way, is steep.

"What did you want to talk to us about?" Peter asks, sliding into lawyer mode.

"Mr. Garrison, Olivia's World History teacher, has brought serious concerns to my attention."

I feel a wave of relief. Missing homework, a falling grade, are concrete problems, more readily addressed than behavioral offenses.

"A number of passages in a recent assignment appear to have been copied directly from an outlet known to produce papers for students," Ms. Stein continues. "We realize that technology has made plagiarism more accessible than ever, but that's all the more reason we must be vigilant. Cheating is something that we take extremely seriously."

"You said the paper 'appears' to have been copied. I assume Mr. Garrison has proof?"

Ms. Stein slides two neat stacks of papers across the desk; one is Olivia's report, the other a printout from an unnamed AI bot. She indicates three paragraphs on each outlined in red and watches as we read, her mouth set in a frown.

I look up first. "I'm sure this is a matter of Olivia not understanding how to cite her sources."

"What does and doesn't constitute plagiarism has been explained numerous times."

"I see the similarities, but I also see discrepancies. You must acknowledge there are gray areas," Peter says.

"I'm afraid Mr. Garrison doesn't agree with you." Ms. Stein leans forward. "Students plagiarize for a variety of reasons—an inability to deal with academic stress, poor time management, a belief that the rules don't apply to them. That doesn't change the fact that it's a blatant act of dishonesty."

"What did Olivia say?"

"She claimed that she mistakenly pasted her notes into the final draft. I've discussed the matter with Mr. Garrison as well as with Olivia's homeroom teacher, Miss Cleary. Miss Cleary objects, but he is willing to let Olivia redo the paper with proper sourcing. I must warn you, if it happens again, our policy is immediate expulsion. In the meantime, Olivia's ability to go on the Forest Valley trip is contingent on satisfactory completion of the assignment."

"Thank you," Peter says, rising. "We can assure you Olivia won't make this type of misjudgment again."

"I appreciate your cooperation," Ms. Stein says. "We'll be watching her closely. Oh, and one more thing, Miss Cleary has barred your family from participating in future bake sales."

Finally, some good news.

"What do you think?" I ask as we walk down the stairs.

"Olivia cheated," Peter answers matter-of-factly.

"You told Ms. Stein there were differences."

"I'll always defend our daughter publicly, especially to that insufferable woman. That doesn't mean I think Olivia is telling the truth. It also doesn't mean that I'm comfortable continuing to defend her if she's lying."

*

Peter summons Olivia to the living room the minute we walk in the door.

"I can't believe they called you into school!" she exclaims, arms crossed defiantly across her chest. "I explained to Mr. Garrison it was a mistake."

"Did it occur to you to talk to us about this?"

"I didn't think it was important."

"What *do* you consider important? Anything?" I demand.

"Olivia, we're trying to understand," Peter says.

"Aren't you supposed to be a lawyer? What happened to innocent until proven guilty?"

"I *am* a lawyer." Peter's calm exterior begins to show signs of fissure. "You haven't told us your side yet."

"I forgot to put in a reference, for fuck's sake."

"It looked like more than a missing citation. The school is willing to give you another chance, but if you don't fix this, they won't let you go to Forest Valley."

"They can't do that."

"They can, and they will."

"If you think I'm going to let Daniel go without me, you're crazy."

"What Daniel Chapman does or doesn't do is not our concern."

"You're worried he'll hook up with Amanda," Maya, who was watching from the hallway, taunts. Her older sister getting in trouble is not the worst thing in her world.

"That's never going to happen," Olivia snaps.

"Can we get back to your paper?" Peter demands.

"Fine. I'll redo it," Olivia tells him before storming out. "I hate you," she mutters as she passes Maya.

*

The next night, Dr. Mendelsohn squeezes us in for an emergency session. He balances his imitation leather padfolio on his lap, listening impassively. He's never opened it, and I wonder if it's a prop or if he scribbles detailed notes after we leave. How else can he keep straight the web of grievances of all the couples who wash up in his office?

"From what I'm hearing," Dr. Mendelsohn says, "neither of you is sure if your daughter is lying, and that's causing some tension."

"I'm willing to accept it could have been a misunderstanding," I answer.

"This isn't the first time Olivia's lied to us recently. Why are you continuing to make excuses for her?" Peter says harshly.

"I'm not."

"You signed the permission slip to let her go on the trip."

"What trip?" Dr. Mendelsohn asks.

"A two-night class trip to the Catskills."

"You don't think she should go, Peter?"

"She's completely obsessed with some boy. I've never seen her so overwrought. Her biggest fear wasn't getting expelled but him going without her."

"Teenage love is by its very nature overwrought."

"I realize that, but this seems over the top, even for Olivia."

"What is it specifically you're worried about, Peter?"

"I don't know," he admits. "My daughter's mind is like the black box they find after an airplane crash. There's useful information in there, but I have no idea how to access it."

"You may not comprehend your daughter's thinking, but what parent of a teenager does? Have you contacted the therapist I recommended for her?"

"Not yet."

"That might be the next step you consider."

"The next step we should consider is moving away from here," Peter says. "This city, this school, the constant pressure it's putting on the kids, and us, to succeed at any cost is going to destroy us."

"Don't you think you're overreacting?" I ask, one eye on Peter and one eye on Mendelsohn, hoping the good doctor will signal his agreement with me. He does no such thing.

Peter turns to face me full-on, frustration scorching the edges of his voice. "I've been telling you this for the past year, but you haven't heard me. I want us to leave the city."

"What makes you think moving would change anything?" I reply, unnerved. Peter seems determined to rip everything I'm desperately clinging to from my grasp. My dreams. My family. My home. "Whatever is happening with Olivia started before she got to Dearborn or met Daniel Chapman," I tell him, ragged with frustration that he refuses to see what I see. "Changing places won't suddenly fix it. It won't change me wanting to start my own business. We have a life here," I insist.

"You hate your job. The tuition is obscene. I no longer recognize my own daughters. It's not the life I want."

There's no rancor in Peter's tone. The words were not said in anger. That's what scares me most.

"Do you mean us? That *we're* not the life you want?"

I search his eyes as my own begin to pool with tears.

There's a long pause. Too long.

"I love you, Kara," he says finally. "I love our family. I want what's best for us. I don't think this is it."

Dr. Mendelsohn shifts his padfolio. "It seems we have gotten to the heart of the matter."

We both glare at his smug little face. He's the only person in the room who views this as progress.

Chapter 18

ABBY

Three days before the murder
Tuesday, October 7

Scott is waiting in a new Italian restaurant on one of the last seedy streets in NoMad. It's only six o'clock, but the room is crammed with people waiting for sourdough pizzas from the open brick oven. It's not the kind of place someone visiting New York once a year would know about without making a concerted effort.

"I'm glad you came," he says, smiling nervously as I take off my jacket and sit across from him. "How are you?"

The notion of us making small talk is absurd. Even the simplest question is loaded.

"I'd be lying if I said things were good. If Rachel has any intention of forgiving me, she's not showing it."

"Give her time. Her whole sense of who she is has shifted. All you can do is let her know you'll be there, no matter what."

"That's hard to do when she refuses to be in the same room as me. Have you talked to her since the two of you had dinner?"

"We speak."

"Ironic, isn't it? I've been there every single day for years, doing all the grunt work. You've been here for one week, and you're the one she's talking to."

"You can't blame her for being curious about me. Besides it's not either/or. That's not what I want."

"What do you want?"

"For us to be a team."

"I'm not sure I can do that."

"Would it be so terrible to try?" He leans forward, his face inches from mine.

It's impossible to look at Scott and not see everything we once were. Or thought we were. The love and the betrayal, the yearning and the loss. All resurrected in a noisy restaurant in NoMad.

"You broke my heart, Scott. I should have been able to get over it sooner, but I didn't."

For so many years, I trained myself to be guarded, to not let anything dent. Certainly not to show it if it does. But I need Scott to know—to truly know—what he did to me. How deep the cut was, how long the healing took.

"I'm sorry," he says quietly.

I believe him. I also believe it's not enough. There's a universe of sorry we haven't gotten to.

He reaches across the table to touch my hand, but I slip my hand away. Trust is too tempting and too dangerous.

"I never stopped thinking about you," he says softly.

"Why did you get divorced?" The question has been ricocheting through my nights. Who was it, if not me? When was it, if not then?

"Elise and I never should have married. We were sixteen when we met. Our families had known each other forever. There was a sense of familiarity that I mistook for love."

The pictures I saw of the two of them posted over the years, their smiles, their laughter, looked an awful lot like love.

"What changed?" I ask, unconvinced.

There is only one thing I really want to hear—that it was me, me all along. That I haunted their marriage the way he haunted my misalliances and solitude.

"We'd been going through the motions for years," Scott says. "I wanted more than that. In the end, she asked for the divorce first."

"Did she find someone else?"

"She says not. Who knows? We both somehow faded from each other's view."

"Was there someone else for you?" I ask warily. There are things I know I couldn't bear, even now. That's one of them.

"If you're asking if I had an affair, the answer is no."

"You had an affair with me," I remind him.

"True."

"What about after that?"

"Not physically, but emotionally, yes, there was someone else."

I bite the inside of my mouth, determined to hold myself in check. I don't know why he's telling me this. I don't know why I'm here. Why I'm letting him do this to me again.

"What happened?" I ask, trying and failing to sound disinterested.

"I'm trying to figure that out."

"Are you still seeing her?" The words come out dry and distanced, my internal shutters slamming closed, locking him out.

"Yes." He smiles. "She's sitting across the table from me."

I exhale, relieved, as the dizziness that was encroaching is replaced by something else. Pleasure, pride. Vindication. Inklings of desire. All of it, as the past and the future, the doubts and the hope that I didn't acknowledge even to myself, collide.

"Scott, we haven't seen each other in seventeen years. We don't even know each other."

It is a half-hearted protest. We both know that.

"The feeling of being with you never left me. You showed me what was possible. I'm not saying we haven't both changed, but the minute I saw the video, I saw the same woman I knew."

"You need to have your vision checked."

"I did everything wrong, Abby. I screwed things up with you and with Elise, but I also screwed things up for myself. The only time I've ever felt completely present in my own life was when you and I were together. That sounds like woo-woo crap, but it's true. I know you think I lied to you when I went back to Hanover and said I needed time to think things over, but it was the truth. I couldn't leave my children. The children I *knew* about," he adds pointedly.

The words slice through layers of scar tissue.

"That doesn't mean I didn't love you," he continues. "I stayed with my wife because it was the right thing to do. Maybe it was, maybe it wasn't. But it's over now." He pauses, pours himself more wine. "What about you? You never married?"

"No."

"Are you seeing anyone?"

There's no simple answer, at least not one that would get me what I want. Assuming I knew what I want. Which I don't. The liminal space with Eliot that holds all the anticipation and none of the wounds. Or this. Whatever this was or is or could be.

"I think so," I tell Scott.

"I have no idea how to interpret that."

"It's new. I don't know what it is yet," I admit. Part of me wants Scott to know that I have options, that other men want me. Part of me wants him to know that the door is also open.

"I'm going to take that as a hopeful sign."

"For who?"

"I'd like to think for both of us." He tilts his face to mine. "You said I don't know you, but I want to. Tell me about your art."

"There is no art. I stopped painting after Rachel was born." There is so much of my life he doesn't see. What I lost, what I had to give up. What I still blame him for.

"Why? You were so talented. I remember watching you when you were trying to work out an image. Nothing else existed for you."

"I had to make a living, Scott. I was, *am*, a single parent."

He suddenly seems willfully naive to me, clinging to a romantic vision of the twenty-two-year-old me in paint-splattered jeans when all I see are the exhausted days spent trying to balance the expenses and the demands. All of it alone. It's hard to remember it's not his fault.

"I would have helped financially if I knew."

"We managed."

"Moving ahead, things will be different. I want to be here for you and Rachel. Have you thought about picking up painting again when she leaves home?"

"I don't know. Maybe some things only make sense at a specific time in your life."

"There are also things that get buried out of necessity. That doesn't mean you can't reclaim them."

"You want me to be the person I was when you knew me, but I've changed."

"I'm not telling you to be or do anything. All I'm saying is that I don't think you should close off the possibility. To anything. No matter what happens, we're tied to each other. We have a child."

"I know that."

"Do you remember that night we went to the Carlyle before I left?" he asks.

"You got so drunk we had to get out of the cab and walk the rest of the way to my place."

"Not my finest moment," he admits. "I was trying to get up the courage to tell you I didn't think I could break up my family."

"But you didn't."

"No, and I've had to live with that. It doesn't seem all that different from the time you came up to Hanover and didn't tell me you were pregnant."

It's a fair point, but I'm not ready to grant him that.

"We're both free now," Scott says. "Why can't we see where it leads us?"

"There is no 'us.'" I'm not sure which one of us I'm trying to convince.

"I'm not pretending to know what will happen, but there's always been an 'us.'"

The magnetic pull is deeper than the ocean. Despite time, despite logic. "I can't go back, Scott."

It's too late. Maybe. Maybe it's too late.

"I'm not asking you to go back. I'm asking for a chance to go forward. Rachel told me about a class trip she's going on. How would you feel about spending time together while she's away?"

"I'm not sure that's a good idea."

"Think about it, okay?"

He reaches over to rest his hand on mine.

This time I give in to the warmth spiraling through me.

Chapter 19

Abby

Two days before the murder
Wednesday, October 8

I stopped going to Rachel's volleyball games midway through the season last year. She had no interest in me witnessing her interminable stretches on the bench, and I was relieved not to watch her trying to hide her embarrassment. But living with Rachel is like living with a ghost of someone you loved and lost. Reaching for her is like reaching for air. I can't bear the thought of her going to Forest Valley with this chasm between us. Surprising her this afternoon is the parental equivalent of the grand romantic gesture.

Dearborn is playing their archrival, Bentley, an all-girls school six blocks away geographically but a universe away philosophically. The competition runs deeper than who has lower admission rates to kindergarten or higher acceptance rates to the Ivies, the largest endowment or the most famous alumni. Bentley is one of the last bastions of blue blood immutability, intent on holding the ever-weakening line against Dearborn's nouveau ascension. The parents and kids pouring into the gym nod politely to each other but separate like guests at a wedding papering over a long-simmering feud.

I get stuck on the staircase behind a group of Bentley mothers in identical ballet flats, gossiping about people I don't know and parties I would never be invited to. I'm trying to maneuver around them when I'm blocked by Amanda, bounding out of a second-floor locker room, followed by the rest of the team, the two coaches clutching notebooks with the Dearborn insignia and, closely behind them, Eliot.

*

The deafening chant of "Defense! Defense!" reverberates through the gym as I find a seat on Bentley's side and look over at Dearborn's bench, trying to catch Rachel's eye. Instead, I see Eliot waving to me from his stance behind the team. I have no idea what he's doing here, but going public is the last thing I need right now. I shake my head to stop him.

Bentley is about to serve when Rachel glances over at the bleachers and smiles. I break into a grin, until I realize it was meant not for me but for Hannah, sitting nearby in an oversized floral dress and black combat boots. Hannah refuses to meet her gaze. Rachel isn't cool enough for even Hannah to acknowledge in public. The only thing worse than the abject pain of high school rejection is witnessing your daughter suffer through it.

When Rachel finally spots me, she glares with unmitigated disgust and turns her attention to straightening her kneepads.

Coming here was an epic mistake.

Bentley scores the first three points and is on its way to a fourth when Amanda, ponytail flying, spikes the ball into an opponent's head, hissing, "Take that, bitch."

She's promptly benched.

Dearborn's head coach directs Eliot to calm Amanda down while the others confer about substitutions. From the corner of my eye, I see Miss Cleary—ever ready to insert herself into a problem—rise from the bleachers and begin to make her way over to Eliot and Amanda. He shakes his head, warning her off. Amanda may be in her homeroom, but it's his job to defuse the situation. Miss Cleary, frowning, reluctantly acquiesces, but she keeps her eyes trained on them as they talk.

By the time Amanda goes back to the bench, she's smiling. I slide out of the bleachers and make my way out.

*

The rest of the afternoon spreads out before me, empty.

I used to treasure the interlude between work and home life, a welcome respite from clients and the endless to-dos of parenthood—Halloween costumes to make, medical forms to sign, after-school classes to arrange, dinners to cook that avoided whatever food group Rachel had suddenly deemed unacceptable. I wish I'd known then that they were not a list of prosaic tasks but a diary of the most precious moments.

There's a text from Rachel when I get out of the subway.

> You don't have to start showing up at games and pretending you care. You're not fooling anyone. I'm having dinner with a friend so don't bother waiting for me.

I will always wait, I want to tell her. As long as it takes. Forever. Instead, I write back, Kk.

I stop at an overpriced gourmet shop to pick up prepackaged sushi to eat in front of the television. I'm staring at the containers nestled on ice, incapable of deciding between salmon or tuna rolls, when Eliot calls.

"I looked for you after the game, but you disappeared. Are you okay?"

"I had some errands to run."

"I saw you shaking your head at me. Did I do something to upset you?"

"No, I was just surprised to see you. I didn't realize you were coaching the girls' team."

"I'm not. At Saint Stephen's, every sports team has an academic adviser. It's part of the whole student-athlete thing. When I told Rita about it, she asked if I'd check out a couple of games and let her know my thoughts. I didn't know Rachel plays volleyball. I'm sorry if I embarrassed you."

"It's not your fault. Rachel doesn't know about us, and I wasn't ready to set off a stream of gossip among the parents."

"I'm still your little secret? That's kind of sexy, at least for a little while."

I laugh. "You know that dinner you promised me? How about tonight?"

Spontaneity is not a luxury allotted to single mothers, but Rachel has summarily dismissed me.

"Really? Sure. How's seven o'clock?"

I put the sushi back and hurry home to change.

Chapter 20

Abby

Eliot is waiting by his apartment door on the third floor of a West Village brownstone, wearing chinos and light-blue shirtsleeves rolled up. He smiles self-consciously and kisses me hello. There's a sweetness to his nervousness that helps ease my own.

"You continue to surprise me," he says, closing the door.

"In a good way, I hope."

"Very, but I would have prepared something special if I had more advanced notice. Is pasta copacetic, or are carbs verboten in this entire city?"

"I'm a firm believer in carb-loading under any and all circumstances," I assure him, despite the fact I've been attempting, with limited success, to eliminate them as part of my turning-forty protocol.

He leads me into the living room, minimally furnished with a charcoal couch, matching side chairs, and a low oak coffee table. Everything is unobtrusive and impersonal, offering few clues.

He watches me take it in, then shrugs apologetically. "It's a work in progress. I've never furnished a home on my own."

"It's a great start."

"You're too kind. You're a visual person. Maybe when I get back from the wilds of Forest Valley, you can come shopping with me."

"I'd like that."

He smiles. Another step forward.

He tips his chin toward the kitchen. "I could use some help chopping."

"At your service."

I follow him into the narrow galley kitchen where the makings of a salad are laid out on a wood cutting board.

"I bought a bottle of wine, if you'd like?" he says.

"You didn't have to."

"I wanted to."

He stirs the pappardelle while I chop red peppers, absurdly anxious about whether my slices are too thick or too thin. "Is this what you wanted?" I ask, holding up a sliver.

He leans over to kiss me. "Definitely."

Everything is corny unless it's happening to you.

We go back to talking, chopping, stirring.

"Why didn't you mention Rachel is on the volleyball team?" he asks.

"It didn't occur to me. It's not a big part of her life."

He puts down the fork he was using to separate the pasta and faces me. "I understand why you haven't told her about us yet, but is it a possibility at some point?"

"Yes. She has a lot going on right now."

This would be the moment to bring up Scott. I let it pass.

"Okay," Eliot says. "We'll have all the time in the world when I get back."

We carry the food to the dining table, where two woven Mexican place mats wait at one end. At the other, there's a laptop and a stack of students' papers peppered with red scribblings.

"I'm sorry," he says, moving them aside. "I haven't gotten a desk yet. I should have put all this away."

"It's fine." I nod in the direction of the papers. "Going old school?"

"I prefer commenting on paper. I like to think there's a better chance they read it."

"How's that working out for you?"

He laughs. "The jury's still out."

"What are the papers on?"

"I'm teaching a class called 'American Nonfiction: Rebels, Conformists and Dreamers.' We're on Emerson and the concept of self-reliance. I gave the kids an assignment to come up with a point of view on whether good old Ralph Waldo is saying your primary duty is to be true to yourself or to fit into the society you find yourself in."

"Are the two always in conflict?"

"You should take my class."

"Only if I can have some private tutoring."

"We can arrange that." He squeezes my hand, his fingers lingering. "Most of the kids gave rote answers echoing what I said in class or whatever they found on Wikipedia, but there's one kid's essay I'm stumped by. I'm not sure if it's a red flag or standard-issue teenage angst. Every school's policy about what to do in these instances is different."

"What do you mean?"

"There's this boy, Daniel. He's one of the smartest kids I've run across in a long time."

"That sounds like a good thing."

"He told me the idea of doing anything to fit into society is anathema to him. What worries me is that he used Dearborn as an example. There's a level of vitriol in his response that I don't know how to respond to. Rita is his homeroom teacher, and she asked me to give him extra attention and keep her apprised of his progress. I thought it was because he's new, but now I'm not so sure. Maybe she senses something troubling about him too."

"Is it Daniel Chapman?"

"Yes, why?"

"His mother is a friend."

"Is there anything I should be concerned about?"

"She hasn't mentioned anything."

"Good. It's hard to know when to raise an alert and when to let kids express themselves. The consequences have proven deadly when you get it wrong." He shakes his head. "Enough about our troubled youth. Let's talk about you."

*

After we carry the dishes into the kitchen, Eliot takes me by the hand and leads me to the couch, kissing me until we're lying half off the stiff cushions. He draws a few inches away, looks at me. "We don't have to . . ."

I pull him back until we're fully entwined, his chest pressed against mine, his hand sliding up my blouse, each step an unspoken acknowledgment that a decision has been made.

This is why I came.

To lose myself.

To leave the past behind.

To see if that's possible.

To see if that's what I want.

We walk hand in hand to his bedroom. One small ceramic lamp on the bedside table casts a truncated conical light. Everything else is bathed in shadows.

He coaxes the rest of my blouse from my jeans and lets it slip to the floor. His forefinger traces the edges of my bra where it curves over my breasts as he kisses my neck, my collarbone. A moan escapes as he reaches to unhook my bra, slips it off my shoulders, his breath shortening. I help with the top two buttons of his shirt and watch as he unbuttons the rest to reveal the trail of light-brown hair on his chest.

"It's been a long time since I've been with anyone," I say hoarsely, all experience draining away.

"Me too," he admits as we fall onto the bed, anticipation turning into avidity.

He slides off my jeans, my thong, kissing my stomach, exploring, learning, while I run my fingers through his hair. All the awkwardness of making love with someone for the first time—*What are the rules now, at this age, in this time, with this person?*—are absent with him. I arch up, feeling him enter me slowly and then powerfully, reaching down to touch me while he moves, taking my pleasure into account. We have yet to learn the specifics of each other's desire, our hands and bodies enacting the sexual trial and error of people new to each other. This? Yes, this.

And I do. Lose myself.

Afterward, we lie on our backs, slowly returning to each other. He plays with a strand of my hair as I lie with my head on his shoulder.

"I can't stay," I say quietly.

"I know." He points to the olive canvas duffle bag in the corner. "I wish I could get out of the trip so we could spend time together while Rachel is away, but no dice. You'll have your two days of freedom, and I'll have God knows what mayhem, but I hope I can see you as soon as I get back."

"It's a date." I sit up and begin to dress, my back to him.

My weekend of freedom includes dinner with Scott.

Chapter 21

Kara

The morning of the murder
Friday, October 10

Pallid gray light filters across the room. I run my forefinger down Peter's chest, our long-established Morse code, but he doesn't turn to me. I don't know if he no longer recognizes the signals or is choosing to ignore them. Since our emergency session with Dr. Mendelsohn, we've been careful with each other. There've been no sudden movements. There've been no clues.

"I'll make breakfast for the girls," he says drowsily.

"Thanks. Maya is sleeping at a friend's tonight, so with Olivia gone, we have the night to ourselves. I made a dinner reservation at Forenzo's." A place we used to go. When things were better.

He looks at me curiously. "It's Friday."

"I know we're supposed to see Mendelsohn again, but we can go after. It would be good for us to go out and try to forget everything for a while."

He sits up and rakes his fingers through his hair, a gesture I've watched a thousand times on a thousand mornings. This time, he avoids my eyes.

"I'm trying, Peter, but you're not making it easy."

"Okay." He relents, swinging his feet to the floor.

I knock on Olivia's door, expecting to find her grumpy about having to wake up earlier than usual, but she's already dressed in a skintight navy top far too low-cut for a camping trip and a thick coat of mascara clumping in the corners. Subtlety is not her strong suit.

"Did you remember to pack a parka and boots?" I ask. "They're predicting a storm upstate tonight."

"They always exaggerate. I'm sure it's no big deal. Is breakfast ready?"

"It should be. Dad's in the kitchen."

"Why are you here?" Olivia asks Maya when she finds her sister already at the table, maneuvering gluten-free Cheerios through a puddle of oat milk, this week's food mandate. "You don't have to be at school for another hour."

"I was up," Maya says defensively, unwilling to admit she's excited to watch the juniors board the yellow buses for a weekend freed from the strictures of school and parents. Soon, it will be her turn to leave.

Olivia shrugs. "Suit yourself. I'm going."

Peter picks up Olivia's bulging backpack to carry it to the elevator while I button my coat.

"I can do that myself," she says, snatching it back.

"Can I at least have a kiss goodbye?"

"You act like I'll be gone forever," she protests, wriggling away from him.

Chapter 22

Abby

Rachel tries one last time to prevent me from going with her to school.

"I don't need you," she insists.

"Parents always come to see their kids off. It's part of the tradition."

"You never cared about traditions before."

Her constant artillery is exhausting. "Let's go."

We ride the crowded subway in silence, grasping separate poles as the train lurches in and out of stations. When we reach Eighty-Sixth Street, she hurries up the long flight of stairs, leaving me to dash after her.

A melee of kids and parents is crowded in front of Dearborn. Rachel sidles over to a group of girls, hoping to be absorbed into their nucleus. They barely acknowledge her. When I spot Eliot coming out of the school, the olive duffle bag that sat in the corner of his bedroom swung over his shoulder, my nerve endings misfire, the urge to connect colliding with the need for subterfuge.

He looks away first, walking over to the constellation of girls Rachel is hovering near.

"We're only going for two nights, ladies," he teases, pointing to their oversized bags.

The girls laugh with the mix of studied cool and yearning to impress they save for teachers they like.

Kara is standing on the outskirts, and I'm about to join her when Scott hurries up the block, carrying a shiny red foil gift bag. He goes over to talk to Rachel, who shows no evidence of surprise or resistance. He only leaves her side when it's her turn to have her backpack checked, her phone tagged and taken away. He's still holding the gift bag as he heads in my direction.

I motion him away from the crowd.

"What are you doing here?"

"Rachel asked me to come."

"Really? She asked me not to." I point to the glossy bag. "Did you forget to give that to her?"

"It's for you."

Inside, there's a mahogany box of watercolors and a pad of thick white paper. My heart swells just a little.

"I thought you might like to play around with them this weekend."

"Scott, I'm not sure I can."

"It's a gift, nothing more."

It's so much more. We both know that.

"I'll see you tomorrow night," he promises.

Chapter 23

Hollis

Daniel is cramming handfuls of clothes into his backpack when Jordan barges into his room without knocking.

"Shouldn't you have done that last night?" he asks, scowling.

"I'm doing it now."

"Please, Jordan," I intercede. "We're already late."

He ignores me. "I'd like a word with you about this weekend," he tells Daniel.

"What about it?"

"You may think you'll be far enough away to do whatever you want with whoever you want, but if you screw up this time, there won't be any second chances."

Daniel glares at him. Sometimes I think he wants nothing more than to prove to Jordan that he's not a total fuckup. Other times, I think he'd rather detonate his father's entire world.

Either way, he wins. Either way, he loses.

He turns to me. "Let's go."

*

The cab jerks forward through the early morning traffic.

"Why do you stay with him?" Daniel asks as he stares out the window, tracing *X*'s through the grime.

"There are things you don't understand," I tell him gently.

"Then explain them to me."

All I've ever wanted is to spare Daniel from the constant vigilance that wends through my days. The never-ending dread of the moment when phantoms become reality, and any hope of connection is lost.

"It won't always be this way," I tell him.

"You're right," he says flatly without turning to look at me. "It won't."

*

Kara, Abby, and I stand together, watching Miss Cleary and the other chaperones form two columns, checking bags for contraband.

"You're acting like we're terrorists," Olivia complains as she hands over her phone.

"Teenagers and terrorists have more in common than people realize," Kara remarks.

"Miss Cleary, you have something on your elbows," Amanda points out to the rowdy amusement of her coconspirators. "Ew, what is that?"

Miss Cleary glances at orange flakes of self-tanner stuck to dry skin and yanks down the cuffs of her cardigan.

"Get on the bus," she snaps.

It's hard not to feel sorry for the poor woman, with her bright-pink lipstick and stiff jeans that look like the tag might still be on. Her hair is lighter this morning, with the telltale jagged streaks of highlights done at home already growing frizzy in the humid air.

"Do you want to hear something pathetic?" Abby asks as the chaperones try futilely to control the cacophony of jibes, taunts, and teasing. "When Rachel went to Forest Valley, I used to sneak a little stuffed animal with a note into her suitcase so she'd find it when she got there. I began to believe if I didn't, something terrible would happen to her."

"You did that this time, too, didn't you?"

"No. She'd be mortified if anyone saw it. It's silly, but I wish I had."

We watch as the last of the kids board the buses, and the doors slowly close.

"Do you think they'll return to us?" Kara asks.

"Of course they'll come back."

"I mean later. Will they eventually return to us as fully formed human beings who don't treat us like infectious disease carriers?"

"I have to believe that. I don't think I could survive otherwise."

The three of us stop talking to wave goodbye as the buses inch down the clogged side street, and our children disappear from view.

Part Two

Chapter 24

Abby

One day after the murder
Saturday, October 11

The ringing phone penetrates the quilt pulled high over my head. I shift position, burrow deeper into the pillows. The insistent tones of the Bach cello suite stop, then after a brief interlude, start again. Defeated, I pry through the smog of sleep to answer.

"Kara? Why are you calling so early?" My brain is foggy, my throat hoarse.

"Didn't the school reach you?"

"Who?"

"The school."

I jolt upright, knocking my elbow against the headboard.

"Why would the school call? Did something happen?"

Kara's breathing is thick, labored.

"Kara? What is it?"

This is the fault line I've been petrified of since the day Rachel was born, the razor-sliced demarcation between before and after. Deep down, I always knew it would come.

"Both of our girls are safe."

"You're sure?"

I need to hear it again. *Our girls are safe.* And then again, repeating it to myself. *Our girls are safe.*

"They're on their way back to the city. There's been an accident."

"What kind of accident?"

"It's Amanda." Kara's voice is riddled with splinters.

"Is she all right?"

"I can't believe it. I just can't . . ."

My relief—*our girls are safe*—begins to give way to the realization that not everyone is safe. "Slow down. You can't believe what?"

"Abby . . . Amanda died."

"What are you talking about?" The words don't add up. I saw Amanda getting on the bus yesterday, blazing with energy.

"The school has been calling everyone since dawn. How could you not have heard the phone?"

"I took an Ambien."

The swirl of Scott, of Eliot, the shifting lure of one dream's resurrection and another's promise churned relentlessly until I reached for a pill to quell it.

I lean back, lightheaded. None of this feels real. None of it makes sense.

"Start over," I say. "What happened?"

"All they said was that it looks like she fell down a cliff or tripped on rocks. Something like that."

"Was anyone else hurt?"

"They didn't mention anyone else, but they didn't say much. They had a lot of calls to make."

"You're absolutely sure it was Amanda?"

"Yes."

I exhale, relieved—not my child, not this time—until the respite shifts into alarm, not as piercing, but alarm, nonetheless.

"Do Bill and Marci know?"

"I'm sure the school called them first."

"Of course."

This is *their* fault line, cleaving their before and an unimaginable after.

"The kids are on their way back. The buses should be arriving at Dearborn in about an hour. I need to talk to Maya before she hears about it from someone else. I'll meet you at school."

*

I clutch my knees to my chest, unable to move.

Finally, I text Rachel. Sweetie, are you okay? Please, please let me know.

No reply comes.

I text Eliot next. I can't believe this. Are you okay? What happened? Is Rachel okay?

He answers immediately. On bus, can't talk. Rachel's fine. It's a nightmare, but . . . His text breaks off mid-sentence.

I dress in a daze, brush my teeth, pull back my hair, and, at the last minute, put on lipstick. I'm surely the most frivolous, callous person in the universe, but when the bus arrives, Eliot will be on it. I'm ashamed, but I don't wipe off the lipstick.

*

I make my way through the cold, bright morning sun, passing women in black leggings clutching their post-workout lattes, glowing with exertion and self-satisfaction, families in dark suits and dresses heading to synagogue; all of them oblivious, actors in a different play, one in which this is a normal Saturday morning in Manhattan. I maneuver around them, irritated by their lack of urgency. I'll only completely believe Rachel is safe when I feel her in my arms.

The block in front of Dearborn is already crowded with parents. Even those who rarely speak to each other hug, bonded by circumstance and shock.

Kara and Peter look drawn, fine lines of worry hatched across their faces. I embrace them both, grateful for the physical contact.

"Did you find out what happened?"

Kara shakes her head. "No one seems to know anything. Only rumors."

"What kind of rumors?"

"That Amanda was out in the woods late at night. You remember how bad the weather was? She must have slipped. That's one of the theories."

We stop speaking as Hollis and Jordan approach.

"I can't get ahold of Daniel. Have you heard from Olivia or Rachel?" Hollis asks anxiously. Her skin is even paler than usual, ghostly.

"They confiscated the kids' phones before they left yesterday," Peter reminds her. "They probably won't give them back until they get off the bus. Dearborn is going to control the flow of information very carefully."

Jordan agrees. "I'm sure the school was lawyered up by sunrise."

The cool assessment is bracing. A child has died. A child we know. Who could have been one of ours. Nevertheless, I'm sure he's right.

"I heard Amanda was alone when it happened," Kara says.

"Where did you hear that?"

Gina Hanson, who's been standing a few feet away, turns around. "I heard a group of them were out drinking in the woods."

"Which kids?" Kara asks warily.

"I assume the same ones who usually engage in that type of behavior," Gina replies tartly before turning her back to us.

"I can't believe she's doing this even now," Kara mutters.

"Ignore her. There's no way she knows any more than we do."

The murmurs continue, everyone searching for an explanation that, however difficult, will be easier to accept than the possibility that what happened was purely random.

"Poor Bill and Marci. It's horrific," another mother says. "Amanda is, was, is such a lovely girl. I can't imagine . . ."

Kara leans her head against Peter's chest as he rubs her back. Hollis clutches Jordon's hand, though it barely stills her shaking. Only I'm alone.

At every screech of wheels, we turn as one, waiting for the buses to come into view.

It's 10:46 a.m. when they finally round the corner of Eighty-Eighth Street and park in front of Dearborn. The school's doors open on cue, emitting Headmaster Nederlander, Adele Stein, and a petite, formally suited woman I've never seen before. They stare straight ahead, scrupulously avoiding eye contact with the parents.

When the bus doors open, the chaperones, led by a stone-faced Miss Cleary, step out, forming two aisles. The children disembark one by one, silent and grim, a shadow of their usual adolescent boisterousness. Two of the chaperones, Wendy Millman and Carla De Santos, remove the kids' phones from canvas bags, checking labels before handing them back, while Miss Cleary remains engrossed in her clipboard, refusing to look up. The process is excruciatingly slow, and as soon as each parent sees their child emerge, they race over to embrace them.

Rachel is one of the last to step off.

I take my first full breath since Kara called, pull her into my arms, and bury my face in her neck, her particular Rachel-scent different from that of her infant self but familiar in a way nothing else ever has been or will be. Her heart pounds against mine.

"Are you okay?"

She nods unconvincingly, and I pull her tighter. I would stay that way forever if I could. I only loosen my hold when her arms drop to her sides, ready to separate.

"You must be tired."

Rachel shrugs, her gaze trained on the ground.

"What happened?" I ask.

"No one knows. They woke us up. And . . . I don't know." Her eyes are glassy, unfocused.

"You don't have to talk now. There'll be time for that. I'm just glad you're home."

Looking over Rachel's shoulder, I see Eliot talking quietly to Adele Stein. He mouths the word "later" before disappearing into Dearborn with Miss Cleary, the tiny woman in the navy suit, and the other chaperones.

"Mom?"

"Yes?"

"Can we go home?"

She wavers, her knees about to buckle, and I put my arm around her narrow waist to support her. She doesn't fight me off.

I say goodbye to Kara and Peter, who have Olivia sandwiched between them, and search for Hollis, but the Chapmans have vanished.

*

As soon as we get home, Rachel goes into her bedroom and shuts the door, exhausted. Exiled, I gather the watercolors strewn about the kitchen table, stash them in the jumble of a whatnot drawer, and pace the perimeter of the living room. On one rotation, I land on the question of where Amanda—her body—is now. The reality that "a girl" can become "a body" in the blink of an eye makes me shudder.

A text from Eliot breaks my ruminations. Sorry I couldn't talk this morning. I'll call you tonight.

It's close to three in the afternoon when I knock gently and go in to find Rachel curled in the fetal position. I lean over to kiss the mossy temple above her left ear.

"You must be starving. Can I get you something to eat?"

"I'm not hungry."

Rachel's shoulder blades, beneath her worn Forest Valley fleece, are achingly thin, sharp enough to puncture my heart. "Sweetie, I know you've been up since dawn, but can you tell me what happened?"

"I don't know what happened."

"Rach, you must know something. What did they tell you?"

"I don't know," she repeats, her rib cage rising and falling with each breath. "I was sleeping, and they came and woke us up and brought us downstairs and asked if any of us had seen Amanda, which was pretty stupid because they already knew she was dead. They asked if anyone had seen her go out, and then it all kind of fell apart."

"What do you mean, fell apart?"

"People were crying, and they told us to pack our stuff. They wouldn't answer any questions. Miss Cleary stood there like a prison guard watching us. Then these other people showed up, like from the camp or the police or something."

"Why would the police be there?" I'm having trouble making sense of the thicket of words. None of it adds up.

"I don't know. They started asking us questions until Miss Cleary put a stop to it."

She blinks to suppress impending tears. I start to press further—*the police? other people?*—but stop. Instead, I curl around her.

Once, I could make everything in Rachel's world better simply by holding her. I try to remember the last time that was possible, but last times are notoriously difficult to pinpoint—the last time you were able to pick your child up, the last time they held your hand crossing a street, the last time you soothed them in the night. I can't locate any of them. I don't know how to make a child feel safe when they've learned firsthand that they're not safe, that they never really were. That no one is. I reach out to hold her anyway.

"Mom," Rachel protests, pulling away, but not before I spot a web of angry red scratches on her right arm, speckled with dried blood.

"Where did you get those?"

"It's no big deal. We were running back from the hike in the rain, and I got scraped by some branches."

"Did you clean them?"

She buries her arm beneath a pillow. "I'm tired. I want to sleep."

"Okay, but we have to take care of those scratches later. Get some rest."

I glance back before leaving, making sure she is truly here.

*

When the phone rings, I pick it up quickly before looking at the number.

"Are we still on for dinner tonight?" Scott asks, cheerful and expectant.

He doesn't know. How could he?

"Abby, are you there?"

"Oh God, I'm sorry. I can't. Scott, something's happened. Rachel's home."

"I thought they weren't getting back until tomorrow?"

"There was an accident." The words clog in my throat. "A girl died."

"Jesus. Is Rachel all right?"

"I don't know. How could she be?"

"What happened?"

"I'm not sure. She's barely talking, and the school hasn't given us any information."

"Why didn't you call me?"

I shut my eyes, breathe. For so many years, I've handled everything alone. Every problem. Every joy.

"I didn't think of it."

"Can I come over?"

"I don't think that's a good idea. Things are confusing enough right now."

"Okay, but you don't have to go through this alone, Abby. I'm here, for both of you."

*

As evening approaches, I bring Rachel buttered cinnamon toast and hot chocolate in bed, the comfort food of her toddler years, and sit with her while she eats. The dried blood is gone from the scratch marks on her arm.

"What happens now?" she asks, bits of brown sugar falling on her lap.

"What do you mean?"

"Do we go back to school on Monday like things are normal?"

I'm as lost as she is. "I don't know," I admit. "We'll have to wait and see."

Her phone vibrates from under the covers, and she picks it up, reads a text, puts it down. Her cuticles are shredded into crimson highways.

"Who was that?"

"Everyone is saying stuff about people."

"Like what?"

"It doesn't matter. It's stupid."

Her phone vibrates again, a parallel universe in the palm of her hand that I have no access to.

*

It's past nine when Eliot finally calls. "Abby?" His voice is so low I can barely hear him.

"Are you all right?"

"It doesn't feel real. Those poor parents . . ." He trails off. "I looked for her, Abby. I went out. I tried to find her, but it was so dark. If I'd known, I would have gone out earlier."

His raw pain fills my bedroom.

"I'm sure you did everything you could. Can you tell me what happened?"

"We're still piecing it together."

"Anything would help."

"We've been asked not to talk to parents, so everything has to stay between us."

"Of course."

There's a long silence, and when he speaks again, it's as if he's talking to himself. "There was a terrible thunderstorm in the afternoon while the kids were out for a hike. Jack Vernon, the head groundskeeper, was leading it. He should have canceled when he saw the forecast, but Rita insisted on sticking to the schedule. We got everyone back to the lodge, and it cleared up by dinner, but the kids were antsy from being inside. They barely made it through the evening performance."

"What performance?"

"This Native American, Chief Little Cloud, was telling them about the history of the land and the Lenape tribe. They had an hour for snacks and free time after that. The kids must have snuck out then."

"It wasn't only Amanda?"

"No, six kids were missing at bed check. Unfortunately, Rita knew but neglected to tell anyone."

"Why would she do that?"

"She probably figured they were out partying and would sneak back in before anyone else found out. This trip was her big chance for redemption in Nederlander's eyes. She wasn't about to get blamed for the kids' shenanigans if she could help it. The only reason I found out was that I heard her in the hallway around midnight and went to see what was going on. She was finally calling Vernon for help. I told her I'd go out to look for the kids while Vernon alerted the rescue team."

"Are you the one who found Amanda?"

"No. I went through the trails, by the lake, anyplace we'd been that day. I keep going over it in my head. If I'd known and gone out earlier or if Rita had called Vernon right away, maybe everything would be different. By the time I got back, all the kids had snuck back in except Amanda. The rescue team found her on the mountain about an hour later."

"Do they know what happened?"

"She was dead by the time they got there. It looks like she slid in the mud, fell a few feet, and hit her head on a boulder."

Amanda's red, red hair, her pale freckled face splattered with mud, her crumpled body. Sometimes images of what you haven't actually seen are harder to shake than those you have. I know instantly this will be one of them.

"What did the other kids say? Didn't anyone see anything?"

"They're scared. They're all hiding something. Drinking, weed. Whatever they went out there to do, they're not about to admit it." He pauses. "How's Rachel?"

"She hasn't really said much."

"Abby, the police talked to the kids before they left Forest Valley, but they're going to question them again, starting with the ones who were out that night. You should prepare Rachel for that."

"What do you mean?"

"I assumed you knew she was one of the kids who snuck out of the lodge."

I flinch, gripping the phone tighter, and swallow hard. "Right, yes, of course," I tell him, trying to keep my voice from cracking. "She didn't mention who the other kids were, though."

"There were four girls and two boys. At least that we know of so far. Rachel, Hannah, Amanda, and Olivia. Daniel and Todd. The boy-to-girl ratio is surprising, but that could mean anything or nothing. Rachel can probably tell you more."

"I'm sure she will. She was so tired, I wanted to let her get some rest."

I don't know if he believes me or not, but my instinct is to protect Rachel, even if I don't know what I'm protecting her from. Protect myself, too, from admitting that Rachel may have been less than honest with me and what that implies about the kind of mother I am. I shut my eyes, replaying my conversation with her, trying to convince myself I missed something as anxiety begins to tunnel between the missing pieces, searching for an explanation.

"Are you still there?" Eliot asks.

"Yes, sorry. I should go check on Rachel," I tell him, part of me already gone.

"Of course." He pauses. "Abby, I wish you were here with me," he says softly. "I realize that's not possible tonight, but what we have, what we started, I don't want to lose that. I know that sounds selfish at a time like this."

"I want that too."

"Can I see you soon?"

"Yes, soon."

I hang up and hurry into Rachel's room.

She's sound asleep, a blanket hiding her face from view.

Chapter 25

Kara

Two days after the murder
Sunday, October 12

Olivia has been locked in her bedroom all day. I can hear her opening and closing drawers, the low hum of her talking on the phone, but except for a few surreptitious trips to the bathroom, she's completely shut herself off since she got back yesterday.

When we first brought Olivia home from the hospital after she was born, we used to sneak into her room on tiptoes, stand over her crib, and marvel at her existence. I would do that now if I could, stand guard, marvel, but the door, despite house rules, is locked. Even Nomi has not been granted admittance, despite her insistent scratching.

"We've given her enough time, haven't we?" I ask Peter when he joins me in the hallway. "I'm worried. She's hardly said a word."

"That's natural. Think what she's been through."

"That's the point. We don't know what she's been through."

"True."

He knocks gently on Olivia's door. "Livvie, can we come in?"

After a long silence, Olivia pads across the floor. She opens the door wearing olive sweatpants and an oversized T-shirt softened by years of washing. Her unbrushed hair hangs below her shoulders, and her complexion is blotchy.

I graze her cheek with the back of my hand, running my knuckles against her skin. "Do you want something to eat?"

She shakes her head.

"Why don't you come out and sit with us for a few minutes?" Peter suggests. "Maybe it will help."

"Help what?"

"I know nothing can change what happened, but sometimes talking can help. If not you, at least it would help us understand."

"I don't know what happened." There's an undercurrent of shakiness in her voice, an echo of how she sounded right before a meltdown when she was little.

"We'd still like to talk."

Olivia slips out of her room without opening the door farther and follows us to the living room, sinking into a chair. She can't admit a longing for comfort, but she wouldn't be here if she didn't somehow need it.

"You've been through a terrible experience," Peter says as we settle on the couch across from her. "We want you to know we're here for you. We can't imagine what you're going through. It's hard enough for us, but you were there."

"I wasn't there."

"I meant on the trip," Peter says calmly. "Do you have any idea why Amanda went out that night?"

"I have no idea why Amanda does anything. *Did* anything."

"We heard she wasn't the only one who left the lodge," I say carefully.

Olivia stiffens. "Who told you that?"

"It doesn't matter." Peter is the only person I've told about Abby's relationship with Eliot.

"Olivia, did you leave the lodge Friday night?" he asks.

"I went out with Daniel. Is that what you want to know?" The rote rebellion is there, but the conviction behind it is gone. She tucks her lips in, struggling for control.

"You knew the rules against leaving the lodge," he reminds her.

"There's no place for us to be alone," she retorts angrily. "Like, ever."

"We'll save that discussion for another day. Where did you two go?"

"Nowhere."

"You have to have gone somewhere."

Frustration is boiling up in both of them, charging the ions. I'm torn between interceding to stop Peter's interrogation and knowing we need answers. He shoots me a warning glance.

"We went to the lake," Olivia says. "It had nothing to do with Amanda. I didn't even know she was gone."

"It has everything to do with all of you," Peter replies. "Do you understand what happened? How awful it is?"

"Of course I understand."

"Did you see Amanda when you went out?"

"No. The whole point was Daniel and I wanted to be alone. I'm sorry about what happened, but I don't know why you're asking me all these questions. I'm tired. Can I go back to my room now?"

"We are not done," Peter tells her. "Other people will be asking the same questions."

"Let her get some rest," I insist.

*

"What do you think 'being with Daniel' means?" Peter asks when Olivia is ensconced once more behind her locked door.

"Exactly what you're imagining."

He groans. "I'm trying very hard not to imagine it."

"Let me know how that goes for you."

He smiles, and our bond, however variegated, tightens.

I never had a first love, that all-encompassing blinding desire that nothing subsequent will ever quite match. I had crushes. I loved—love—Peter. But it's a reasonable, adult love. The force of what Olivia feels for Daniel is something altogether different and impenetrable.

"She doesn't seem to be absorbing that someone has died," he says.

"She must be in shock." I'd like to believe that's all it is. I'm not sure I do.

"Maybe."

Olivia has become in many ways indecipherable, and I wonder, not for the first time, how someone who has been lodged in your heart since the second they were born can drift and drift until all you recognize are their outlines. Maybe I wasn't paying close enough attention.

"It's weird, but I have no idea what she believes. We haven't talked about it in years."

"Talked about what?" Peter asks, baffled.

"What happens when someone dies."

It's one more thing that got overlooked in the daily busyness of our lives. God, not God. Afterlife, not afterlife. All of it missing from any discussion in our nonobservant home. I don't even know what I believe.

"Do you remember when my father died?" Peter asks. "Olivia must have been around four. We told her grandpa would always live on in her heart. She looked aghast."

A look of terror had crossed Olivia's face. "He's too big to live in my heart," she protested.

Was that the last time we broached the subject? No one close has died since then. It was a talk easily relegated to some future moment that slammed into us so much sooner than expected.

"We might need some expert guidance on this one."

"I'm not sure Mendelsohn is the right man for the job," Peter says.

He reaches over and pulls me to him, and I nestle into his chest, comforted by the strength of his arms. There's no protection against sadness or fear, but there is, however fleetingly, solace.

We close our bedroom door and make love wordlessly, clutching each other not with the desire of our early years or the efficiency of overtaxed parents when lovemaking is one more to-do but with the desperate fervor of two people who have somehow escaped unscathed.

Chapter 26

Hollis

Four days after the murder
Tuesday, October 14

Despite the Xanax I washed down before I brushed my teeth, my legs jiggle uncontrollably beneath the marble table. The collar of my black coat dress rubs against my neck, irritating the skin. The last forty-eight hours are a blur—Amanda's death, the hospital's decision to hold my mother, Adam's text last night after I didn't show up for the meeting on Saturday.

> Are you fucking kidding me? You promise me you'll help, then you pull a no-show? You've gotten away with lying and manipulating your entire life. It's time to pay.

I force myself back to the present, sitting with Abby and Kara in the back of Café Simone, stirring our cappuccinos with tiny silver spoons.

"I don't know how Amanda's parents will get through this." I hear my own voice as if through a mist.

It's a morning of dreaded what-ifs, of clinging to what you have and bargaining with whatever power you believe in not to take it away.

I hugged Daniel tightly before he left for school and promised I'd see him at the service. Though I'd assumed families would go together, Dearborn announced the junior class would travel to the funeral home together with support provided by their staff. Whether the show of unity was deemed best for optics or the emotional well-being of the students is debatable, but it wasn't presented as a choice.

Daniel nodded dully as I kissed him goodbye, barely hearing, dark circles carved beneath his eyes. He's been strangely robotic since he returned. Jordan chooses to view it as a rare demonstration of self-control. I wish that's what it is.

"Do the Carters have other children?" I ask.

"An older son in college, Josh," Kara answers.

"Have either of your girls talked about what happened? Daniel's been so withdrawn."

"This is the first time Rachel has had someone she knows die. I would say she isn't acting like herself, but I don't know what 'herself' is anymore." Abby shakes her head. "When did our own kids become a guessing game?"

"Maybe they always were, and we were too busy to notice," Kara replies.

"I googled how to speak to your child about death," I admit. "I know that sounds pathetic."

"I've googled far worse," Kara says. "Did you learn anything useful?"

"The article was meant for younger children. It said to answer any questions they have in clear, simple language, but Daniel refuses to talk about that night. If I try to press him, he walks away. I still don't understand what happened. Do you?"

Kara begins to recite the litany of rumors circulating online and off. "Amanda was drunk. They were all drunk. She had a fight with one of the girls and ran off on her own. She had a fight with one of the boys. She snuck off to throw up because she's bulimic and passed out. She was hooking up with someone. They were all hooking up. They were taking Ecstasy. Take your pick."

"How could the other kids leave her there? That's what I don't get," Abby says. "Why didn't anyone go for help?"

"Olivia said she was with Daniel the whole time. She said they'd been shut in all afternoon because of the rain and wanted to get some air. Is that what Daniel told you?"

"Yes, he said they didn't know anyone else had left the lodge."

Kara nods, reassured. "At least they were together."

*

The yellow buses that Dearborn arranged to transport the junior class from school are parked in front of the funeral home, the brilliant color shocking against the line of long black sedans. We walk through the foyer with its plush maroon carpeting, deep-gray walls, and decorous chandeliers to take our place behind other parents making their way to the seats, heads bent.

Dearborn teachers and administrators take up the second and third rows, where Miss Cleary, dressed head-to-toe in black, is sitting beside the new English teacher, her head tilted to his. Behind them, Amanda's classmates, the girls in dark dresses, the boys in button-down shirts, a few in blazers, sit upright and quiet. I search for Daniel and try to catch his eye, but his gaze is locked on the coffin in the front of the room. To the left, there's a large picture of Amanda propped on a stand, her flaming red hair in a high ponytail, her slim arms aloft, frozen in time. On the other side of the coffin, there's a collage of photographs of her at various stages, in a wading pool surrounded by palm trees, playing volleyball, shimmying at her disco-themed sweet sixteen party, with her parents on a Caribbean beach, all of them dressed in white.

Bill and Marci Carter, the older brother Josh, grandparents, and relatives file solemnly in.

Once they're seated, Bill Carter runs his hand up and down his wife's narrow back, trying to comfort her, but there's no comfort to be had in this room. Josh Carter, his ginger hair cut close to his head, surveys the audience, biting his lip, and turns back to his family.

The rabbi steps up to the podium and clears his throat.

"Today, we've come to say goodbye to a daughter, a granddaughter, a sister, a friend," he begins. "I've known Amanda Carter since she was an infant in her mother's arms. She was a remarkable young woman, filled with goodness and grace, with wisdom far beyond her years."

Daniel's back remains locked as a ripple of sobbing passes through the girls, a communal outpouring that feeds on itself. The rabbi's words do not fit the Amanda I met at the safety walk, but it's the Amanda they're claiming now. The boys, glancing furtively at Todd, the stoic athlete, take their cue from him and remain stone-faced.

"We search for answers that are hard to find at times like this," the rabbi goes on. "An innocent life snatched from us far too soon. We question meaning, we question God. I ask you instead to treasure the moments we had with Amanda, to burnish those memories, and to know that she will live on in the many people she touched. Do not doubt that Amanda's life, though brief, had importance. Pray for her soul and know that she is in a better place. And pray for her family, who need our love and support in this most difficult of times. Bill, Marci, Josh, we are united with you in grief now and in the days and weeks to come."

Josh Carter gets up to speak next. His eyes, swollen and bloodshot, scan the room, searching for an explanation of why these kids lived and his sister did not.

He begins to speak, but the words get snarled as he chokes back tears. He bends his head, his shoulders heaving with the effort of each breath, starts again.

"My little sister could be the biggest pain in the butt." Nervous laughter fills the room. Josh tells stories of how Amanda once put her pet frog on a diet, how she dreamed of becoming a songwriter, how, let's be real, she liked a good party. "It's impossible to find anything to be grateful for," he says, glancing at the rabbi. "Amanda is going to miss out on so much, and we're going to miss out on so much that she would have done. I don't believe in silver linings. I think that's just bullshit we tell ourselves." He looks at his parents unapologetically. "I'm sorry, but it is, and no words from someone who barely knew Amanda are going to change that."

The rabbi, expressionless, leads Josh back to his place beside his parents. His father puts his arm around him. Marci Carter, her face buried in her hands, doesn't move.

The flower-draped coffin is borne slowly out.

*

The kids cluster in groups on the street, prolonging the moment they'll have to board the buses to take them back to Dearborn. Headmaster Nederlander stands with school officials for a few minutes and then hurries off, away from parents' questions he cannot or will not answer, away from explanations he doesn't have.

Daniel and Olivia emerge together, heads touching as they talk quietly, separated from the others.

"I'm glad they're helping each other through this," I tell Kara.

She nods distractedly and turns to Abby.

"Who's that man Rachel is talking to?"

Rachel is standing on the outskirts of the crowd, speaking with a stranger in khaki pants and an ill-fitting brown tweed blazer.

"I have no idea. I'll be right back."

As Abby approaches, Miss Cleary races over, grabs Rachel firmly by the elbow, and pulls her away. She stands guard, hands on her hips, until Rachel has safely boarded the bus.

"Who was that?" Kara asks when Abby returns.

"A reporter from *The New York Times*."

"What's he doing here?"

"White girl from elite private school dies on class trip? Of course he's here."

"He looks young enough to be one of them," Kara says, eyeing the reporter still hovering on the outskirts.

"And smart enough to use that to his advantage. Rachel should have known better than to talk to him," Abby says, shaking her head.

"I don't think any of them know which end is up."

"I'm not sure any of us do."

We watch as the buses pull away and the Carters climb into the long black limousine that will drive them to the private burial, their faces hidden by the darkened glass windows.

Abby, Kara, and I stand in muddled silence before hugging tightly and going our separate ways.

*

I call Jordan as soon as I'm out of view. I have strict instructions never to bother him at the office for trivial matters, but I'm certain he won't consider a nosy reporter from *The New York Times* a trivial matter.

And then I try once more to call Adam to explain why it was impossible for me to go to Harkendale on Saturday morning.

His phone is disconnected.

Chapter 27

Abby

Eliot is sitting at a small table in the West Village restaurant where we had our first real date. The familiarity is comforting on such a discomfiting day. He's still wearing his blazer from the funeral, but the tie is gone. His eyes are hooded with exhaustion.

I rest my head in the crook of his neck as we hug, my mind a kaleidoscope of images I can't shake: The flower-draped coffin. The Carters, bent over in grief. The muffled sobs. Miss Cleary, snatching Rachel away.

"Have you slept at all?" I ask, taking a seat beside him.

"Not really. I keep thinking how this all might have been prevented."

"It's not your fault."

"Yes, but rational and emotional are two very different things."

It's late afternoon, and the restaurant is nearly empty. I would kill for a glass of wine, but when the waitress comes over, I order my third cappuccino of the day before turning back to Eliot.

"I can't imagine what it must have been like to go back to school after the service. Why didn't they cancel classes for the day?"

"There was some discussion of it, but the logistics would have affected too many kids and their parents. The workloads will be adjusted, and grief counselors will be in place at the school, which may be more beneficial than sending the kids off on their own. Plus, maintaining architecture is crucial to getting children through a crisis."

"Architecture?"

"Structure. Kids need reassurance that class bells still ring at the same time and teachers are still waiting for them in the same rooms."

"Don't they also need to know they can be open about their feelings?"

"It's a tough balancing act. It seems harsh, but Amanda's desk was removed, and the school cleaned out her locker on Sunday. They sent a box with her notebooks and the rest of her belongings to her parents."

"It must have been dreadful for the kids to find an empty space where Amanda used to sit."

"Sometimes there are no good options."

"Have you been through the death of a student before?"

"There was a suicide two years ago at Saint Stephen's."

"That's awful."

"Yes, but sadly more expected. There's a lot of training around it. That's not the case here."

I rest my hand on his. "How are you holding up?"

"We've been so busy dealing with the potential ramifications, I haven't had time to absorb it all. Dearborn is instituting major damage control. Their PR guy, Tom Hennessy, is overseeing the flow of information to the press, and they've hired an outside lawyer, Charlotte Colson."

"You'd think they would have bigger concerns than public relations."

"Reputations can take decades to recover, and they're desperate to avoid Dearborn being a stand-in for every private school morality tale. There's a lot at stake: school rankings, the endowment, a drop in applications. But more than that, they're terrified of being sued by the Carters. The lawyer, Colson, is a cool customer. She keeps referring to Amanda as 'the girl,' as if not naming her will make it feel less real."

"It feels pretty damn real to me."

"It feels pretty damn real to them too. The police talked to us and the kids before we left Forest Valley, but that was merely for immediate information. Colson has already started meeting with each of us to 'firm up' where we were that night, starting with Rita."

"Because she didn't call the Forest Valley rescue team as soon as she realized kids were missing?"

"Yes, and because she was in charge of all the arrangements, including safety precautions. If the Carters sue for lack of adequate supervision, the school is going to need a scapegoat. They're also questioning the Forest Valley staff to see if the accident can be blamed on some misjudgment on their part."

"How is it their fault?"

"I don't think it's anyone's fault. The sad truth is accidents happen. It poured that afternoon, and the grounds were basically a mudslide. Colson is looking into why the trail where they found Amanda wasn't roped off considering the conditions and how rocky it is. There's also the fact that Forest Valley has one thousand acres, and no checkpoints to prohibit access. Anyone could have gotten on the property. It might have had nothing to do with Dearborn. If all else fails, they'll smear Amanda. We've seen that happen before."

"Are you serious?" Still? This is still going on? It shouldn't shock me, but it does.

"Unfortunately, yes. The kids signed an honor code before the trip. Amanda left the lodge despite the rules. They'll dig up any other infractions, start a whisper campaign. They won't go there unless they have to. The blowback would be too severe, but they'll keep it in their back pocket. What has Rachel told you?"

As the names of the kids who left the lodge became public, Rachel had no choice but to admit she was one of them. She was sorry she didn't mention it earlier. She should have, she said, but it was all so much. Besides, she didn't think it mattered. She never saw Amanda. Rachel, a girl who has no experience getting in trouble, who I've never had to discipline or ground, hunched over as she told me. All I had to do was shake my head in disappointment to make her wince.

"She said some of the girls had been teasing Hannah, and she went to make sure she was okay. Do you know anything about that?"

"Not the specifics. I'd gone up to my room, but according to Rita, there was an incident after the performance during snack time. From what I hear, Hannah stuffed some extra cookies in her pockets, and they fell out in front of everyone. I gather some of the girls were pretty nasty about it, including Amanda. They do seem to pick on Hannah a lot."

"They still go to her house when it suits them. I don't know why Hannah puts up with it."

"Most teenagers will do anything to belong even if it means being used, but resentment has a tendency to fester. It was nice of Rachel to go check on her. You've raised a sweet kid. Luckily, all she got was a few scratches. Rita said they were nothing too serious. It could've been worse."

The air catches in the back of my throat. Rachel told me she got the scratches running back from the hike. We were both so tired, though, there's a chance I misunderstood.

"Can you stay for dinner?" Eliot asks.

"I wish I could, but I need to get home. I don't want to leave Rachel alone for too long right now. I know it seems like I keep running out on you, but it won't always be this way. I promise, I'll make time for us."

"It's okay." He takes my hands in his. "Abby, as horrible as this is, your daughter, the school, everyone will move on."

"Except the Carters."

"Except the Carters," he agrees.

We gather our things and linger outside the restaurant on the dusky West Village street. Smoke from a nearby falafel truck wafts around us, then dissipates.

"Will you be okay?" he asks, his lips close to mine.

I nod.

"Are *we* okay?"

"Yes."

We kiss one last time, but it's impossible to lose myself in it.

*

Rachel is sprawled on the living room couch with her laptop when I get home.

"Are you doing homework?"

She shrugs. "Sort of."

"I thought we could order pizza for dinner and watch a movie."

She looks at me suspiciously. "It's Tuesday."

We'd long ago developed the ritual of eating pizza in front of the television on Sunday nights, sitting cross-legged on the floor together. When Rachel was little, she would inch closer if the movie scared her until she was sitting on my lap without acknowledging it, intimacy achieved in increments. Sometimes, I put on a scary movie to feel that closeness.

"I think an exception is in order."

When the margherita pizza comes, I put two slices on each of our plates and settle down beside her, biding my time, while we decide on a movie.

Halfway through the opening credits, I ask as offhandedly as I can, "Sweetie, can you tell me again why you left the lodge that night?"

Rachel's eyes remain glued to the screen. "We went over this already. I was looking for Hannah. Some kids were teasing her about stupid stuff, totally body-shaming her. They were such bitches. I wanted to make sure she was okay."

"Was she?"

"Not really. I mean, she had a right to be angry."

"Was Amanda one of the kids giving Hannah a hard time?"

"She's the one who started it. I don't know why everyone always follows her like they have no brains of their own."

"Did anything else happen when you went out?" I ask carefully. "Did you fall?"

"No, why are you asking me that?" she asks suspiciously.

She's slipped past the age when she was willing to take any question at face value. Even the simplest inquiry is an intrusion. Every conversation is a calculation—how far to push, how far to recede—on both our parts.

"I thought maybe that's how you got those scratches," I suggest.

"I told you, I got them when I was running back to the lodge in the rain. Can we drop it?"

Retreat seems like the safest option.

For the next hour, we lean against the couch, picking at the pizza. Slowly, Rachel inches over until our knees are touching.

I shut my eyes, trying to imagine what it would be like to never again feel her breath so close, her flesh against mine. It's unthinkable.

When the closing credits roll, we clear our plates and withdraw to our separate rooms. I consider calling Eliot to ask why Rita told him Rachel got the scratches when she left the lodge, but intuition tells me not to.

Chapter 28

Hollis

Six days after the murder
Thursday, October 16

Jordan is scrupulous about maintaining relationships with editors at all the top media outlets. He's skilled at feeding them information they didn't know they needed and mining them for information they don't know he needs. His mastery worked to cataclysmic effect during his first divorce, forcing his first wife to flee to her hometown in Michigan. That's not something I'm prone to forgetting, though I appreciate it now.

He managed to get tipped off about the story about Amanda Carter's death set to run in *The New York Times* soon after I told him about the reporter at the funeral. Despite applying increasing pressure, though, he was unable to pry loose the specifics.

When the story posts soon after five in the morning, he reads it quickly before handing me his iPad.

*

Student at Elite New York City School Dies Under Mysterious Circumstances
October 16
New York

The students and faculty at the tony Dearborn Academy on Manhattan's Upper East Side have been shocked by the death of one of their students on a junior class trip to Forest Valley Camp in the Catskill region of New York state. Amanda Carter, 16, died last Friday night on the campgrounds in what at first appeared to be an accident. A representative of the investigative department of the Sullivan County Sheriff's Office who is not authorized to speak on the record has told this reporter that the incident is considered "suspicious." According to the source, the initial examination of the crime scene along with preliminary findings from the medical examiner indicate that Ms. Carter died from repeated blunt force blows to the back of the head. The nature of the resulting skull fracture, including the pattern of the wounds and the prone position Ms. Carter was discovered in, is not consistent with a fall. The final autopsy and toxicology results will not be available for several more days, but it is likely Ms. Carter died instantly. Reached via email, Detective Ned Bremmer stated, "We will not classify the death until we have completed our investigation." No suspect has been named. Representatives of Dearborn have released a brief statement: "We are cooperating fully with the Sullivan County Sheriff's Office and look forward to a speedy conclusion to this investigation. We have no further comment at this time and ask that you give the Carter family privacy."

The campgrounds, which include steep mountain trails marked with large rocks, were said to have been particularly slippery after a storm, and the terrain is known to be difficult under the best of circumstances. Forest Valley's head groundskeeper, Jack Vernon, who led the Dearborn students on a hike earlier that day, has insisted that all safety measures were in place.

Classmates, teachers, administrators, and family members gathered on Tuesday for Ms. Carter's funeral service. Friends described her as a talented athlete and a popular class leader. Replying to a reporter's questions, Ms. Rita Cleary, a Dearborn teacher and organizer of the trip, stated all necessary precautions were taken. She refrained from going into further detail. Ms. Carter is survived by her parents, William and Marci Carter, and one brother, Josh Carter.

This is a developing story.

Jason Blakely

The article is accompanied by a photo of the gathering outside the funeral home. Rachel, Miss Cleary, and a number of other students can be made out in the crowd. Thanks to Jordan's intervention, Daniel is nowhere visible.

Within two hours, an email from Dearborn arrives, announcing a meeting at six that evening for all concerned parents.

*

Dearborn's auditorium is filled with as many fathers as mothers, an exclamation point on the gravity of the situation. The stately hall, scene of so many Christmas pageants and high school musicals, is rife with distrust that could easily tip into open hostility.

The anxious murmuring stops as Headmaster Nederlander takes to the stage. The school administrators in the front row straighten their backs. Miss Cleary, seated behind them, leans forward and whispers something to one of the other chaperones, who makes no show of hearing her.

"Thank you for coming this evening," the headmaster begins. "This is a difficult time for all of us. The entire Dearborn family is in mourning." He clears his throat, scanning the sea of parents. "Adele Stein, our head guidance counselor, will outline the steps we are taking to support your children through this tragedy, but I would first like to make one thing clear. The story in today's newspaper was not only premature but irresponsible and based on unconfirmed sources. We have every reason to believe that Amanda's death was due to an unfortunate accident on campgrounds that were not properly safeguarded by the camp staff." He glances down at his notes. "We have called in Charlotte Colson, Dearborn's outside counsel, to speak with you tonight and answer any questions you might have. As you can imagine, this development has been deeply disturbing to the Carter family. They greatly appreciate your thoughts and prayers, but I hope we can all agree to give them privacy. I will now turn it over to Ms. Stein."

The guidance counselor steps up, cloaked in layers of somber chocolate-brown muslin.

"As Headmaster Nederlander made clear, we're here to assist you in any way we can. Grief counseling is available twenty-four seven, not only for your children but for you. We are taking steps to ensure that this investigation will be as minimally disruptive to our students' lives as possible. That said, it may contribute to a sense of uncertainty and distrust in our community. We encourage you to be mindful of your child's use of social media, where rumors can masquerade as fact," she continues. "I thought it would be helpful to describe some signs of distress in your children to be on the lookout for, including loss of appetite, withdrawal, mood swings, and nightmares. We suggest that you take extra time to talk with your child about what has happened. Reassure them that you are doing everything you can to keep them safe and that Dearborn is committed to that as well. Any changes in behavior that seem extreme or do not abate should be brought to my attention. My door is always open."

Jordan is growing increasingly impatient, his fists clenching and unclenching. "How long are they going to dance around the real reason we're here?" he mutters.

His question is answered when Dearborn's lawyer, Charlotte Colson, strides up to the podium and introduces herself. "I'm sure you all want to get home to your families, so I will be brief. Beginning tomorrow, a detective from Sullivan County will be at Dearborn to conduct interviews with everyone who was on the trip or might otherwise have information. We are cooperating fully with the investigation and expect it to be brought to a rapid conclusion. We have also instituted our own review to look into Forest Valley's safety measures and uncover any lapses that might have occurred. We have canceled all class trips until we are satisfied with the results. Now, I'm happy to take your questions."

Todd Hanson's father bolts from his seat. "The newspaper report did not make this sound like an 'unfortunate accident.' Are our children at risk of further violence?"

Finally, the yearning for reassurance and the distrust of anything we'll be told are both out in the open. Parents shift in their seats, their attention laser-focused on the lawyer, waiting for answers.

"I must warn you not to jump to conclusions based on one poorly sourced story. There's no conclusive evidence that Amanda's death was due to an act of violence. Regardless, Dearborn continues to place the utmost importance on the security of all our students while on school premises and will take all necessary precautions."

Jordan shoots up. "Our children are minors. I presume parents will get prior notice and be able to accompany them to meetings with the detective?"

"I cannot reiterate this enough, your children are not, I repeat not, under investigation. They are being questioned as witnesses in the hopes that they can provide useful information. There is no law stating that an adult must be present for that," Ms. Colson replies.

"I'll take that as a yes," Jordan retorts. "Is Dearborn itself, and the clear lack of supervision that occurred, being investigated as well?"

"As I said, we are cooperating fully, but I take exception to your characterization. There is no evidence that our chaperones were at fault in any way."

A grumbling ripples through the room. Of course, Miss Cleary and the rest of them were at fault. It was their job to watch over our children, and they failed. Catastrophically.

Before the next question can be asked, a young man in gray slacks and a white button-down shirt rises from the front row and steps onto the stage. Ms. Colson does a poor job of hiding her displeasure but is forced to make room for him.

"Do you mind?" the young man asks, polite but insistent. "It might be helpful if I said a few words."

"Of course."

"Thank you." He turns to face us. His close-cropped hair is the color of burnished copper. A smattering of freckles bridges his nose. "Good evening. I'm Detective Ned Bremmer from Sullivan County. I will be the person speaking with your children. First of all, let me express my sincere sympathies. There is no tragedy that touches our hearts as deeply as the loss of a child. We intend to proceed with the greatest sensitivity and will work closely with the Dearborn staff to ensure that we are operating in accordance with best practices from an investigative as well as compassionate standpoint. That said, we will follow the investigation wherever it might lead. To that end, I'd like to clarify some of what you've heard."

Nederlander stares at the floor, his jaw clenched.

"I agree that the report in this morning's newspaper was premature, and my department will do everything possible to prevent further leaks, but the basic facts were correct. Initial autopsy results suggest that Amanda Carter's death was due to repeated blows to her head. We are in the early stages of the investigation, but we do not believe this could have been accidental."

I clutch Jordan's hand while all through the room others do the same, turning to each other, to the detective, and to Nederlander, who was blatantly trying to hide the facts from us. Facts that shock and scare every single person in this room, inconvenient facts, but facts nonetheless. Anger is brewing in every parent's face. You can see its reflection in Nederlander's eyes.

The detective waits for the room to settle. "I'd like to take this opportunity to ask that if your child tells you anything that might be useful, please come forward," he continues. "You are our greatest resource. We have set up an anonymous tip line, and all communications will be kept strictly confidential."

The headmaster, who has had quite enough, steps up to intervene before the audience can turn on him.

"Thank you, Detective Bremmer." Nederlander looks out at the parents. "Your children will be informed of this procedure by their homeroom teachers tomorrow. Any questions or concerns should be directed to Tom Hennessy, our head of communications." He signals to the Dearborn staff to rise, closing the meeting to further questions, leaving us adrift.

*

We follow the stream of stunned parents out of the auditorium. The school staff, including Miss Cleary, have stayed behind, which spares me from having to pretend to have anything more than a cursory relationship with her.

We find Kara and Peter standing on the sidewalk.

"If that was meant to reassure anyone, I don't think it worked," Kara remarks. "I can't believe the school knew this and didn't tell us. You have to wonder what else they're not saying."

"At least the detective seems like a straight shooter," Peter says.

Kara shakes her head. "It's so hard to believe. Who could have done something like this to Amanda?"

"Has Abby learned anything more from Eliot?" I ask.

"Who's Eliot?" Jordan asks.

"One of the other chaperones," Kara adds hastily. "He was as surprised as everyone else when he read the story, but I didn't have a chance to catch up with her tonight. She ran out before the meeting ended."

I turn to Peter. "You're our resident lawyer. Are you going to let Olivia talk to the detective?"

Jordan frowns, displeased that I've asked another man for advice.

"Yes," Peter replies, "though I won't allow it without being present."

"What do you think they'll be questioned about?"

"Their whereabouts, if any of them was with Amanda or knows who was, for starters."

"Didn't they already ask the kids all that before they left Forest Valley?"

"I'm sure the scene was chaotic, and information may have changed."

"Has your daughter said anything more about that night?" Jordan asks.

"The only thing she's said is that she and Daniel were together."

"Exactly. Once they explain that to the detective, we'll be done with this."

With that, Jordan indicates it's time for us to leave.

*

"I'm going to call Harriday before Daniel speaks to anyone," Jordan says as soon as he closes the Uber door.

Harriday is our lawyer. Jordan's, really. And Daniel's. "Is that necessary?"

I know the answer. I wish I didn't.

"We don't know what is or isn't necessary yet. And I want to talk to Miss Cleary as soon as possible. In the meantime, remind Olivia's mother to get the partnership agreement I sent them back to me. Tell her as soon as I have it, the money for the app is ready to go."

Whatever happens, whatever is necessary, Jordan will handle it.

I try to be reassured. And turn a blind eye to the maneuverings I claim to find so distasteful.

There's only one thing that matters now.

Chapter 29

Kara

Olivia, making a rare appearance outside her bedroom, is waiting for us when we get home.

"So, what did they tell you at this big meeting tonight?" she asks while we're hanging up our coats, feigning a sarcasm that rings hollow.

"The newspaper story was right. Amanda's death wasn't an accident. There's going to be a detective in school tomorrow," Peter tells her. "Why don't we sit down? There are a few things we need to go over."

"Like what?"

"Like what you were doing that night."

"I already told you."

"Tell me again."

"Daniel and I were together. Last time I checked, that's not against the law."

Peter manages to maintain the calm demeanor he's acquired through years of litigation. His lack of visible emotion or judgment is a strategy designed to avoid putting Olivia on the defensive. I agreed on the way home to trust his methods, but it's not easy. It's all I can do to keep from screaming at her. *Don't you see how serious this is? Can't you tell us, please,* please, *you had nothing to do with what happened?*

"This detective, Bremmer, is going to want more details than that. Is there anything you're not telling us?" Peter asks calmly.

"Are you asking me to describe *exactly* what Daniel and I were doing?" Olivia retorts, certain Peter would not appreciate those particular details.

However hard it is for me to accept that Oliva might be having sex—*might be*—it's harder for Peter. Maybe it always is for fathers. He shakes his head, refusing to take the bait. I know him, though. It will burrow in, uprooting his notion of Olivia as still young, still his.

"Olivia, you're not doing yourself any favors with this attitude," he continues, exasperation beginning to poke through. "These are exactly the types of questions you're going to be asked. Are you sure you didn't see Amanda at any point?"

"No."

"I'm assuming Daniel will say the same?"

"Why wouldn't he? It's the truth."

Good, I think. *Great. Are we done now?* Daniel and Olivia were alone together. What happened is horrible, *beyond* horrible, but it has nothing to do with our daughter. My pulse begins to slow for the first time since we got home. I'm ready—more than ready—to accept Olivia's answers as final.

Peter refuses to be as easily satisfied. "Where did you two go?" he continues.

"I'm not sure. It was dark. Somewhere near the lake," Olivia answers dismissively.

I want Peter to stop now, just stop. Olivia has told us enough. What does he think can be gained by poking further and heading into territory we may not be able to find our way back from?

"I think we've heard enough for tonight," I interject.

They both look at me as if they've forgotten I'm in the room.

"I'm handling this," Peter snaps at me impatiently.

I glare at him, seething at being reprimanded in front of our daughter, but remain rooted as he continues his interrogation. Whatever he asks, whatever she answers, I need to hear.

He turns back to Olivia. "What time did you get back?"

"How should I know? They took our phones."

"You and Daniel left together and came back together?"

"We wanted to be alone. Why is that so hard to understand?"

"I'm trying to understand. I'm also trying to understand why you seem so unconcerned about what happened to Amanda."

"It sucks, but it had nothing to do with me."

"'It sucks'?" Peter repeats, incensed. "Your classmate died, and all you can say is 'it sucks'?"

He looks at Olivia, wondering what, if anything, can break through to her. Nothing, it seems.

Olivia has been exhibiting every one of the warning signs Ms. Stein listed tonight for the past two years, but there's something new lurking behind her scrim of bravado, a corrugated hardness that baffles and troubles me.

"Are we done?" she asks, standing up. "I need to finish my homework."

"One more thing," Peter calls after her. "Under no circumstances are you to speak with the detective alone."

She slams her bedroom door, lost to us.

I leave Peter on the couch, his head in his hands, and retreat into our bedroom. I would slam the door, too, if I could, slam it shut against my willful, impenetrable daughter and my dogged, stubborn husband, slam it against everything that's already happened and everything to come.

But I don't.

A few feet away, the sound from a video trickles out of Maya's room, where she's been holed up since we got home. Poor, placid, note-taking Maya, perpetually hiding from us. I don't blame her. I should go into her room, comfort her, at the very least show curiosity about her day. And I will. Tomorrow.

I leave the door ajar and curl up on the bed, waiting for Peter to come back to me, too spent and too scared to hold on to anger.

*

Within hours, online, local, and cable news outlets across the country pick up the story of the beautiful redheaded sixteen-year-old who was killed on a class trip. The reporting replicates and mutates, depending on the source: privileged kids who think the rules don't apply to them, an innocent girl's life violently snatched from her, the scandalous lack of oversight. Underlying each recounting, there is the search for an explanation—lax parenting, rough sex, drinking, drugs. Dearborn parent chats teem with rumor and outrage, suspicion and blame, though the object of the wrath varies; the school, the chaperones, Forest Valley, the kids who were out that night, their names ricocheting about.

"One of us should take the girls to school," Peter suggests over breakfast the next morning.

We're gentler with each other, both exhausted from last night's battles. Peter did what he had to do, not in the way I would have, but in the way he believed was best for Olivia. I recognize that. It doesn't make me happy, but nothing would. We have no choice but to stumble through this together.

"I'll do it," I tell him. "I have an early meeting at work."

"You can't be serious?" Olivia protests.

"It's going to be mayhem," Peter tells her.

"You're being ridiculous."

"I'm being a parent."

*

A scrum of news crews is circling the entrance to Dearborn when we arrive. Two extra security guards in red jackets push intruders back, forming an aisle to let rattled kids scurry through. The young reporter Rachel talked to at the funeral stands at the edge, taking notes.

It's a scene you see on the news. At other schools. With other families. Now, us.

Olivia hurries over to Daniel, and the two of them walk into school holding hands, a world unto themselves, leaving Maya to brave the corridor alone.

When both girls are safely through the door, I turn to leave and find Abby watching from half a block away.

"Where's Rachel?" I ask.

"Inside. I had strict orders not to come any closer."

"Olivia and Maya weren't thrilled either. They don't understand how quickly something like this can spin out of control."

"Eliot told me Nederlander is going to do everything in his power to make this go away as fast as possible. The way they're handling this is unbelievable."

"It's hard to make a girl's death simply go away," I remark.

Abby is waiting for more—a shared sense of outrage, any information I might have picked up, a theory that might make sense of any of this.

Instead, I tell her I have to run and ask if she got Hollis's text about signing the partnership papers last night.

"Yes," she answers, "but don't you find the timing a little surprising considering everything going on?"

"Jordan's a businessman; he likes moving quickly. Abby, sign the papers, okay? We're running out of options."

The urgency is duc to more than financial duress, though that is real enough.

For the first time, it's not something I'm comfortable trying to explain to Abby.

Chapter 30

Abby

Ten days after the murder
Monday, October 20

Scott has called twice since the newspaper story about Amanda's death, anxious for details, offering to help, asking when he can see me. He's been checking in with Rachel as well, though she's as opaque with him as she is with me, rebuffing even rudimentary inquiries with one-word answers.

"I wish you'd told me about the meeting at Dearborn. I would have come," he said when we spoke Thursday night. "This concerns me too. She's my daughter, and I would prefer it if you no longer made unilateral decisions."

Inserting Scott into that world would require an explanation I have yet to formulate. I don't have a ready-made narrative for Rachel to offer her friends about the sudden appearance of her father. I don't have a viable explanation for Eliot that wouldn't shred what we've started. There probably isn't one.

"Let's get through this first," I told Scott. "I'm not sure Rachel is prepared to tell people about you yet."

"Are you sure you're not the one who isn't prepared?" he asks, his patience diminishing.

"I'm not sure of anything."

*

The time comes sooner than I'd hoped.

An email from Dearborn shows up Monday morning, at 8:17 a.m., while I'm making a second cup of coffee.

> Dear Ms. Ettinger,
>
> As we announced at the meeting last week, we are working closely with authorities to gain a fuller understanding of what happened at Forest Valley and will be speaking to each of the students who were on the trip. Detective Bremmer has requested a meeting with your daughter, Rachel, after school tomorrow at 4:30 p.m. in room 412. You are welcome to join her should you choose to. I will assume the time is confirmed unless I hear otherwise.
>
> Thank you,
> Adele Stein

I read the email twice, text Kara, then Hollis.

Neither has received a similar request.

Eliot is in school and not answering his phone.

I hesitate, then call Scott.

"I've checked with two other mothers. No one else's kid has been summoned," I tell him.

"I'm sure they're going down the list. I'd like to come with you, though. I've spent my entire career in academic environments. I have a sense of how these things work. Schools like Dearborn operate by their own set of rules. Their goals are not always what they seem."

It isn't a question, and I don't protest.

*

"Nice outfit," Scott remarks when we meet outside Dearborn. "Going for sexy librarian?"

I dug a pencil skirt out from the back of my closet and a navy silk blouse that I hoped would read "responsible mother."

"Too much?"

"You look good."

Even now, his smile scrambles the molecules. It would be so much easier if it didn't.

Scott, in a charcoal blazer and light-blue shirt, looks reassuringly professorial.

"This feels like the parent-teacher conference from hell," I murmur as we make our way in, passing a tide of students jostling and teasing each other as if a child, one of their own, hasn't died. Only the noticeably beefed-up security gives a hint that anything untoward has happened.

"I spoke with Rachel last night. I wanted to let her know there's nothing to worry about. All she has to do is tell them what she knows," he replies.

"What did she say?" I ask nervously.

"Not much. I seem to have lost my favored nation status."

*

We pause outside the closed door of room 412.

"Where's Rachel?" Scott asks.

"She said she'd meet us here. Maybe she's already inside."

He knocks lightly.

A voice coming from the other side answers. "Come in."

Detective Ned Bremmer rises from behind his desk and leans over to shake hands.

"You must be Rachel's parents. Thank you for coming."

There are three empty chairs crammed around the desk. Charlotte Colson, the lawyer, rises from the fourth and introduces herself with none of the false bonhomie of the detective.

"We're still waiting for your daughter," Ms. Colson informs us in a clipped tone.

Scott looks at his watch. "She's only four minutes late."

Detective Bremmer shrugs, unconcerned. "In my experience, kids have a fluid sense of time."

There are no papers on the desk aside from a single folder and a spiral notebook open to a blank page. The only personal touch is a silver-framed photograph of the detective and a young woman with waves of long blond hair, both of them young and smiling and new. He follows my gaze. "My wife, Susanna," he tells me. "I'm still getting used to saying that. It's only been three months."

"Congratulations."

We sit in an uncomfortable silence until Rachel finally walks in, taking the smallest possible steps. She offers no apology for being tardy as she settles on the edge of the sole empty chair.

I try unsuccessfully to cue her to appear more amenable.

"Hello, Rachel. Thank you for coming," Detective Bremmer begins. "I'm sure this is a hard time for you."

"It's okay," she mumbles.

The detective turns to Ms. Colson. "Charlotte, I was wondering if you'd mind? I'd like to speak to Rachel and her family alone."

The lawyer's pinched face constricts further. "I'd prefer to stay."

"I'll fill you in afterward," he insists.

He waits until she's closed the door.

"School authorities give me the heebie-jeebies," he tells Rachel conspiratorially. "Maybe I'm getting flashbacks of my own misspent youth."

There's absolutely nothing in Detective Bremmer's demeanor to suggest he's had a misspent moment in his life.

"I appreciate all the help you can provide as we try to make sense of what happened at Forest Valley," he continues.

"I don't see how I can help. I didn't see Amanda."

"Sometimes the most inconsequential things end up being useful. I understand that on the night Amanda died, you were one of the six kids who left the lodge?"

Rachel manages a reluctant half-nod.

Despite knowing this, I'd been holding on to the irrational hope that it was a misunderstanding and this entire meeting would prove unnecessary. Magical thinking is second nature when it comes to your child.

"Who did you leave the lodge with?"

"No one."

"You ventured out alone? That must have been scary. It's awfully dark there at night. I get ridiculously nervous when I can't see where I'm going."

"It was all right."

"You're obviously braver than me. Do you remember what time you left?"

The detective's smooth tone sets my teeth on edge. I hope Rachel can see it for what it is—a ploy—but there's a differential between her intellectual savvy and her emotional intelligence. The cost until now has been her lack of close friends. The danger is far greater here.

"I don't know," she answers. "I didn't have my phone."

"Maybe we can piece the time together if we look at the activities schedule."

Bremmer opens the folder and pulls out a neat stack of papers. "I gather that the afternoon hike and evening entertainment were the only planned activities that took place," he says. "I've spoken with Jack Vernon. You remember the Forest Valley guide? We went over the paths you took on the hike. The man is a marvel. He knows every inch of the grounds like the back of his hand, but I'll bet you know the area just as well. I've heard you've gone there for a number of summers. How many is it, five?"

"Six," Rachel corrects him.

"You must love it there."

She nods but offers nothing more. She doesn't tell him that she dreams of camp during the winter months. That she packed for the summer weeks before she had to. Or that, despite that, she has never stayed in touch with a single person she met there for reasons she is unwilling to explain.

"I understand the hike was cut short by the rain."

"It was pouring. We could've been killed by lightning."

"I'm sure you were soaked. I gather you all changed clothes, then went to dinner. What happened after that?"

"There was that performance thing."

"Chief Little Cloud. Were you present for that?"

"It's not like we had a choice," she snaps.

I bite the inside of my cheek and glance at her, trying to send the message to be polite. Notes are being taken, scores are being kept. She ignores me, looking straight ahead. All I can do is stand by and watch her teetering on the edge of a cliff, unable to give her a hand.

"Then what did you do?"

"There was free time and snacks."

"Is that when you left the lodge, Rachel?"

Scott interrupts before she can answer. "Detective, I hope you're looking into how any of the kids could have left if there had been adequate supervision."

"This is a murder investigation, Mr. Ettinger. We're looking into everything."

The word—*murder*—cuts through the air. The certainty of it. Amanda's head smashed, bloodied. Rachel flinches. We all do.

"Mr. Amberson," Scott corrects him.

The detective makes a note. "It appears the back door wasn't locked because Miss Cleary was worried it would be a fire hazard. Speaking of Miss Cleary," he says, turning back to Rachel, "all of you who were out that night are in the same homeroom. You must know each other very well. Have a special bond."

Rachel shrugs.

"When they told me how small the class size is here, I couldn't believe it. I went to public school where there were at least thirty-five of us in every class."

"I went to the same kind of school as you, not Dearborn," I interject, grasping at any opportunity to establish an alliance. I have so little control in this meeting, none. Not over the detective's questions, not over my daughter's answers.

Bremmer nods politely. "Getting back to what we were talking about, Rachel, you say you left the lodge after the performance. Can you tell me where you went?"

"I don't know. Like you said, it was dark. Some field."

"You didn't recognize it from all your years at Forest Valley?"

"They all look the same at night."

"Can you tell me why you would go out in the dark on such a wet night?"

"I went to find Hannah."

"Yes, she was one of the girls who also left the lodge. I gather that Hannah was bullied by Amanda and a number of the other girls. Wasn't there an issue about cookies or cupcakes, something like that? Were they teasing her about her weight?"

"Yeah, it was gross. Who does that?"

"That must have hurt Hannah. What happened when you found her?"

"We talked for a while."

"Hannah must have been very angry with Amanda."

"She had a right to be. I know I'm not supposed to say anything bad about someone who died, but what Amanda did was disgusting," she says vehemently.

Her anger is justified. Surely the detective would agree. It's not a portent of anything more.

"Bullying is inexcusable under any circumstance," Detective Bremmer says. "How long would you say you were with Hannah?"

"I don't know. Not that long."

"Did you happen to see Amanda while you were out?"

"No, I didn't see anyone."

"What did you and Hannah do after you talked?"

"We went back to the lodge."

Bremmer glances down at his notes, then back to Rachel.

"Miss Cleary said you came in alone."

Scott jiggles his left foot, stops. There's a curve in the road ahead. Rachel instinctively starts to move her forefinger to her mouth to gnaw a hangnail but quickly puts it down. She sees the bend too.

"We walked in separately," she says.

There's the same slight tremor in her voice that's been there since she was a toddler when she told me something that hovered between an excuse and a lie. I used to find how easy it was to recognize reassuring.

"Did you see Hannah enter the lodge?"

Rachel shakes her head.

"Do you know where she might have gone after the two of you spoke?"

"She was going to follow me back. Like I said."

The detective pauses to make another note before continuing.

"I understand Miss Cleary cleaned up some scratches on your arm when you got back. How did you get those?"

"I got them earlier," Rachel answers, squirming in her seat.

"Miss Cleary seems to think you got them while you were out at night."

"She's wrong."

Miss Cleary is almost always wrong, about everything. But there's something in the way Rachel hid the scratches when she got home, the way she cleaned the dried blood off them herself, that makes it hard for me to know what to believe.

"I see. Well, it was awfully slippery. Let's go over everything to make sure I have it straight." He runs his right forefinger down his notes. "Amanda was teasing Hannah, and Hannah got upset and ran out. You went to comfort her, and then you came back to the lodge. Is that right?"

"That's what I told you."

"I gather Amanda was something of a class leader. What do you call it, an alpha girl? I don't know a lot about teenage girls, but if memory serves, girls like that can be hard on each other, and on teachers. My mother is a teacher. The stories she can tell." He shakes his head. "Did Amanda have a beef with Miss Cleary?"

"I mean, sure. She made fun of her, but everyone does."

"What about you, Rachel? Did you have a more personal reason to be upset with Amanda?"

Rachel eyes him suspiciously. "What do you mean?"

"I'm sure it's nothing, but I heard she said something to you on the bus ride to Forest Valley that might have been upsetting."

Rachel gnaws at a hangnail on her left thumb.

Bremmer looks at us. "This is a difficult conversation. Perhaps it would be best if I had some privacy with your daughter?"

"We're not going anywhere," Scott answers firmly.

The detective turns back to Rachel. "People overheard you two having a disagreement. Can you tell me what made you so angry with Amanda?"

Rachel, flushed, shakes her head, refusing to answer.

"We're done here," Scott says, rising and indicating for us to follow.

Bremmer stands up as well and slides a card with his cell phone number across his desk in Rachel's direction. "If there's anything you want to tell me, you can reach me any time."

Scott grabs the card and slips it into his pocket.

"Don't say a word," he warns as we make our way to the staircase.

*

"Rachel, do you want to tell us what your argument with Amanda was about?" Scott asks when we are safely outside.

She hisses at him with pure venom. "I don't have to tell you anything. I barely know you. I don't even know why you're here. Besides, it doesn't matter what Amanda said to me. I'm not the one they should be talking to."

"What do you mean? Who should they be talking to?"

"Daniel and Olivia. I know they're lying about that night. I heard them talking about it at the funeral."

"Rachel, are you sure you know what you're saying?" I ask.

She glares at me. "I hate you. Everything you do makes my life worse. Because you lie about everything doesn't mean I do."

She tears off down the street, her backpack swinging wildly from her shoulder. Rachel, the person I love most in the world. Who I only want to protect. And who I'm losing.

Desperate, I'm about to take off after her when Scott stops me.

"I think it might be best if you let me handle this."

Admitting he's right is one of the hardest things I've ever had to do.

I nod reluctantly and turn to head in the opposite direction when I spot Eliot, standing in front of Dearborn's doors, observing us closely.

Chapter 31

Abby

I would walk away if I could.

I would go back in time and tell Eliot about Scott when I should have.

Instead, all I can do is stand, paralyzed, waiting for the pieces to shatter.

Eliot and I find a spot a few feet from Dearborn where the buildings meld into brownstones, their window boxes beginning to turn brown in the autumn air.

"You didn't tell me you were coming to school today." His words barely disguise the question lurking within.

"The detective asked to meet with us."

He's barely listening. "Abby, the man you were with. I saw you talking to him in front of school the morning we left for the trip, and now he's here with you. Who is he?"

I grind a dried leaf into the pavement with the tip of my shoe until it turns to powder. The time bomb that's been ticking since the evening Eliot and I met at the bar after I dropped Rachel off for dinner with Scott has stopped. I knew it would at some point. Still, I'm not ready for it. Not now. Not like this.

"He's Rachel's father," I say quietly before summoning the nerve to look at him.

"I don't understand. You told me you never saw Rachel's father after she was born, that he was totally absent from your lives."

"I hadn't seen him in years. Do you remember that accelerator program I went to? He was one of the judges. I had no idea he'd be there." Maybe. Maybe that will be enough.

"That's why you blew me off that night?"

"I'm sorry."

He looks down the street, then back to me, thrusting his hands into his pockets. "Is he in your life now?"

"He's in my daughter's life."

"That's not what I asked."

No matter what I answer, I'll be betraying someone: Eliot, Scott. I don't want to be disloyal to either of them. I don't want to lose either of them.

"I don't know," I admit.

He rocks back and forth before speaking. "I've been honest with you about everything. You know my history. You know what my ex-wife did. You must realize how important trust is to me."

"I was going to tell you, Eliot. There's just been so much going on."

Which is true. I wish he could understand that. It's also true that I was a coward, unwilling to risk the chance at an intimacy I didn't think I'd find again.

"When?" he asks.

"Soon. Now."

I can see it instantly, before he says another word. I can feel the disintegration. It's over.

"I can't do this," Eliot tells me. "I can't be with someone I don't trust."

"Please, try to understand," I beg. "Rachel didn't know about him. I had to talk to her first."

The words slip out before I can shape them, ripping open the last seam of the story I'd stitched together for him.

"How could she not have known? Did he desert you?"

"Not really," I hedge. As if I still have a chance.

"He either did or he didn't."

I'll lose Eliot, but I have no choice. There's no way to rewind everything I said—or didn't say. There's nowhere to go.

"He didn't know about her until a few weeks ago," I admit. "We'd broken up by the time I got pregnant."

"Are you saying you never told him you had his baby?"

He stares at me with confusion and something worse, distaste.

Tears cluster in my eyes as I grasp at one last chance—however slim—to make him understand.

"I thought it would be better that way. I made a mistake. I wish I could change it."

He shakes his head in disbelief, his lips curling down.

"Say something," I plead.

"I wouldn't know where to begin."

He turns to leave when I put my hand out to stop him. As painful as it is to lose him, there's something that pains me more, enough to eradicate any last shred of pride.

"Eliot, wait. I get it, I really do. When you're ready, I'll answer any questions you have and tell you anything you want to know." I pause, ashamed, but not enough to stop. "I realize I have no right to ask a favor, but if you could do one thing for me until then?"

His muscles tense. "What?"

"It's about what happened that night. Rachel said she overheard Olivia and Daniel agreeing to lie."

"About what?"

"I'm not sure. Something to do with Amanda."

"Is that what Rachel told the detective?"

"She said it after we left his office. Olivia's mother, Kara, is my best friend. I don't know what to believe."

"Rachel might have misunderstood. Maybe she has a thing for Daniel, and she's jealous," he says dismissively.

"She's never mentioned that." It's possible, of course, but unlikely. At least I think it is.

"Did you mention every crush you had to your mother at sixteen? Bremmer has a lot of people to interview. Why don't you wait before doing anything? I have a feeling they have a better idea of what happened than they're letting on."

"Are you sure?" A tiny flicker of light opens up.

"I'll see what I can find out, if that's what you're asking. I want to help them figure out who's responsible for what happened to Amanda, but it doesn't change the rest. It doesn't change us."

"I understand. Will you at least consider giving me a second chance?"

An infinity of time passes before he answers.

"I'll be in touch."

*

I'll be in touch.

Something a recruiter says after a bad job interview. Something I say every year to Debra Seymour after her annual party.

"I'll be in touch" is what you say before you walk down the street and turn the corner, taking all hope for a future with you.

Chapter 32

Kara

Twelve days after the murder
Wednesday, October 22

When the downstairs intercom rings at half past seven on Wednesday night, I assume it's a food delivery person with the wrong apartment. New York may be a city of random encounters, but there remains an inbred suspicion of spontaneity. People don't show up at each other's apartments unbidden. They don't call without texting first. I press the button on the intercom to tell whoever it is they've made a mistake. Instead, a vaguely familiar face pops up on the tiny video screen.

"Can I help you?"

"Good evening, Mrs. Strickland. I'm Detective Bremmer of Sullivan County. I believe your daughter's school mentioned that I might be speaking with her?"

His appearance is so out of context that it takes me a beat to make the connection. When I do, my stomach drops. I know that Rachel and others have met with the detective at Dearborn, but no one mentioned him showing up at their door. There's no universe where this can be good.

"I was hoping I could talk with Olivia for a few minutes," the detective continues when I don't answer.

I have no choice but to let him in.

Peter, in the living room studying a report on water scarcity in Somalia, looks up. "Who was that?"

"That detective we saw at the school meeting."

Peter immediately puts down his iPad. "What's he doing here?"

"He wants to speak to Olivia."

I try to gauge from Peter's expression how alarmed I should be. His brows, knit in puzzlement, do nothing to reassure me.

"Go tell Olivia to stay in her room," he says abruptly. "I'll let him in."

Peter's usual confidence in his ability to defuse any situation with authorities is nowhere in sight. I hurry to Olivia's bedroom, wondering what would happen if we locked the door and refused to come out. Forever. Unfortunately, this is not a realistic scenario. Instead, in as calm a voice as I can manage, I tell her that the detective has come to speak to her. For a split second, Olivia's face registers alarm before she masks it with her current default mood—insolence. I pretend to ignore it, reluctant to instigate a fresh battle, and tell her to stay put until we give her a signal to come out.

By the time I get back, the detective is at the front door talking with Peter.

"What can I do for you?" Peter asks brusquely as I join the two men.

"I was hoping to speak with Olivia. I've found that kids can be more comfortable outside the confines of school. It feels less official. Is she home?"

"But this is an official visit," Peter reminds him. "Can you tell me what exactly you want to talk to her about?" He has yet to open the door enough to let the man in.

"It's important that we find answers to what happened on the class trip. I'm sure you would expect the same diligence if, God forbid, it had been your child who was killed. I would appreciate any help your daughter can provide."

The thought—*what if it was my child*—wakes me in the night, rattles me during meetings. But it wasn't. My child is in her bedroom, about to be questioned by a police detective, and I have no idea how to protect her.

Peter, accepting we have no choice, acquiesces. "I'll go get Olivia."

He disappears into the back of the apartment. It's clear from the amount of time he's gone that warnings are being issued, guidelines are being expressed.

Flustered, I go into hostess mode as if that will somehow morph this into a social call. "Can I get you something to drink?"

"I'm fine, thank you. Do you mind if I sit? It's been a long day."

His face, his voice, everything about the man, is resolutely neutral except for his eyes, as he takes in the room. I follow his gaze to the paw prints on the couch, the labyrinth of unopened mail on the coffee table, all the things it's too late to neaten up.

He's settled on the couch when Peter returns, trailed by a reluctant Olivia in sweatpants and a T-shirt. Her expression is inscrutable, her eyes cast down.

Bremmer rises to greet her. "Hello, Olivia."

"Hi," she mumbles.

"Thank you for talking to me. I know you must be busy. From what I gather, Dearborn gives a ridiculous amount of homework. Maybe it's an exaggeration, but I hear three, four hours a night. Is that true, Olivia?"

His blatant attempt at disarming Olivia irritates me. I hope she's smart enough not to be fooled. Luckily, she distrusts all adults on principle.

"I guess," she shrugs, choosing the chair farthest from him. Nomi, not known for her friendliness to strangers, hides behind her feet, eyeing the detective, her whiskers twitching.

"I won't take long," he promises. "I only want to ask a couple of questions. I'm hoping you can help me understand a few things I'm a bit confused about. Is that all right with you?" he asks, as if inquiring what ice cream flavor she prefers.

"I already told your people everything I know."

"I appreciate that, but let's go over it again."

He pulls a little pad out of his pocket.

Olivia looks at it as if it's an ancient artifact rather than the prop I know it to be.

"Remind me, who did you leave the lodge with?" he begins.

"No one," she answers flatly, as if that will be enough to settle the matter.

Bremmer smiles slightly. "So odd, isn't it? All six of you who went out that night seem to have gone alone. I suppose you were breaking the rules and didn't want to get caught, is that right?"

"Maybe," Olivia answers.

I glance at Peter, who's watching closely, straining with the effort it takes to stay silent.

"Here's one of the things I'm confused about," Bremmer says. "I thought you told the security people you spoke with Saturday morning that you were with Daniel Chapman. Are you saying you weren't with him?"

My pulse quickens. It's obvious he's setting a trap, purposefully trying to force my daughter into contradicting herself.

"I'm sure everyone was too upset to think clearly that morning," I interject.

"That may be true," he tells me. "That's why I'm here. Olivia, can you help me understand?"

"I was with Daniel," she answers cooly. "We met up outside the lodge."

"Where exactly was that?"

"Where the path begins."

"And then what did you two do?"

"We went to the lake."

Olivia's tone is clipped, the answers too neat. The detective doesn't know her the way I do, though. There's a chance he'll mistake her lack of hesitation for honesty.

"I imagine it was very muddy after all that rain," he posits.

"We sat on our jackets."

"Were you with Daniel the whole time?"

"Yes," she replies firmly.

"How long were you together?"

"I don't know."

For the first time, uncertainty creeps into Olivia's voice. She shifts her legs, accidentally kicking Nomi, who scampers away. I want to reach over and still her hands, remind her to breathe normally, make eye contact, but she isn't looking at me.

Bremmer remains unfazed. "Would you say an hour? More?" he asks.

"Something like that."

"Did anyone see you?"

"No."

I sigh loudly. *Of course no one saw them,* I want to chide him. *They were teenagers, sneaking around to do God knows what. Can we leave it at that?* Instead, I cluck my tongue like an old lady.

Bremmer pays no attention. Peter and I have been relegated to mute witnesses, our presence necessary but unappreciated. Acknowledging us in any way would break his rhythm, which he has no intention of doing.

"I understand you came back to the lodge separately," he tells Olivia. "I assume for the same reason. You didn't want to get caught?"

"I guess."

Bremmer nods. "Let me make sure I have this right. You went out alone. You met Daniel out of view of others to go to the lake, and at some point, you don't know when, you came back alone. Can you tell me what you two were doing by the lake?"

With every observation that piles up, the snags become more obvious.

"We were hanging out," Olivia replies vaguely.

Bremmer's voice shifts, becoming almost gentle. "Olivia, I realize there might be things you're embarrassed to say in front of your parents. Would you like to talk alone?"

I'm about to object—there's no way in hell I'm going to leave her alone with this man—but Peter beats me to it.

"Olivia, stay right where you are," he orders her.

The detective's gaze remains fixed on Olivia. "Is it possible that you got the time confused? Or could you be mistaken about where you met Daniel?"

Olivia shifts her legs again but says nothing.

"Where are you headed with this?" Peter interrupts.

Bremmer ignores him. "Olivia, think hard, is there any chance you didn't walk to the lake with Daniel?"

I've had enough of this, more than enough. "What makes you think our daughter isn't telling you the truth? Olivia is not a liar," I say, so vehemently I almost believe it.

"I never said she was," he replies equably, looking at me fully for the first time. "I'm only trying to figure out what happened." He turns back to Olivia. "Is there a possibility that you didn't walk to the lake with Daniel but met him there later? Or didn't meet him at all?"

I wait. Peter waits. Bremmer waits. But Olivia refuses to answer.

"Okay, let's move on then," the detective says finally, looking down at his notepad. "Are you sure you didn't see anyone else by the lake or on your way back? What about Chief Little Cloud?"

"Who?"

"The evening's performer."

"Why would I have seen him?"

"We're trying to confirm his whereabouts. Did you notice Amanda speaking with him after the performance?"

"I told you I didn't see her."

"You're right, you did say that. Would you say you had a good relationship with Amanda?"

I tense up again. The volatility of their not-quite-friendship has the potential to spark an eruption from Olivia that would not be beneficial.

She realizes this as well. "We didn't really hang out," she answers indifferently.

"Who did she hang out with?"

"Lots of people."

"Is it possible Daniel Chapman was one of them?"

"What? No, that's ridiculous," Olivia exclaims, her anger slicing through the air. "He thought she was a spoiled bitch. I told you, Daniel and I were together."

Bremmer doesn't say *aha*. He doesn't need to. "Did you and Amanda have something of a disagreement about Daniel before dinner?" he asks.

Peter's eyebrows rise. This is the first we're hearing about this, but it doesn't seem beyond the realm of possibility. At all.

"Who told you that?" Olivia demands.

"It's something I heard along the way. I could be wrong."

"You do realize anonymous tip lines are notoriously unreliable," Peter informs the detective in his most condescending lawyerly tone.

Bremmer's façade finally cracks. "In fact, they're often quite useful. But if you must know, this information came from one of the chaperones," he replies impatiently.

"Miss Cleary?" I ask incredulously. "That woman overreacts to everything. Ask around about the alarm bells she set off last year with that 'no touching on school grounds' nonsense."

That particular alarm bell went off when she found Todd and Olivia making out in the hallway, but I see no reason to provide further ammunition.

"Ma'am, I'm trying to find out what happened." Bremmer turns back to Olivia. "I understand you and Amanda weren't close, but if you had to guess, who do you think she was with that night?"

"I heard she may have been with Todd. They used to be a thing."

"Yes, the track star. Didn't you date him too?"

This is too much. Too intrusive, too judgmental. Too male. "My daughter's dating history is not relevant here," I tell him firmly.

Bremmer considers this, nods almost imperceptibly, and changes course. "Olivia, can you think of anyone who would want to hurt Amanda?"

Peter's legal reflexes kick in. "Detective, it seems safe to assume whoever attacked Amanda was stronger and, in all probability, larger than her, wouldn't you agree?"

"Not necessarily," Bremmer replies calmly. "Amanda was hit from behind. If she was taken by surprise, especially if she'd been drinking or taking drugs that diminished her reaction time, the perpetrator would not have had to overpower her. Size, strength, and sex are not determining factors in this case. In fact, there's no evidence of defensive wounds."

The clinical way he dismisses Peter's argument—the careful inclusion of details about how Amanda died—makes my blood run cold. Clearly this was his intention. He turns to Olivia. "Did you or any of the other kids have alcohol or marijuana?"

"That's enough," Peter says. "You don't need to answer that, Olivia. This conversation is over. I'll show you to the door, Detective."

"All right, we can continue this talk another time," Bremmer says, smiling politely as he rises. His butt is filmed with Nomi's white fur from the couch. None of us points this out.

"My daughter has already told you everything she knows about that night," Peter insists.

"That may be, but in my experience, memories, especially after a violent incident, can return in bits and pieces. It's one of the reasons trauma is so hard to treat. Some memories are impossible to forget, others impossible to remember."

"You do realize it's illegal to question my daughter without an adult present," Peter reminds him.

"Of course, though there's no law against people of any age coming forward of their own volition with information. It's something Olivia might want to consider. It could make things go easier in light of new evidence." He pauses. "You should know that we've recovered fabric fibers from the undergrowth near where Amanda was found. Our forensics team is examining the DNA now, but we do know this: It came from more than one individual. You can expect a follow-up on this."

"Good night, Detective." Peter locks the door behind him.

By the time he turns around, Olivia has vanished into her bedroom.

"Do you think I should call Hollis and see if Bremmer went there too?" I ask.

"That's the last thing you should do. Don't you get it, Kara? If Daniel has no alibi for all of his time, neither does Olivia. This could come down to his word against hers."

*

For the rest of the evening, Peter and I avoid looking at each other. Neither of us wants to ask the question haunting us both: *Do you believe Olivia is telling the truth?*

It's after one in the morning when I climb out of bed, tiptoe down the hallway, pull the clothes Olivia wore on the trip out of the laundry bin, carry them to the washing machine, and run the cycle twice.

Chapter 33

Hollis

Thirteen days after the murder
Thursday, October 23

The last stragglers from after-school activities have drifted off to tutoring sessions, away games at the hill schools, or the steps of the Metropolitan Museum, leaving the halls unnervingly quiet as we stand outside of Detective Bremmer's office, waiting to be summoned. Daniel, leaning against the far wall, sways slightly from side to side, avoiding our eyes.

"Don't forget what I told you," Jordan warns him. "You're to say as little as possible. Do you understand? Let me handle this."

Daniel doesn't acknowledge hearing him.

"Thank you for coming on short notice," Detective Bremmer says when we enter room 412 and take our seats.

"You implied there was some urgency." Jordan sits ramrod straight, his feet planted wide apart, staking out his territory.

"Unfortunately, the timing is not completely within our control."

"What does that mean?"

"We prefer to take time developing a case to make sure it's rock-solid before taking action. The problem," the detective says, shaking his head disparagingly, "is leaks. Upstate, we wouldn't have this type of situation, but the rules appear to be different here. Despite the fact that we have asked people not to speak to reporters, that request has not been honored."

"I hope you're not implying that has anything to do with us."

Jordan's demeanor, so intimidating to subordinates, has the opposite effect here. I shoot him a warning look that he chooses to disregard.

"As I was saying," Bremmer continues, "there's more media scrutiny around this case than any of us would like. It's come to our attention that the reporter from *The New York Times* who first wrote about the incident is poking around and has obtained certain information."

"What type of information?"

"I'm not at liberty to share the details, but I've impressed upon him that Daniel is a minor, as are others involved. There's no law prohibiting journalists from talking to teenagers though. We may disagree over the ethics, but I have no power to stop him. I've asked him to withhold publishing for a few more days as a professional courtesy, but there are no guarantees."

"Perhaps you're not applying the right type of pressure."

The detective ignores Jordan and looks directly at Daniel, who forces himself to meet his gaze. "I appreciate your cooperation, Daniel. Here's what I want to talk to you about: Once the mud dried on the mountain, certain objects were found near Amanda."

"What type of objects?" Jordan demands.

"Dad, will you be quiet," Daniel, who had been picking at a hangnail, insists.

I remain silent. For once, I'm on Jordan's side. I'm more than willing to have him prevent Daniel from talking. The risk of anything he might say is all too evident.

"Object might be the wrong word. A marijuana joint. The stub of a joint to be precise. The initial toxicology report shows there was THC in Amanda's system. Daniel, we have reports that you were heard making plans with Amanda."

Daniel opens his mouth to speak, but Jordan shuts him down. "Be quiet." He turns to the detective. "You can't seriously be basing assumptions on hearsay?"

"Mr. Chapman, I'm here to talk to your son, not you," Bremmer answers firmly. "If this continues, I'm going to have to ask you to leave."

A smile sneaks across Daniel's mouth. It's so rare that anyone stands up to Jordan.

Bremmer turns back to Daniel. "I know you'd like to clear this up as much as we would. How would you feel about taking a DNA test?"

"You said yourself the joint was covered in mud," Jordan says before Daniel can answer. "I find it hard to believe there would be any DNA on it."

"You'd be surprised by the technology our labs have today. I don't understand it myself, but there we are," Bremmer replies.

"Are you asking others to take DNA tests?"

"I can't share that information with you."

"Well, I have some information to share with you. That Indian performer Forest Valley hired? You haven't managed to locate him yet, have you?"

"Native American," Bremmer corrects him dryly. "Why do you ask?"

"I had my people look into him. You'd think they might have considered doing a background check before letting him near our children. You must know about his arrest record."

The detective, so even keeled until now, can't hide his annoyance. "We don't need 'your people' looking into anything. Any interference on your part will not only hinder our investigation, it could have serious consequences." He leans across the desk, focused only on Daniel. "There's something else you should know. Your friend, Todd Hanson, saw you coming down the mountain where Amanda was found."

I stare at a tiny smudge on the silver-framed photograph on Bremmer's desk, determined not to waver.

"Todd and I aren't friends," Daniel says. "He thinks I stole his girlfriend. He'd say anything to get back at me."

"You seem to be missing the point," Jordan informs the detective. "What was the Hanson boy doing on the hill? Are you getting a sample of his DNA?"

"We're looking into every possibility." Bremmer turns back to Daniel. "When you say you stole his girlfriend, do you mean Olivia Strickland or Amanda Carter?"

"Olivia."

"Thank you for clearing that up. Is there a chance that Olivia believed you were cheating on her with Amanda, and the two of them argued about it?"

"I wasn't cheating on anyone."

I take a shallow breath, remembering Amanda in Dearborn's lobby telling me she was "a good friend" of Daniel's. The same afternoon I went home to find him with Olivia when he promised me everything was "cool."

"That's not what I asked," Bremmer says. "Can you remind me where you met Olivia? I gather you left the lodge separately."

"We met by the lake."

"Perhaps I wrote it down wrong, but Olivia told me that you met by the path and walked to the lake together."

"That's what I meant," he answers too quickly.

"Did you happen to see the other two girls who were out, Rachel Ettinger or Hannah Streitfeld?"

"No."

"So you have no idea if they were together or not?"

"I didn't see anyone except Olivia."

"All right, Daniel. That's enough for today. Why don't you go home and think things over? You can give me your answer about the DNA test in the morning. It could clear this whole thing up for you."

"You have our answer," Jordan says.

"I can get a court order if necessary. Oh, and one more thing. I know that Daniel's records from his previous school were sealed, but we can get a court order for that too."

Jordan rises and looms over the detective's desk. "You'll find that people who threaten me end up regretting it."

*

We're a full block from Dearborn before Jordan turns to Daniel. "How stupid are you?"

"Jordan, please, that's not going to help anything."

"Tell me, if you were to take that DNA test, which you most certainly will not, what would it show?"

"Calm down," I warn.

He ignores me, continuing to scowl at Daniel. "What exactly happened up there? Because if it was anything like before, I'm not sure what I can do."

"I don't need you to do anything," Daniel retorts angrily. "I'm not like you."

Jordan glares at him before turning to me. "I told you to get that Cleary woman to come over. We need to talk. I'm going back to my office to make some calls."

Daniel waits until he's out of sight before speaking.

"I didn't hurt her, Mom. I know how it looks, but I never hurt her." His voice is straining at the seams.

"Your father will take care of it."

Daniel starts to walk away, and I follow when, out of the corner of my eye, I spot Adam, watching us from under an awning across the street.

Chapter 34

Abby

Fourteen days after the murder
Friday, October 24

The watercolors Scott gave me have remained untouched since the night of the trip when I sat at the kitchen table dipping my brush in a mug of water, making faltering strokes. It was awkward, my fingers unsteady, the brush too wet. The fusion of vision and execution that was rare enough when I painted regularly remained frustratingly out of reach. I haven't picked them up since.

Scott and I have barely spoken since he took off after Rachel the afternoon we met with Bremmer. "Whatever Amanda did or didn't say to Rachel, she's not in the mood to trust your version of anything," he informed me. He didn't ask for details about Eliot, and I gave up trying to explain. "Now is not the time," he said dismissively before hanging up.

The support he promised that day has proven to be provisional.

I've written more texts to Eliot than I can count. Apologizing. Trying to explain how something I was certain was long gone, a nonissue, is suddenly very much an issue. That I miss him. I haven't sent any of them. I wait to hear from him, looking for signs from the universe like a teenager checking every horoscope until she finds one that tells her what she longs to hear.

I force my attention back to designing banner ads for a dessert food truck, already a week late. The montage of cupcakes, waffles, and cannoli refuses any attempt to instill harmony. The colors are wrong, the shapes misaligned. When the phone rings, I'm grateful for an excuse to take a break.

"Can you talk?" Kara asks.

"Sure. Is everything okay?"

"I don't know. It's about that detective from Dearborn."

"What about him?" I ask warily.

My report to Kara of our meeting with Bremmer was an outline without color or details. I certainly didn't tell her what Rachel claimed out on the street, that Olivia and Daniel are lying. I'd like to think that, without tangible proof, I was protecting Kara, but I was also protecting Rachel. It never occurred to me that she might find out about it from someone else.

"He was here two nights ago."

"At your apartment?"

"Yes. Did he come to you?"

"I told you, we met with him at school. Why would he come to your apartment?"

"Olivia said she was with Daniel, but for some reason, Bremmer didn't seem convinced. Peter doesn't want me to tell anyone, but I'm worried."

I nestle the phone between my ear and shoulder while I fumble for my AirPods.

"What makes Bremmer think Olivia wasn't telling the truth?" I ask carefully. "Did Daniel say something different?"

"I don't know what Daniel said. Bremmer implied it came from one of the chaperones. It's got to be that fucking Cleary. She's had it in for Olivia since the staircase incident last year. The fucking cupcakes didn't help."

"What cupcakes?"

"Never mind. It has nothing to do with this. Let's just say Miss Cleary is not the biggest fan of my family."

"Did Bremmer tell you it was her?"

The pieces are slowly fitting into place no matter how hard I try to resist the connections.

"Who else could it be?"

"He wouldn't," I mumble. I can't believe that he would do that, that he resents me that much.

"What are you talking about?"

I push my laptop aside and pace the tiny kitchen.

"Eliot."

"What about Eliot?"

"Rachel might have mentioned she thought Daniel and Olivia weren't being completely truthful," I say tentatively, though there's no way to defuse it. It would be useless to try to explain that my only concern was turning Bremmer's attention away from Rachel. I didn't stop to consider the consequences for Kara. I'm not sure it would have stopped me.

Kara's tone grows harsh. "Are you saying Rachel told the detective that Olivia is lying?"

"No, she didn't do anything like that," I assure her.

"Then what are you saying?"

"Rachel brought it up after we left Bremmer's office. I didn't want to upset you for no reason, so I asked Eliot if he could find out what was going on. He promised he wouldn't say anything to Bremmer."

"Let me get this straight. Your daughter is an emotional basket case because you've been lying about who her father is for her entire life, so she made up some bizarre story, and instead of coming to me, you went to your boyfriend. We've known each other for years, and you've known him for, what, one month?"

"Kara, if Olivia is covering something up for Daniel, she could be in trouble, and if Rachel knows about it, she would be too. Think about it, how well do we know Daniel? Hollis has been so cagey about why he left his last school."

"What makes you so sure Rachel is right? She's always been jealous of Olivia. Maybe if she wasn't so desperate for friends of her own, she wouldn't lie about other people."

Every accusation is targeted precisely at the soft spots Kara knows exist.

"That's not fair," I protest.

"You don't have the right to talk to me about what's fair. Do you have any idea the position you put us in?" Her anger is escalating, a torrent now.

"I would never do anything to hurt you."

"You just did. I'm so sick of all your drama. You can rip up the partnership agreement. We're done, Abby."

She hangs up before I can say another word.

*

I put the phone down, stunned.

This is what Kara really thinks of Rachel: that she is friendless. Desperate. A basket case.

I remember all the times Kara complained about Olivia, her missing nights, her intransigence, all the panicked phone calls when Kara confided her fears and frustrations. She wasn't looking for verification. She was looking for a friend. There's a lot I could have said about Olivia—true things, hurtful things. How she flings herself at one boy after another, turning the dial up way too high to get a reaction. How she's flailing in plain sight. But I didn't. I wouldn't. I thought that was part of the deal.

I rub a drop of coffee from the table as my anger shifts to Eliot. Who I confided in. Who I trusted. And who went behind my back.

I reach him while he's walking to the subway on his way to school.

"We need to talk."

"Can it wait?"

"No. I told you what Rachel said in confidence. I very clearly asked you not to say anything to anyone. How could you have gone to that detective?"

Eliot waits for cars honking to stop before answering. "I didn't say anything to Bremmer. I wouldn't do that, Abby. All I did was ask Rita if she thought there was a chance that Olivia or Daniel might be lying. She knows them better than I do. I told her to keep it between us. I never mentioned Rachel's name."

"Why would you have gone to her without telling me?"

"Because I believe what Rachel said is probably true. I don't know Daniel Chapman well, but something isn't adding up. I also believe the Carters deserve an answer about what happened that night. I should have spoken to you, I'm sorry, but the school is pressuring the police to wrap this up quickly, and I didn't want you or Rachel to get caught in the cross fire. I was trying to protect you."

"Protect us from what?"

An ambulance screeches by, the city's soundtrack turning up and down at will.

"Hannah didn't back up Rachel's story," Eliot says when the siren fades. "She claims she never saw Rachel that night."

Chapter 35

Abby

There must be some mistake.

Some reason Hannah is lying.

Hannah and her party house and her truant parents, always a convenience, never a cohort. I used to feel sorry for her, but I wonder if she's been lying in wait all this time, hanging on until the right moment to strike.

Rachel has already left for school, and the apartment is eerily silent except for the whoosh of street cleaners making slow progress up the block.

For so long, it's been Kara who guides me through parental quagmires, who listens and advises me about what to do, what to think.

It's hard to believe that's over, that *we're* over, severed when I need her most.

I go into the bathroom and splash cold water on my face before calling the one person who, despite my pride, I may still be able to turn to.

"This isn't a good time," Scott says when he picks up.

"It's about Rachel. We need to talk. Please. I'll meet you anyplace you want."

"That's not possible."

"What do you mean, it's not possible? It's important. It's about that night."

"I'm up in Hanover."

"You left without telling me?"

Again. He is doing it again. It's unbelievable. Except it isn't.

"The professor taking over my classes asked if I could confer with a few of my graduate students, and it coincided with an important departmental meeting."

I collapse onto my bed, sucker punched. "You promised I wouldn't be alone. That you would be here for me. For us."

I never should have trusted him. Only a fool believes people change.

"I have responsibilities, Abby, and you made it clear you have a boyfriend," he says icily.

"I'm not sure I do, and even if I did, this is different. Rachel is our daughter."

It's the first time I've referred to Rachel as "ours." It stops us both.

Scott's voice softens, not completely, but enough. "Is she all right?"

"I don't know. What did Rachel say to you after we met with Bremmer?"

"We've been over this. She refused to tell me anything about an argument with Amanda."

"Even if it happened, Rachel would never do anything to hurt anyone. You know her, she's not like that."

"I don't know her. You made sure of that," he says bitterly.

"Are you saying you believe she could be involved in what happened?"

"It suddenly seems like you do."

"I could never believe that," I insist.

"What is this about, Abby?"

I take a deep breath, reluctant to give the words substance. "Hannah told the detective she never saw Rachel that night."

"How do you know?"

"Eliot told me."

"Your teacher boyfriend?"

"He was trying to help."

"Who is this Hannah, anyway?"

"She and Rachel were never friends before this year. Her parents are divorced, and they rarely come to school events. All I know is they're loaded. The school publishes a list of donations to the annual fund drive, and Hannah's family is always near the top. I'm talking six figures, but that's the extent of their involvement with Dearborn or, as far as I can tell, their daughter. Hannah has been a target for the other kids, but I have no idea why she would hold that against Rachel."

"Okay, I'll be back as soon as I can. In the meantime, don't say or do anything until we have more information, and tell Rachel not to speak to anyone, including Hannah. I'll get the name of a lawyer."

*

This is what I didn't tell Scott: Rachel has taken to biting her lower lip until there are dark tunnels through the skin. That she's been crying out in her sleep. That I found her naked in the empty bathtub at three in morning, rocking back and forth. That I followed her to her room and, with my ear pressed against the door, heard her make a call.

"I swore I would do anything to protect you," she said angrily. "You were supposed to do the same."

I couldn't see her throw her phone across the room, but I heard the crash.

I didn't tell Scott that I have no idea what to believe.

Chapter 36

Kara

The muddy brown and black triangles in the painting above Dr. Mendelsohn's desk are the same. The floral cube of tissues on the end table is the same. Dr. Mendelsohn, with his studiously neutral expression, the same. Only we are different.

After we hem and haw through the obligatory "how was your week?" prelude, Dr. Mendelsohn presses for sore spots. "During our previous sessions, we've been exploring the possibility of you leaving New York. Have you thought further about the topic?"

"Other things have taken precedence," Peter answers.

"Can I assume certain news stories I've heard are impacting your family?"

"If you're talking about what happened at Dearborn, yes."

"Would you like to share your feelings about that?"

I thought shrinks were supposed to be like juries, sequestered from outside information, but even Dr. Mendelsohn is hungry for tidbits.

"Olivia was on the trip where Amanda Carter died," Peter says. "The two girls were friends."

"I wouldn't say they were exactly friends," I interject.

"Their relationship was complicated," Peter admits. "They were competitive with each other socially, but they kept each other within view. They mattered to each other in that sense."

"Rivalry is common among high school girls. They often measure their self-worth in comparison to others."

"That propensity is not limited to teenage girls. Regardless, Olivia doesn't seem appropriately shaken by what happened."

"We try not to use words like 'appropriately' here," Dr. Mendelsohn says. "Is it possible she's in shock?"

"Anything's possible," Peter answers curtly.

"It would help me understand your concerns if you went into a bit more detail," Dr. Mendelsohn suggests.

The details *are* the concern. Olivia told us she left the lodge with Daniel. She told Detective Bremmer she left alone. Olivia and Daniel are both lying, according to Abby. Rachel may be the one lying out of spite, but I can't get the conversation out of my head. I told Peter about it the minute I got off the phone, though I was too ashamed to include the harsh things I said about Rachel, and we agreed not to mention it to anyone. The only thing certain is that not all of it can all be true.

I wait to see if Peter will explain any of this. Instead, he replies, "Olivia is not particularly communicative at the moment."

"Your daughter has been through a frightening event. You've brought up her drug use in the past. The propensity to self-medicate can become exacerbated in stressful situations. I suggest you encourage Olivia to see a therapist on her own."

"We're doing that," Peter assures him.

This is news to me.

"Excellent. In that case, let's get back to the two of you."

"Unfortunately, we need to end the session early tonight," Peter says, standing up to leave. "A client meeting came up at the last minute. We should have told you before we got started."

*

"Why did you tell Mendelsohn we got Olivia a therapist?" I ask as we walk through the ornately grilled lobby door.

"For the same reason I ended the session before you brought up Olivia's fuzzy memory about that night. We'll get her the help she needs when the time is right, but if she says anything to a psychiatrist that might implicate her in Amanda's death, they would be legally obligated to report it."

"Are you saying you think she did something she could be implicated for?"

"I'm saying we can't take the risk."

Despite all of Peter's strictures about right and wrong, actions and consequences, he is choosing to protect Olivia and our family. I wasn't sure he would.

We walk half a block, lost in our own thoughts.

"Do you remember the time we broke up?" I ask.

We'd moved from Michigan to New York and were discovering the city together. Three-dollar happy hour drinks at Saint Mark's Place. Free nights at the Whitney. Our first real jobs, with all the excitement and uncertainty that brings.

"I remember that it lasted exactly two months and four days. What I don't remember is *why* we broke up."

It started as a minor argument about paying off our student loans that spiraled into disagreement about our entire financial, logistical, and emotional trajectory. We didn't have enough ground beneath our feet to realize that sometimes it's better to hit pause rather than let a single moment determine your future. It felt, too, like a failure of nerve to marry the guy I met at nineteen without first exploring this vast new city and its infinite possibilities.

"I hated every minute of it," I tell him.

I despised dating and the painstaking process of trying to make other people understand who I was when there was already someone who did. It took me two months to realize it wasn't a failure of nerve. It was luck that we found each other. It still is.

"Let's never do that again," I say.

"I don't plan on it."

"I did hear you about wanting to leave the city. I understand what you think it's doing to us. I want you to know that. But if we do leave, I don't want it to feel like I'm giving up. I still want to start my own business."

"You could try viewing it as a step forward rather than a retreat."

"I can try, but I can't guarantee I'll get there."

"I'll take it."

Peter smiles and leans over to kiss me on the temple.

I would freeze time if I could. Right now, on West Ninety-Second Street, the trees of Riverside Park behind us, the turrets of the grand prewar buildings ahead of us, walking home with Peter beside me. Before whatever might happen next.

I put my arm through his as we make our way home.

Chapter 37

Hollis

At precisely seven o'clock, Michael, the night doorman, calls to announce that Miss Cleary is downstairs. He's checked her ID, he informs me. Twice. Ever since I spotted Adam lurking under an awning, I've instructed the building staff to be scrupulous about not sending anyone up without prior notice, including relatives.

Every shadow bears his profile, every sudden movement makes me jump, but I haven't seen him again. I haven't heard from him. That only makes me more nervous.

"I'll handle the teacher," Jordan says when I go to let Miss Cleary in.

"It'll go better if I put her at ease first."

"Trust me, she's not going to be a problem," he snaps.

Nevertheless, he returns to the living room.

I open the door to greet her. The jagged highlights she debuted the morning they left for Forest Valley haven't been touched up, and dark roots fringe her tired face.

"Thank you for coming tonight, Miss Cleary. I know this is a difficult time for you and everyone at Dearborn."

She steps tentatively into the foyer. I wonder if she's comfortable anywhere outside of her Dearborn. I doubt it. Even there, her attempts to win acceptance and respect or, barring that, adherence to her decrees, have met with ill-concealed derision. Instead of changing course, though, she's like a tourist in a foreign country who thinks if they only speak louder, they will eventually be understood. This is exactly what Jordan is counting on.

"I'll always make time for Daniel, but I assumed we would postpone our tutoring sessions for another week or two," she says as I hang up her coat. "The students have been granted extensions on all their assignments."

"I'm aware, but we wouldn't want Daniel to fall behind. He hasn't been at Dearborn long enough to have the same support system as other kids. When colleges look at transcripts from junior year, they may not take the circumstances into account. Can I take your things? My husband would like a word with you before you meet with Daniel."

I lead her into the living room, where Jordan is waiting.

"Hello, Mr. Chapman. I understand you'd like to speak to me. Is Daniel having any problems I should be aware of?"

Jordan regards her with a stony expression. "That's what you're here to tell us."

"I don't understand."

"You've disappointed me, Miss Cleary. I thought we had an understanding. Your job, your sole purpose, was to give us fair warning about anything to do with Daniel. What do you think we've been paying you for?"

Miss Cleary's broad cheeks redden precipitously. "I don't understand."

I sympathize with her but not enough to have postponed this meeting. My cooperation was tacit approval of Jordan's tactics. I didn't ask for specifics.

"What I can't figure out," Jordan continues, "is what you have against us."

"Why would I have anything against you?" she stammers. "I'm here to help you in any way I can."

"I suppose you consider going to Detective Bremmer and telling him, erroneously I might add, that Daniel is lying is helping us? If so, you're even more deluded than your reputation has led me to believe."

"I would never do that," she protests.

"My sources say otherwise. Don't make this worse for yourself."

"I can explain," she says hurriedly, her voice rising an octave. "I'm on your side. I've been working to shield Daniel."

I've been standing with my arms crossed in front of my chest, letting the encounter unfold—until now.

"Shield him from what?" I ask anxiously.

"Mr. Handley, Daniel's English teacher, came to me with some concerns. For some reason, he thought Daniel and Olivia Strickland weren't being completely truthful. I told him he was mistaken, that Daniel is a good kid. I wasn't sure he believed me, so I went to Detective Bremmer to set the record straight."

"Handley? Isn't he the one dating that girl's mother?" Jordan asks.

I didn't set out to betray Abby's confidence, but her post about dating a teacher came up when I showed her app to Jordan. I wanted to demonstrate how universal the confusion about dating is, regardless of age. It seemed inconsequential, but Jordan stores bits of information in his pockets like stones, ready to be weaponized without warning.

"What girl's mother?" Miss Cleary asks, blinking rapidly. "You must have the wrong person. Eliot Handley is not dating anyone. Certainly not a parent."

"He's seeing one of my wife's friends. The woman with the idiotic app I got roped into, Abby Ettinger. Her daughter was on the trip."

"Rachel?"

"This Mr. Handley must have made up the story about Daniel to protect his girlfriend's daughter. Surely that must be obvious to everyone. And what about this Olivia? I'm sure you know more about her that the authorities would be interested in. You're going to fix this, Miss Cleary," Jordan orders her.

She rocks unsteadily on her scuffed heels. "What can I do?"

"You have access to school records. You have the detective's ear. You'll find a way. Do you know what will happen if I tell Jerome Nederlander that you're tutoring Dearborn kids for extra money? That you're writing their papers for them and forging their college applications? That you're taking money in exchange for bullshit recommendations?"

"I've never done any of that."

"You've done plenty of other things. We both know that. There's no need to go into the rather unsavory details now, but rest assured, I will if I have to."

"What do you want?" she stammers. The scarlet in her cheeks has vanished, replaced by a sickly gray.

"You were the one responsible for watching our children. You were the one who left the back door unlocked. You were the one who waited to alert security. This is not going to go well for you." Jordan looms over her. "You will make sure Daniel is safe, whatever it takes, or pay the price. On the other hand, if you do the right thing, there will be a sizable reward. The choice is entirely up to you. Am I making myself clear?"

I've rarely been witness to the nuts and bolts of Jordan's maneuverings. They've taken place in boardrooms and clandestine meetings, where they remained vague and easier to ignore. The full force of them is chilling.

Miss Cleary, shell-shocked, nods.

"Good. There's no need to meet with Daniel tonight. He decided to go out for a run at the last minute. My wife will see you out."

Chapter 38

Abby

Rachel is picking at her breakfast, taking mouselike bites of toast, when I sit down beside her, cradling my coffee mug in both hands.

"Can we talk for a minute?" I ask.

"I'm going to be late for school," she answers without looking up.

It takes all my willpower to ignore her dismissiveness. Nothing makes it harder to play the long game than teenage impudence. But there's too much at stake to respond.

"That detective hasn't asked to speak with you again, has he?"

She glances up suspiciously.

"You told me not to talk to him."

"Has he spoken with Hannah?"

"How should I know?"

I'm not sure if Rachel knows about Hannah's conflicting account of that night. I've been too scared to confront her. Even the simplest question—what she wants for dinner, what book she's reading—pushes her further away. I was hoping—irrationally—that Hannah's version of events would change or prove to be irrelevant. That the discrepancy would close up on its own. None of these things has happened.

"Rachel, Hannah told people she never saw you that night. Do you have any idea why she would do that?"

"I have no idea why Hannah does or doesn't do anything." Rachel pushes her plate away and stands up. "It's just like you to believe her and not me." Her eyes fill with angry tears. She wipes them away with the back of her hand.

"I didn't say that. Please, I'm trying to understand."

"Well, you don't. You never will."

I take a breath, defeated. How do you warn someone if they don't believe anything you say?

"I don't want you talking to Hannah until this gets straightened out," I tell her.

"Not a problem," Rachel retorts.

*

I put the breakfast dishes in the sink and call Scott. Twice.

He doesn't pick up or answer my texts.

Finally, I call Dartmouth and get put through to his department assistant.

"Professor Amberson is on temporary leave," she replies curtly. "He hasn't been in his office for two weeks."

"Can you give him a message when he stops in for the department meeting?"

"There's no department meeting on the calendar. I'm sorry, but I have to take another call."

*

I stand in the living room, paralyzed, more alone than I've been since the endless nights when Rachel was an infant and I paced the apartment at three in the morning while she wailed. The exhaustion and helplessness, the desolation and feelings of abandonment, come flooding back. I thought I'd left them behind, but they were just waiting for the right moment to overtake me.

Every tie is loosening.

Gone, or almost gone.

Scott. Kara.

There is one person left.

I have little hope that he'll say yes, but I summon what mettle I have left and text Eliot, asking if we can talk.

Four hours later, he answers. That would be a good idea.

*

Eliot is waiting for me at the back of a small East Village café when I arrive. The morning sun has given way to bluster, and the rich scent of espresso fills the small, low-ceiling room. Indie rock plays softly, but not softly enough, in the background.

He's studying the handwritten menu as I sit down.

"Thank you for coming," I tell him. I wasn't sure he would.

He nods. "I was going to reach out to you."

"Were you?"

"Yes."

I'm not ready to hear whatever he has to say. I don't think I can bear it, not yet.

The waiter comes over, takes our order.

"I'm sorry I snapped at you about going to Bremmer," I begin.

"It was never my intention to hurt you, Abby. I stupidly misjudged what Rita would do, and I shouldn't have said anything to you about Hannah. She's still claiming she never saw Rachel, but her story is all over the map. She was binge-eating in the woods, she was crying alone behind the dining hall. It's squishy, but it may not be relevant. They're more interested in Daniel. You were right, he and Olivia have been lying."

The rat-a-tat pulse banging inside my chest begins to ease. We are safe, almost safe.

"Are you sure?"

"They found a joint near Amanda's body, and they think Daniel was with her. He's refusing to take a DNA test."

"What about Olivia?"

"I'm not sure. There are a few theories floating around. Daniel and Amanda were high, and their sex got out of hand. They got in a fight when Amanda threatened to tell Olivia about them, and it got out of hand. Olivia found the two of them together. Who knows? I told you I saw red flags with Daniel before the trip, but it turns out I'm not the only one. It's the strongest lead they have, and they're determined to wrap this up quickly."

"'They' meaning the school, or 'they' meaning the police?"

"Both."

"How do you know all this?" I ask, puzzled.

"Dearborn is not averse to letting certain information leak if it will help them put this whole thing to bed and avoid liability. From what I understand, the police still haven't found the performer from that night, Chief Little Cloud, to get his statement. And the groundskeeper's wife was out of town, so no one can vouch for his whereabouts between dinner and the time Rita called him about Amanda's disappearance. My point is Rachel is not their main concern. I hope this eases your mind."

I nod slowly, sifting through the cat's cradle of possibilities to make sure none can be wrapped around my daughter. For the first time in days, my breathing starts to normalize.

"It does. Thank you," I say finally.

I put my cup down, waiting for the next part, the one where he severs what's left of our relationship.

"Is that all you wanted to tell me?" I force myself to ask.

"Isn't that enough?"

"Yes."

He rests his elbows on the table. "Abby, I've been trying to understand what you told me, or didn't tell me, about your past, but I'm having trouble with it."

Here it is, then. The ending. I'm not sure why I let myself hope it could be otherwise.

"I'm sorry. I wish I had told you about Rachel's father from the beginning, but I hadn't told anyone. I know that's not an excuse."

"What happened that was so terrible you felt the need to hide it?"

There were no monsters, no crimes. I wish there had been. It would make it easier to explain.

"I was twenty-two when I got pregnant. I knew Scott was married, but I thought he was separating from his wife. That turned out not to be the case. I didn't handle it well, to put it mildly."

"Is that why you never told him about Rachel?"

"He had another family, an entire life someplace else."

It was so clear to me then that I didn't owe Scott anything. It's so clear to me now what I owed both him and Rachel.

"It's the ongoing-ness of it that I'm struggling with," he admits. "It wasn't a onetime mistake. It was a choice you made every day."

"At some point it stopped being a choice and became my life."

"It was always a choice," he insists. "What about now?"

"He wants to have a relationship with Rachel."

"What about the two of you?"

"It was all so long ago. I don't even remember who I was then."

"That's not an answer."

"It's complicated."

"You seem to specialize in complicated. This is your chance. Are there any other skeletons you want to come clean about?"

"Isn't that enough?"

"More than enough."

He leans close enough for me to see the uncertainty in his eyes. "You asked me the other day for a second chance. Is that still what you want?"

"Yes," I answer hastily. "If that's what you want," I add more cautiously, embarrassed by my neediness.

It takes him a long time to answer, too long.

"After my divorce, I didn't know if I would ever find someone again. I was trying to make peace with that and build a new life. Then I met you, and for the first time, I had a sliver of hope that there might be another way."

"If it matters, I felt the same way about you. I still do."

The truth is all I have left to offer him.

Eliot takes a deep breath, exhaling slowly.

"I have to know there are no more secrets between us."

"No more secrets," I assure him. "We can start slowly, rebuild. Whatever you want."

A smile gradually creases his face. "I'd like that."

It doesn't sink in at first. Then he reaches across the wobbly table to kiss me, and tears of relief threaten to spill over. I hold him close to keep him from seeing them.

Chapter 39

Hollis

When Detective Bremmer calls early that Friday evening after Miss Cleary has left, I insist Jordan put him on speaker.

I knew we couldn't avoid him forever. Still, the call still lands like punch.

Bremmer doesn't pretend to be friendly. We're beyond that now. "I was expecting to hear from you about Daniel's DNA test," he says.

"Were you?" Jordan replies. "I can't imagine why. We made our position quite clear."

"You should know that further information has come to light."

I look at Jordan questioningly, but he turns his back to me.

"Go on," Jordan says.

It's obvious he doesn't know what Bremmer is referring to. It's so rare for Jordan to be caught off guard, I instinctively sit down to brace myself.

"We already have an eyewitness who saw Daniel heading down the mountain," Bremmer begins. "Your son was overheard making plans with Amanda. We've recently learned of past incidents that point to a pattern of violent behavior. And," he pauses, "Daniel's alibi has holes in it. The girl he says he was with, Olivia Strickland, has provided a different account of events."

My mouth goes dry. I knew there was a chance the detective would uncover what happened before, despite Jordan's assurances it was buried. But as long as Daniel and Olivia were together by the lake, it shouldn't matter. Now, without warning, that's gone, leaving Daniel stranded. I look helplessly at Jordan. There must be something he can say to dismantle the narrative Bremmer has glued together.

"None of that constitutes hard evidence," Jordan replies. "You have an unreliable witness, a joint covered in mud, and records that I seriously doubt would be admitted as evidence. Correct me if I'm wrong, Detective, but you still haven't located a murder weapon, have you? I believe I heard that from the pattern of blood splatters, it was probably a large rock, isn't that right, Detective? I seriously doubt your chief is going to start dredging the lake for it."

"Where did you get that information from?"

"That's irrelevant," Jordan replies superciliously.

"I'll tell you what we do have, Mr. Chapman," Bremmer says angrily. "DNA from the sweatshirt Amanda Carter was wearing the night she died. If Daniel doesn't submit to a test voluntarily, I'm prepared to get a court order."

"That would be a violation of my son's rights."

"You're welcome to present that case to a judge, but you'll have a much better chance at a deal down the road if Daniel turns himself in voluntarily. We can arrange to do it quietly, or I can have my people show up at Dearborn Monday morning. My guess is you'd prefer not to have that kind of publicity, but that's up to you and your son."

"If you go ahead with this, I guarantee your career will be destroyed," Jordan warns, the cords in his neck bulging.

It's the absolute wrong tack, but it's too late to stop Jordan.

"You have until Monday morning," Detective Bremmer says calmly before the line goes dead.

*

I follow Jordan as he storms into Daniel's room, where he's sitting cross-legged on his bed, oblivious, noise-canceling headphones glued to his ears that he only grudgingly lowers.

"That detective called. I'm going to ask you one more time. If you were to take a DNA test, what would it show?"

"You seem pretty convinced what it would show." Daniel frowns. "It would be nice if you had a little faith in me for a change."

"It would be nice if you gave me reason to."

"Please, both of you, stop," I beg.

The war between Jordan and Daniel is so deeply embedded, neither acknowledges me. Crouched in their corners, eyeing each other, they've refused every attempt I've made to coax them to common ground, even temporarily. The only thing they have in common is a fierce and blinding stubbornness.

Daniel starts to put his headphones back on when Jordan yanks them out of his hands.

"Are you sure you were with Olivia the whole time?"

Daniel's eyes narrow. "Why are you asking me that?"

"The detective implied there's a problem with your alibi."

I wait for Daniel to tell us the detective is wrong. That Olivia is, for whatever reason, lying. That it's all a mistake. Instead, he stares sullenly at the quilt and says nothing at all. I can't will him to speak. I can't will this not to be happening. Any last scraps of hope disintegrate.

"I don't want to know what happened," Jordan continues. "It's better legally for your mother and me *not* to know. Maybe you wanted to screw the Carter girl, and it got out of hand. Maybe she provoked you. Maybe you were high and weren't aware of what you were doing. Harriday will lay out our options, but you're damn well going to listen if he thinks it's advisable to turn yourself in this time."

Any of the options seems horrific. Any of them seems possible. That's what scares me the most.

"Why would I turn myself in if I didn't do anything?"

"You did something. We're going to meet with Harriday first thing tomorrow morning. In the meantime, I suggest you get your story with Olivia Strickland straight."

"Fine."

Daniel puts his headphones back on, the music so loud I can hear it from three feet away.

*

Jordan goes into the study to make a series of calls. There are strings to be pulled, connections to be activated.

Helpless, I lie on top of the bed, staring at the ceiling.

Despite all the years I spent preparing for this—not this precisely, but something like this—it turns out preparation is a fool's game.

The first time my mother attacked someone, we had no idea of the warning signs. The second time, we sensed the air pressure dropping and thought we could wait it out. I swore never to make that mistake again, but there's no proof that Daniel is like my mother. Aren't all teenagers unstable to some degree, hormonally addled and prone to impulsivity?

I find the burner phone hidden in my lingerie drawer and email Dr. Akoris, asking for a call in the morning. It's urgent, I tell her.

She texts back within the hour that she can make time to speak, but if I'm worried about Adam, he's been allowed at Harkendale on a probationary basis. He's been there for the past two days.

It wasn't Adam I was calling about.

It's close to midnight when Jordan climbs into bed beside me, sets the alarm on his phone, and shuts his eyes.

"Promise me you'll get Daniel whatever help he needs," I whisper.

"That's exactly what I've been doing."

*

I slip out of bed as the first light filters in, make myself a cup of coffee, and sit in the kitchen watching the numerals on the microwave click slowly on. Harriday agreed to see us at eight thirty this morning, despite the fact that it's Saturday. He prepped with Jordan at Thomasville. It's the kind of thing these men do for each other. At seven, I go to the cabinet and pull out flour and vanilla. It's been years since I made banana pancakes, Daniel's favorite breakfast from childhood, and I have to look up the recipe. I'm not sure how much comfort I can offer, but I can at least provide ballast. When the pancakes are done, I stack them on a plate and pour an extra dollop of maple syrup on top before carrying them down the hallway.

There's no answer when I knock on Daniel's door. I'm glad he was able to get some sleep. I turn the knob with one hand, balancing the plate of pancakes in the other, and walk quietly in.

The room is empty, the bed untouched.

I check the bathroom and kitchen, then circle back to his bedroom, trying not to panic. He must have gone out for an early morning run to burn off stress before meeting with Harriday. I open the closet door. His running shoes are gone, along with his backpack. I hear Jordan shower, go into the kitchen, and get coffee. He is freshly shaved, his wet hair perfectly combed, when he finds me in Daniel's room.

"Where is he?" he asks gruffly. "I want to remind him to wear a suit."

"He went for a run."

"You're telling me he's not home?"

"He'll be back."

"Do you know how many strings I had to pull to get Harriday to meet with us? Every time I think Daniel can't fuck things up any further, he does."

"He's scared, Jordan. I'm sure he'll be back any minute."

"Are you? I'm not."

"Please, don't give up on him. Whatever happens, he's our son."

"We've tried to help him for years. I fail to see what good it's done. He's making his own choices now. It's out of our hands."

"How can your own son ever be out of your hands?"

Jordan leaves without answering.

*

The appointed time with Harriday comes and goes.

Finally, I get my phone. Kara and I haven't spoken since the investigation began. I don't know why Olivia changed her story—*why she would do that to us*—but finding Daniel is all that matters.

"I'm sorry to bother you so early, but is Daniel there?"

"Why would he be here?"

"I thought he and Olivia might have gone out for a walk or to get coffee."

"I haven't seen him."

"If you do, can you ask him to call me?"

"Is everything all right?"

Nothing is all right. For any of us.

"I need to talk to him."

"Okay. I'll let you know if I hear anything."

"Thank you."

I curl up on Daniel's bed, clutching the phone, and wait, the pancakes growing cold beside me.

Chapter 40

Kara

Fifteen days after the murder
Saturday, October 25

I haven't seen Olivia since last night, but I would have heard her go out. Surely, I would have.

I hurry down the hall, refusing to give in to the impulse to run.

There's no answer when I knock on her door.

Her room is empty.

Blood throbs in my temples as I step into the hallway to find Maya watching me, her blue plaid pajama top misbuttoned, one of her little notebooks in hand.

"Do you know where your sister is?"

She shakes her head unconvincingly.

"Maya, it's important. Where's Olivia?"

She points reluctantly to the bathroom where Nomi is standing guard, whiskers twitching at the muffled sobs coming from behind the closed door.

"Honey, can I come in?"

"Go away." The words are fractured by gasps.

I test the doorknob, relieved to find it unlocked.

Olivia is sitting on the edge of the bathtub in sweatpants and a long-sleeved T-shirt, her eyes wild with anguish. Crimson blotches of blood are soaking through the fabric of her sleeve.

I stare at the blood, aghast, then at her face, then the blood again.

"Olivia?" I ask, too horrified to fully comprehend what I'm seeing.

"I told you to go away."

I take small, creeping steps, avoiding any sudden movement that would betray my terror or cause her to do further harm, until I reach the edge of the tub. She doesn't fight me when I reach—slowly, carefully—behind her and find a razor in her right hand.

I pry her fingers loose one by one, gingerly, as if detonating a bomb, and take the razor, exhaling only after I place it out of reach on the bottom shelf of the vanity and turn back to Olivia.

I shut my eyes, pull her into my embrace, shaken to the marrow. "Oh, honey."

I stifle a sob as I kiss the top of her head, breathing in the scent of her scalp, the lavender soap on the sink, the iron of her blood.

"I wasn't trying to kill myself if that's what you're worried about," she says defiantly.

I tighten my arms around her, avoiding the wounds, and kiss her again. "Do you know how much I love you?" I ask, tears spilling out. "Infinity."

She nods. At least I think she nods. She may just be shaking. I hold her for a long time before letting go.

All the fight has left her. She watches dispassionately as I push up her left sleeve to reveal fresh crosshatches scaling her forearm. The flesh of my flesh.

Wincing, I unspool sheets of toilet paper and blot the beads of blood.

"Does it hurt?" I ask, because it is the simplest question I can think of.

She shakes her head.

The wad of toilet paper is speckled and soggy when I throw it into the trash and reach for a hand towel. Olivia examines the blood staining the fabric as I work in silence, unspoken thoughts cascading. *Why? How long? When? How could I have missed it?* And this: *I'm sorry, I'm sorry, I'm sorry.*

I rinse the towel, start again. "Did something happen to make you do this?" I ask carefully.

Olivia pulls away angrily.

"He left. That's what you wanted, isn't it?"

"What are you talking about?"

"Daniel. He's gone. Are you happy now?"

"How can you ask that? Of course I'm not happy. Whatever hurts you hurts me double. All I've ever wanted is for you to be okay." I search her crumpled face, powerless. "But why this?"

It takes an eternity for Olivia to answer in a ruptured voice. "I never felt anything before. I was always playacting. I used to think there was something wrong with how I was made. Like, what if I could never feel things the way other people do? It's like I was always watching myself but not *in* myself. Daniel made me feel everything I thought I couldn't."

"I wish you had told me. I promise, you will feel again, without having to hurt yourself."

"You can't promise anything. You don't know anything."

"I know that your father and I love you. We're going to get through this as a family. Whatever you need. Whatever we need to do."

She stiffens. "Do you have to tell Dad?"

"I think so, yes."

I open the medicine cabinet to find an ancient tube of antibiotic cream, squeezing whatever I can out of it. When I'm done, Olivia pulls down her sleeve.

"Can I have a minute?"

"I don't think it's a good idea for you to be alone right now."

"I'm not going to do anything. I want to change before talking to Dad."

I grab the razor and leave the bathroom door open.

*

Maya is waiting in the hallway. She rips a page from her tiny notebook and hands it to me.

"It's not the first time," she says quietly.

Written in black ink in Maya's exceedingly neat block print is a list of dates that go back six months. March 30, June 21. June 22. August 13. There's a gap from the second week of school until today. When Olivia was with Daniel.

I stare at the slip of paper, trying to remember where I was on those exact days, how I could have missed every sign. My child, slicing into her skin.

"Why didn't you tell me?"

"I'm telling you now." She was keeping her sister's secrets after all.

"You should have come to us. Olivia needs help."

I stop. It's not fair to blame Maya when I was blind myself.

"I'm sorry," I tell her, wishing I could take the words back. "None of this is your fault."

Maya, eyes watering, nods and retreats to her bedroom.

Olivia is studying herself in the bathroom mirror with a distant expression when I go to her room to check for sharp objects and find her phone, open to a text from Daniel.

> I have to go. It's the only way. I never should have asked you to cover up for me. I'm sorry. I love you.

Chapter 41

Kara

Olivia, wrapped tightly in her long-sleeved waffle bathrobe, trudges reluctantly into the living room.

"Livvie, why don't you come sit with us?" Peter suggests, patting the couch. Behind his glasses, his eyes are hazy.

She shakes her head and sits in the armchair across from us.

"Okay." He sighs. "I want you to know we love you, and we'll always be here for you, no matter what. Do you understand?"

She doesn't respond.

"I'm sorry if there's anything we did or didn't do that made you think you couldn't talk to us or ask for help. You and your sister are the most important things in the world to us."

His words swirl around me. There's only Olivia's arm, the blood-stained towel, the razor.

"Is there anything you want to tell us?" Peter continues.

"Not now," she mumbles.

"Hon, I'm sure this is overwhelming. We'll be here when you're ready, and we have the name of a therapist who'll help us all navigate this. Your well-being is our first priority, our *only* priority. There's something we do have to talk about now though."

"What?"

He opens his hand to reveal Olivia's phone. The screen saver is a picture of Olivia and Daniel, arms around each other, a cluster of elm trees behind them.

"Where did you get that?" she demands.

"I found it on your bed," I tell her.

"You had no right."

"Under the circumstances, you can understand why Mom felt it necessary. She saw the text from Daniel."

Olivia shifts her legs, shifts them again.

Peter remains preternaturally calm. "Do you know where he is?"

"If I knew where he was, I'd be with him." All the yearning in the world is lodged in her voice.

"Honey, can you tell us what Daniel meant about asking you to cover up for him?"

Olivia picks at her chipped purple nail polish.

"Do you understand that if you're lying for Daniel, you could be in serious legal trouble?" Peter asks.

"He didn't do anything," she protests. "Not what people think, anyway."

"You don't know that," I tell her.

"I know Daniel," she insists, still defiant, still blinded.

"Do you?"

"He loves me, and I love him."

I shake my head, powerless against her obsession with Daniel. It obliterates all reason.

Peter takes a deep breath. "Is there something about that night you haven't told us? Something you'd like to correct?"

"He wanted to get high. It was no big deal," she blurts out. "It's only because he was kicked out of his last school for getting caught smoking. It's so stupid."

"Were you getting high with him?"

"No."

"I need you to walk me through precisely what happened," Peter tells her.

Olivia is on the verge of breaking apart.

"Peter, can't we do this another time?" I beg.

"I wish we could, but no. Olivia, tell us again what happened that night, step by step."

"Daniel said he needed some space to be alone and asked me to meet him at the lake. I didn't want to press him. I didn't want to be that kind of girl. He was at the lake when I got there."

"So you didn't walk there with him?"

"Not really."

The wavering in her voice mirrors the wavering in my chest.

"You either did or you didn't."

"I told you, I met him there."

"Why did you lie?"

"Because if he got caught smoking, he'd get kicked out of Dearborn, and I might never see him again."

There's no room for logic in first love. Consequences are irrelevant. I never should have underestimated it.

"I wish you'd told us the truth to begin with," Peter says.

He waits for an apology, at the very least an acknowledgment, that doesn't come.

"Olivia, we'll be by your side the entire time, but you have to tell Detective Bremmer that you made a mistake."

"Why?"

"Because if not, you could be considered an accomplice."

"Daniel didn't do anything."

"That's not for us to figure out. My job, *our* job, is to protect you. Why don't you get dressed? I'm going to make some calls, and then we'll face this together."

Olivia, expressionless, untangles her legs and walks slowly out of the room.

*

I bury my head in Peter's neck, feel his heart beating rapidly against mine.

"How could we have been so blind?" I moan.

He doesn't respond. There is no answer, or there are too many.

"I'm going to call a criminal defense lawyer I know before we talk to Bremmer," he says, straightening up.

"What makes you think Bremmer will believe Olivia once he realizes she's been lying to him this whole time? He'll assume she had something to do with it."

"We have no choice. We'll call the therapist Mendelsohn recommended right after I speak with the lawyer." He kisses the top of my head. "It's a good sign that she left the bathroom door unlocked. She wanted us to find her."

I don't see good signs in any of this.

*

An hour later, after speaking to the lawyer, Jason Rubin, Peter calls Bremmer and puts him on speaker.

"Detective? This is Peter Strickland, Olivia's father. I have information that might help you, but first I need to know that my daughter will be granted immunity."

"I can't promise that until I hear what she has to say."

I wave my hand, mouthing *no*. Peter turns his back and continues to speak methodically, using the precise language Rubin prescribed.

"Olivia remembered certain details incorrectly."

"Go on."

"She didn't walk with Daniel Chapman to the lake. She met him there."

"I already know that," the detective replies. "What I don't know is why she lied."

"She's a teenager. He's her first real boyfriend. She loves him and thought she was protecting him. It seems Daniel Chapman was kicked out of his previous school for drug use. He asked her to lie for him because he was getting high. He played off of her fear that he would get expelled from Dearborn. She knows what she did was wrong. She's willing to talk to you and answer any questions."

"I appreciate that, but there's one problem, Mr. Strickland, aside from your daughter's prevarications."

"What's that?"

"The reason Daniel Chapman was forced to leave his last school had nothing to do with drug use."

Chapter 42

Hollis

Jordan left the house as soon as he realized Daniel was gone. He didn't tell me where he was going, and I didn't ask. I'm better off alone, with my fragile faith and my fears.

Saturday afternoon trickles into Saturday evening. Every minute takes an hour. Every hour takes a day. I've left eleven phone messages and fourteen texts for Daniel.

I carry my phone to the bathroom, to the kitchen where I stand before the open refrigerator, unable to eat, to my bedroom where I find the engraved locket with a snippet from Daniel's first haircut in my jewelry box and hang it around my neck. He was almost two, sitting in one of the red trucks in the kids' salon, his hair the color of wheat before it began to darken.

It's close to midnight when Jordan returns to find me exactly where he left me.

"Nothing?" he asks.

I shake my head.

He goes into the bedroom and closes the door, while I sit, while I wait, while I bargain, and I pray.

*

I would tell Daniel to keep running if I could, as fast and as far as possible, even though I know there are things it's impossible to outrun no matter how hard you try.

I would tell him there's help, though I've learned how capricious it can be.

I would tell him anything to keep him safe.

*

It's not quite dawn when my phone rings. I must have drifted into a light sleep and, after searching frantically, find it lodged in the crack between couch cushions. It takes me a few seconds to realize it's the burner.

"I can't do this now," I bark at Adam before he can speak.

But it's not Adam who answers. It's Daniel.

"You can't do what, Mom?" he asks angrily.

"Daniel, thank God. Where are you?"

An eternity passes before he answers.

"Near Grand Central Station. Meet me behind the library in Bryant Park. Come alone."

*

The sky is bathed in pearly-gray demi-light when the cab drops me off in front of the library's two majestic lions, Patience and Fortitude.

I hurry around to the park, past the deserted Grill and shuttered coffee carts. The benches are empty save for a homeless man covered in a tattered navy blanket, his belongings held together with fraying gray electric tape. Halfway down the gravel path, I spot Daniel, huddled and shivering, his backpack beside him.

The breath wedged between my ribs rushes out in a tidal wave of relief.

I walk as quickly as I can until I'm by his side, hugging him.

He slithers out of my embrace, reluctantly moving his backpack to make room for me to sit. I try to put my hand on his thigh to keep him from vanishing into thin air, but he pushes it away.

"I was so worried, Daniel."

He'll never fully understand, not in his bones. No child can.

"I'm sure you were," he replies coldly.

"Where were you?" I ask cautiously.

There's only one person Daniel could have gotten the burner phone's number from: Adam. Only one place he might have gone: Harkendale.

"I went to talk to Teddy Finster," he says.

I rear back, surprised.

"Why would you go see Teddy after all this time?"

"I had to make things right. Dad never let me apologize for what happened. Harriday said it would be an admission of guilt, but I *was* guilty." Daniel's eyes are older than old, rubbed dry. "I never should have agreed to that deal. I've regretted it every single day. I don't want to be that person anymore."

"It was for the best."

He bristles. "For who? Me? Dad?"

"Everyone."

"Do you want to know what really happened? I decided to come home a day early for Christmas vacation to surprise you and found Dad in our apartment screwing another woman. In your bed. Not any woman, Teddy's mother. My fucking cocaptain," he spits out indignantly.

I squeeze my eyes shut. Shocked but not shocked. I had no illusions about Jordan's infidelities, but I was willing to absorb the blows because I thought I was the only one he was hurting. It was the price I was willing to pay to protect Daniel, the life I constructed for him. Jordan—heedless, selfish—made a mockery of even that.

"I'm so sorry," I tell Daniel quietly. "I had no idea."

"Dad made me promise to cover for him," Daniel continues bitterly. "He said it would hurt you too much if you found out."

I learned long ago that being forced to hold on to secrets is a special form of poison. It seeps past brain barriers, dyes every thought with guilt. It breaks my heart that Jordan used me as an excuse to do that to his own son.

"Dad never should have made you lie for him. That's too much for you to carry around."

"Teddy's a dick," Daniel says. "He loved to go around telling everyone I was only at Thomasville because of my family's money, going off about the fucking Chapman Student Center. I always ignored it, but we were at practice after Christmas break, and he started up again. I told him to ask his mother what she thought about the Chapman money. All I remember after that is I began pummeling him and couldn't seem to stop." He pauses, catching his breath. "Teddy's father wanted to press charges, but Dad threw enough money at the Finsters and the school to keep everything quiet."

"I didn't know," I tell him when he's done.

"You didn't want to know." He turns to face me, straightening his broad shoulders. "I thought you were different than Dad, but you're as bad."

"What do you mean?"

"I know about your mother. Your brother followed me after school the other day. You told me Adam lived on the West Coast, that you had a falling-out. He's been an hour away this entire time. You said your mother died."

He looks at me, waiting to see if I'll refute any of it, hoping that I will, then looks away.

"I didn't believe him at first," Daniel continues, "but he showed me pictures. He gave me the number of your burner phone. How could you abandon your own family?"

His eyes are wide as a lost, scared little boy's. If I could abandon my own family, I could abandon anyone, even him. There's no ground beneath his feet, nothing and no one he can hold on to, much less believe in.

"I didn't abandon them," I tell him. "I've been paying for my mother's care since I was seventeen. I go up to see them when I can, but she needs real help, more than Adam can provide."

"All you've ever cared about is what other people think. That's why you lied about her all this time. That's why you want to keep her locked up."

"I know that's what Adam believes, but it's not true. I want her in a place where she can be looked after properly."

"Then why have you hidden her all this time?"

"I was trying to protect you. The one thing I wanted most in life was to give you the stability I never had. My mother wreaked havoc on my life. I thought when I moved to New York I could start over, but she stalked me wherever I went. I found her raving in the street outside my office with a kitchen knife. Did Adam tell you that?"

"He said you exaggerate."

His outrage is beginning to weaken. There's still some small part of him that wants to be wrong.

"Adam romanticizes her condition."

"What exactly is her condition?"

"Schizophrenia. Schizophreniform disorder, to be precise."

"What's the difference?"

"There's a spectrum. If my mother takes her medication and keeps up with therapy, she can function enough to get by without being a risk to other people or herself. The problem is she doesn't like the side effects. As soon as she feels better, she goes off the meds, and it all starts up again."

"Is it hereditary?" he asks anxiously.

"There's a genetic predisposition, but that doesn't guarantee anything. They're still trying to figure out the triggers, but they do know that having a steady home life can make a difference."

"Is that why you stay with Dad, because you're scared I could end up like her?"

"At first I was scared *I* would. Then, yes, it was something I thought about. That's one of the reasons it upsets me when you get high. Drugs can be a tipping point. But you're not like her, Daniel."

"You have no idea what I'm like." He picks up his backpack. "I'll meet with Harriday, but this time it will be on my terms."

"Promise me you'll listen to what he has to say," I beg.

"I'm not promising anything."

"At least come home and get some rest before we go see him."

"There's someplace I need to go first."

"I'll come with you."

"I have to do this alone."

He stands up, slinging his backpack over his shoulder. "One more thing. When this is over, I want to meet my grandmother."

He waits until I nod, then walks out of the park while the sky gradually lightens, and the city begins to stir.

Chapter 43

Kara

Sixteen days after the murder
Sunday, October 26

All through the night as I slid in and out of sleep, I tried to trace the skein of the last few years to figure out where it went wrong. Where *I* went wrong. To locate the blind spots and see now what I couldn't see then. Twice, while Peter slept, I climbed out of bed and peered into Olivia's room to make sure she was sleeping, safe. We insisted she leave her door ajar, but how long can we keep that up? It can't remain open forever.

Peter and the girls are still asleep early Sunday morning while I sit in the living room, hugging my knees to my chest.

All the dreadful things I said about Rachel, all the pain I inflicted, come flooding back. I'm not naive enough to think you ever forget bricks thrown at your child, but if nothing else, I need to tell Abby that Rachel was telling the truth about Olivia and Daniel. I owe her that.

After breakfast, eaten in shifts, no one waking at the same time, no one able to look at each other, I ask Peter to skip his bike ride and stay home for an hour. Neither of us wants to leave Olivia alone in the apartment. We'll have to at some point, but not yet. For now, we'll spell each other the way we did when the girls were little and we each needed a pocket of time to ourselves.

*

The girls are in their rooms, and Peter, dressed, is researching the causes of adolescent cutting, accumulating facts and therapeutic options. I kiss him goodbye and am getting my coat when the doorbell rings. I glance at Peter to see if he asked the lawyer he spoke with to come over, but he shakes his head. The bell doesn't ring again. Relieved that someone had the wrong apartment, I open the door to leave.

Daniel is standing in front of me, disheveled and pallid.

I freeze, blocking his entry.

"What are you doing here?" I demand.

"Can I talk to Olivia?" His voice is hoarse, beaten down.

I stare at him, dumbfounded. "Absolutely not. You are never to speak to my daughter again."

"Please. It's important."

"You need to go home, Daniel. Does your mother know where you are? She's frantic."

"I have to talk to Olivia first."

Before I can slam the door in his face, Olivia emerges from her bedroom, followed closely by Peter.

"You have to leave. Now," Peter demands.

Daniel peers around him. "Olivia?"

"Dad, please."

Peter stands his ground but, fearful of sending Olivia, with her fresh wounds, into a deeper spiral, grudgingly yields.

"Whatever you have to say, you'll do it in front of us."

Daniel turns to Olivia. "I'm sorry," he begins haltingly. "I never meant to involve you in this or get you in trouble."

Olivia, expressionless, listens closely.

"You asked my daughter to lie for you," Peter interrupts. "Don't you consider that involving her?"

Daniel ignores him, speaking only to Olivia. "I *was* with Amanda," he admits. "She got weed from someone, and we went to get high up on the mountain. That's it. Then I went to meet you by the lake. She was alive when I left her."

"You were with Amanda?" Olivia repeats, stunned. "You told me you went to the lake to get high alone."

"There was nothing between me and Amanda, but everyone heard the two of you arguing after dinner. I didn't want to make it worse."

Olivia searches him, wanting to believe, not quite believing. "Amanda told me you were going to ditch me for her."

"That's ridiculous. She had weed, and I wanted weed. That's all it was."

Peter has heard enough. "Even if you're telling the truth, which I seriously doubt, Olivia lied to the police for you. Do you have any idea how much jeopardy you put her in?"

"I never meant for any of this to happen." Daniel leans against the doorframe to steady himself. "I didn't think anyone would believe me if they found out I was with Amanda."

"You convinced Olivia to say she was with you because you told her you were kicked out of your last school for drugs. That's not true either, is it?"

Daniel, taken off guard, leans against the doorframe. "No."

"What really happened?"

He shuts his eyes, steeling himself before answering.

"I was struggling academically. Things were bad at home."

"Your grades are not the point here," Peter says brusquely.

"I got in a fight. This guy on the track team was saying things, and I wasn't thinking. I sort of lost it. I guess I hurt him pretty badly."

"You guess?"

"I did. The school was willing to keep it quiet after my father made a big donation and paid the other kid's hospital bills, but they wouldn't let me back."

"You got away with it because that's what your family does. That's not going to happen this time," Peter says angrily. "I'm not going to let my daughter become collateral damage."

Olivia, transfixed, hasn't taken her eyes off Daniel. "How could you have left yesterday without telling me?"

"My father is pressuring me to turn myself in. I needed to square something first."

"Why would you turn yourself in if you didn't do anything wrong?" Olivia asks.

"I haven't decided what to do." Daniel, exhausted, inches closer to Olivia. "I meant it when I said I love you. You believe that, don't you?"

"That's enough," Peter says, stepping between them.

He slams the door shut before Olivia can answer.

The problem with love is that it makes you believe anything.

Chapter 44

Abby

The Midtown streets are littered with last night's trash as I head to the coffee shop nestled between vacant office buildings. The location seemed an odd choice until I realized it's precisely halfway between our apartments.

Two waiters sit at a booth in the back, scooped over their phones, while I pick seeds off a pumpkin muffin, nervously arranging them in a semicircle around the edge of the plate.

When Kara walks in, I catch her eye and return to tidying the ring of seeds while she settles across from me. Her hair hangs limp, unwashed. New lines fan out from her eyes.

"I was surprised to hear from you," I admit after a waiter drags himself over to take her order.

"I owe you an apology." She props her elbows on the table, struggling to get the words out. "You were right. Olivia was covering up for Daniel. He was with Amanda that night."

"Are you sure?"

"He admitted it this morning."

"Why did she lie?"

"Because she's in the throes of first love, which is its own form of madness. Daniel told her he needed some 'space' to be alone. He left out that 'space' meant getting high with Amanda. He swears he left her alive."

"Do you believe him?"

"I don't know what to believe. I've been wrong about so much. He beat up a kid pretty badly before. How do we know that's not what happened this time?" Kara squeezes her eyes shut for a moment. "Olivia's been cutting herself. I didn't see it, Abby. She's been doing it for months, and I had no idea. I was so busy trying to rein her in, I never considered the *why* behind her behavior."

"I'm so sorry. Is Olivia okay? Are *you* okay?"

"I don't even know what okay would look like. I sensed something was wrong, but I had no clue how bad it was. What kind of mother does that make me?"

"None of this is your fault."

"We tell ourselves that, but is it true?" She sighs. "I never should have said what I did about Rachel. I was scared and angry, but that's not how I really feel."

"I know." It will be stitched into the quilt of our friendship, a piece of it but not the only piece. "I'm sorry too. I should have talked to you before going to Eliot."

"I almost feel sorry for Hollis."

"Do you? There's a good chance Daniel killed Amanda."

"I'll never forgive him, no matter what he did or didn't do, for involving Olivia, but it's not Hollis's fault. I used to think we had more control over our children. I'm beginning to wonder if we have any. Maybe none of us know what our own kids are capable of."

There's so much I want to tell Kara. About Rachel rocking back and forth in the bathtub at three in the morning. About Hannah claiming Rachel is lying. But I can't. Not until I'm certain this is over. Instead, I say, "I know."

"Are things any better with Rachel?" she asks.

"I'm not sure she'll ever forgive me for not telling her about Scott, but it's more than that," I admit. "You were right about some things. I do think Rachel is lonely and has trouble making friends. She never fit in at Dearborn. I don't know if it's something in her or something in them. Maybe it doesn't matter."

"It always matters. Don't make my mistake, Abby. Go home and talk to her. Keep talking until you get through."

"That assumes she'll talk to me at all, which is doubtful."

"What about Scott?"

"He left. He said he would be here for us, and then he bolted as soon as it got complicated. He told me he went up to Hanover for meetings, but when I called the school, they said he hadn't been there."

"I'm sorry. You deserve better than that."

Another thing we tell ourselves.

"I'm sure he'll come back. If not for you, for Rachel," Kara says.

"It's hard for me to imagine how that would work."

"They may have to figure it out on their own."

"Because I've done enough damage?"

"I didn't say that. There's your relationship with Scott, and there's Rachel's. They're not the same thing. What's going on with Eliot?"

"Shockingly, I think we're going to be okay. At least there's a chance. I was furious with him for going to Miss Cleary without telling me, but we both made mistakes."

"No offense, but in my humble opinion, not telling Eliot about your child's father is a wee bit worse."

I can't help but smile.

"Point taken, but luckily, he appears to be a very forgiving man. He wants to take me away for my birthday to an inn in the Hudson Valley. Kara, I'm a single parent. No one has ever taken me away for a long weekend. Ever."

"I hope you said yes."

"I did, but I keep waiting for him to change his mind."

"Abby, I know you've been burned before, but at some point, you have to risk opening up and trusting someone."

"I'm working on it. How are things with you and Peter?"

"He wants us to leave New York," Kara says quietly.

"Because of Olivia?"

"Because of everything. He's determined to fix things, and moving is his solution. I don't know whether it would be better or worse for Olivia to leave Dearborn so late in the game. Part of me just wants to get her away from Daniel."

"But you love the city." I can't imagine New York without Kara. She is home to me.

"I have to do what's best for my family. I only wish I knew what that is." She pauses. "Did you rip up the partnership agreement for Jyst?"

"No, I couldn't bring myself to do it."

"Neither could I," she admits. "We definitely can't take money from Jordan Chapman, but I'm not ready to give up."

I look across the table and see all the hours we spent planning and practicing, creating and almost birthing it together. "Neither am I."

Kara's face lights up behind the veil of fatigue. "I've missed you," she says.

"I've missed you too."

The waiters in the back raise their eyes curiously when they spot us holding hands across the table.

Chapter 45

Hollis

The soundproofed conference room on the forty-fifth floor of Harriday, Renstein, and Lowe is empty on Sunday afternoon, the chairs neatly lined up at the long mahogany table in the conference room, the video screen dark. There are no assistants at the desks outside of the closed office doors, no associates slavishly racking up billable hours.

Bob Harriday stands to greet us when we enter his corner office with its spotless wraparound windows overlooking the tip of Manhattan.

"Jordan, good to see you."

The two men shake hands with the easy familiarity of old prep school buddies bound by shatterproof loyalty and a shared conviction that rules are designed to be skirted. History has proved them right for as long as either can remember.

Harriday, a sparse ring of graying hair around a bald dome, is wearing a charcoal suit jacket and an open-neck shirt. Daniel immediately loosens the tie Jordan ordered him to put on as the four of us settle at a large round glass table.

"Thank you for seeing us today," Jordan begins. "I apologize for having to reschedule our appointment."

"I understand this is a trying time. Can I get you anything to drink before we begin?"

Jordan answers no before I can ask for a glass of water. Parched by nerves, I bite the tip of my tongue, hoping to spur enough saliva to suppress a cough. Daniel, staring out at the ferries crisscrossing the East River between Wall Street and Brooklyn, doesn't acknowledge the question.

"Let's get started then, shall we?" Harriday suggests.

There's no tape recorder, only a legal pad and a black enamel pen that Harriday grasps in his left hand before turning to Daniel.

"Your father has kept me apprised of developments, but I'd like to hear your version of events. Why don't you start with what motivated you to leave the lodge? I assume you were aware that it ran counter to rules specifically stated in the honor code you signed."

"My motivation was to see my girlfriend."

Harriday is far too battle-tested to react to adolescent insolence.

"By girlfriend, who do you mean?"

"Olivia Strickland."

Daniel's faux formality, his curt answers, are the compromise he's made with himself. He's here, but he's not playing the game. Not yet anyway.

"From what I understand, you also saw the dead girl, Amanda Carter."

"I saw them both."

Harriday, stone-faced, takes notes that, despite my best effort, I can't read.

"Can you tell me the precise time and place you saw each of them?" he asks.

"I don't know the exact time. I saw Amanda first, and then I went to find Olivia."

"Where did you meet with Miss Carter?"

"Halfway up a trail on the mountain. Maybe three-quarters."

"Which mountain? I gather there are quite a few on the property."

"I don't know the name of it. The one near the lake."

"Was your meeting with Miss Carter premeditated?"

Daniel frowns, irritated by the lawyer's tone. I don't like it myself. Especially not the word *premeditated* and all that it infers.

"Amanda told me she had some weed, and we arranged to meet up."

"So it was premeditated."

"You're making it sound like I knew what was going to happen."

"Son, I'm not going to ask you what you did or didn't do in the presence of your parents. You will only be protected by client-attorney privilege when we speak alone. For now, I'll lay out how a prosecutor would present their case. You left the lodge against clearly stated rules to go to a prearranged rendezvous to take drugs with a girl who subsequently died in a violent manner. As far as we know, you were the last person to see her alive. In all likelihood, your DNA will be on the joint they found as well as on the girl's clothing. You not only lied about your whereabouts to the police, you coerced your other so-called girlfriend to provide you with a false alibi."

"It's not like that."

"What part, exactly, is not like that?"

"Olivia and I *were* together by the lake."

"Let's talk about that. You can't be sure of Olivia's whereabouts before or after you met her since the two of you left the lodge and returned separately. From what your father told me, there are witnesses to a loud argument she had with Miss Carter. Olivia is an emotionally unstable young woman who has been in trouble in school including, according to a source at Dearborn, a reported incident of lying. She is widely known to have been jealous of your relationship with Miss Carter. We might say to an obsessive degree."

I should interrupt his characterization of Olivia or at least shade it. I don't.

"What are you implying?"

"I'm merely suggesting that you don't know where Olivia was or what she may have done. Our job is to explore the possibility of establishing reasonable doubt. That said, it will not be an easy task." Harriday puts down his pen. "With the potential DNA, the false alibi, an eyewitness who saw you coming down the mountain, and your previous, shall we say, proclivities, you have very little chance of being acquitted should this go to trial."

I despised this man last year. I despise him now. More than that, I distrust him. He's Jordan's ally, not necessarily Daniel's. But I don't have an alternative.

"The so-called eyewitness is Todd Hanson, who thinks I stole his girlfriend," Daniel says. "He would say anything to get back at me. Besides, I didn't see him, so how can they be so sure he's telling the truth about seeing me?"

"The prosecutors will claim that you were high on drugs and incapable of accurately remembering what you saw or did."

The walls are closing in.

"You're supposed to be helping us," I plead with Harriday.

He ignores me. I'm extraneous to him, someone to work around. For all I know, Jordan warned him of that ahead of time.

"Would you like to step outside and get some air?" Jordan suggests.

"No, I would not like to step outside and let you decide Daniel's future without me."

"I'm the only one deciding anything," Daniel insists.

"For argument's sake, let's look at the pros and cons of potential deals," Harriday suggests. "There's no clear motive to prove premeditation, but the prosecution could argue that you killed Amanda to prevent her from telling Olivia about your relationship. They could go for manslaughter in the second degree. If they try you as an adult, which they very well might, that's fifteen years to life. You have no prior arrests, thanks to your father. I'm confident we could negotiate that down, but you're still looking at substantial jail time. We could try a rough sex defense, but with no evidence of intercourse, that would be difficult. Regardless, the tides are turning against that type of argument."

"What do you recommend?" Jordan asks.

"I don't see self-defense as an option, but a case could be made that Miss Carter, who we know had a fiery temper, provoked you, causing you to have a sudden outburst that blinded you to the ramifications of your actions. That could bring the charge down to criminally negligent homicide. If you turn yourself in and we negotiate a plea deal, you could get off in a year or two with probation and some fines, which your father has agreed to handle. You'd still have your whole life ahead of you."

"And if I don't go along with your plan?" Daniel asks.

"You can choose to roll the dice, but I don't like your odds." Harriday lowers his voice, leaning closer to Daniel. "Son, one of the most important lessons you'll learn in life is that whatever did or didn't happen, the truth is not as powerful as perception. Once you accept that and use it to your advantage, you get to write the rules."

"Those are your rules, not mine," Daniel says bitterly.

"They're the world's rules."

Harriday sits back and crosses his arms, frustrated by the naivete of his client.

"There's one option you didn't bring up," I venture.

The men eye me condescendingly, doubtful that anything I say could be of value.

"What might that be?" Harriday asks skeptically.

"What if Daniel has a medical condition?"

"What type of medical condition?"

I take a deep breath, unsure how far to go. According to Dr. Akoris, even if Daniel has the first signs of schizophrenia—which we're not at all certain of, she reminded me—he wouldn't go free if he was found guilty. He would end up institutionalized. Often, for longer than a prison sentence, with little chance of negotiation.

"It's a hypothetical," I say. "If you could look into it for us."

"You're going to have to give me more to work with than that," Harriday replies.

I begin to speak, then stop.

Harriday is about to lay out next steps when his cell phone rings. He pulls it out of his pocket, raising one eyebrow.

"Excuse me. I need to take this."

He remains seated, listening intently and taking notes.

After two long minutes, he hangs up and turns to Jordan.

"That was good news. We've got what we need," he says. "We have a way out."

Chapter 46

Abby

Kara is right. I can't continue to ignore Rachel's cries in the night. Or her obfuscations during the day. She may not like me pushing—and pushing harder if I have to. I may not like what she has to say, if she says anything at all. But it's far riskier to do nothing.

I call out her name as soon as I open the front door.

There's no answer, only the low murmur of a man's voice coming from the kitchen.

I hurry back to find Scott, leaning against the counter, holding a glass of water, with Rachel beside him.

"What are you doing here?" I demand, baffled.

I thought he was gone for good. All the anger at him for leaving and at myself for trusting him again is still coursing through me. I can't rectify the turbulence with suddenly finding him here. Within reach.

"I asked him to come," Rachel replies.

"What's this all about?"

I'm the third wheel. In my own home. With my own daughter.

"Rachel wouldn't tell me until you got here," Scott says.

I turn to look at her.

"Can we sit down? There's something I need to tell you both." Her tone is studied, serious. Too serious.

We follow wordlessly as she leads us into the living room and waits until we sit down.

She squares her shoulders, her hands on her narrow hips.

"I lied to you," she begins. "That detective did ask to speak to me again."

"Okay," I say carefully, trying to disguise the panic mushrooming within.

"Don't worry, I didn't talk to him," she snaps peremptorily. "And I'm not going to talk to that lawyer I heard you calling either."

"What did you want to tell us?" Scott asks calmy, trying to defuse the tension.

I thought that was over, the chance of "us." I try, briefly, to decipher his expression, but whatever he did or didn't mean will have to wait.

Rachel begins to bite a hangnail but stops herself, braiding her fingers through each other. "I know why Hannah is lying."

"Go on," I urge.

She looks from one of us to the other. "You have to promise you won't tell anyone."

"That depends on what you have to say," Scott answers.

Rachel stares at him, considering her options. "Hannah and I were together," she says.

"That's what you've said all along," I remind her.

"I mean *together*, together. I did go out to find Hannah after Amanda made fun of her," she continues. "I stayed with her until she calmed down. We were lying behind the trees that border the lake when I got the scratches."

"Are you saying you and Hannah are a couple?" Scott asks.

She looks at him as if he's from another planet. "A couple? I don't even know what that means. We've been together before, if that's what you want to know."

I stare at her, the daughter I thought I knew down to her very molecules, and realize I didn't—*don't*—know her at all. She didn't trust me enough to show me, and I was too ignorant to see.

"I'm so sorry," I tell her, my chest cracking open with regret.

"For what? I'm not ashamed of who I am."

"That's not what I meant. I'm sorry you didn't feel you could tell me."

Her eyes begin to glisten as we look at each other across the divide of our own making.

"Rachel, you have to tell the detective," Scott says, bringing us back to the situation at hand. Amanda, Hannah.

"I already told him we were together."

"I mean the whole truth."

"Don't you get it?" she exclaims, tears of frustration spilling from her eyes. "I can't out Hannah. When the police came that morning and asked us where we were in front of everyone, she lied because she didn't want people to know about us."

"I understand how hard this must be," Scott says, "but that doesn't excuse Hannah's actions. She's had plenty of opportunity to correct her story. She has to go to the detective and tell him the truth. If she doesn't, you do."

"Outing people against their will is unacceptable," Rachel informs him. "Hannah's parents don't know, and she's terrified of them finding out. I'm only telling you because you didn't believe me."

"Of course we believed you," I assure her.

She scowls. "Right." She turns to Scott. "You said you want me in your life. Well, this is who I am," she says, daring him to accept her. Daring us both.

"I'll always want you in my life, Rachel. That's why I'm here. But we have to talk to the detective."

"You don't get to decide that. Neither of you do. I just thought you should know."

She stands up and races from the room, leaving us alone, the specter of what she told us hovering in the air.

*

For a long while, I sit completely still, my head spinning as I rummage through the past searching for what I missed. It's too soon to reconstruct the pieces. For now, they're scattered on the floor, waiting to be put back together into a new shape.

"You had no idea?" Scott asks quietly.

"None."

"She didn't merely come out of the closet, she blew down the goddamned door."

It's beyond sad that Rachel felt she could only tell us her truth when she was cornered.

"What do we do?" I ask.

Having Scott here, asking him what to do about *our* daughter, is the one thing I never thought I'd have. I want to cross the room and have him hold me to make sure he's really here. I also want to push him away before he can leave again. Because he will. That's what he does.

"I have to believe part of the reason Rachel told us is so that we'll do what she can't. What did you tell the lawyer when you called her?" Scott asks.

"Nothing. I left a message asking for a time to speak."

Scott considers this. "Rachel is going to have to tell Bremmer."

"Why? It will still be her word against Hannah's, and it might not matter anyway. Kara told me Daniel admitted he was with Amanda."

"That doesn't mean he'll confess to killing her. Either way, Bremmer needs an accurate record of everyone's whereabouts."

"We can't force Rachel."

"In the long run, she'll understand it's for the best."

"I'm not sure we'll make it to the long run," I tell him.

He looks at me quizzically. "We have to," he says.

I meant with Rachel. At least I think that's what I meant.

"I didn't think you were coming back," I admit.

"I told you I would."

"When I called Dartmouth, they said you weren't there."

"I went to talk to my ex-wife. I wanted her to know about Rachel before I spoke to my kids."

I wrap a strand of hair around my forefinger, trying to interpret what he's saying, what it means.

"Why didn't you tell me?" I ask.

"I wasn't sure how it would go. They weren't easy conversations, but at least now they all know the truth."

It's everything I wanted. Or thought I wanted. Scott, in our lives. Us, in his.

Before Eliot.

It's too much for now.

There's something more important.

"I need to talk to Rachel alone," I tell him.

Chapter 47

Abby

Rachel is on her bed, the lights off, dusk dimming the room, when I slip in and sit cross-legged beside her, our knees grazing, nerve ending to nerve ending.

"You know that I'll always love you no matter what," I tell her.

She nods but doesn't answer. All the adrenaline it took for her to tell us is gone.

"You said I don't know who you really are," I say softly. "I want to, if you'll give me the chance."

She listens closely. Not pushing me away. Not speaking.

"How long have you known?" I ask.

"That I'm gay? I've always known I was different," she begins slowly. "Then two summers ago, I kissed a girl at camp, and everything began to make sense."

"Is that why Forest Valley is so important to you?"

"Every summer, there's a campfire ritual. We each share a secret no one can ever tell outside the circle. It's like a sacred oath. I told people so I could be myself there."

All the pictures that Forest Valley posted at three in the afternoon, Rachel's joy shining through. It wasn't the swimming hole or the field games or the talent nights that made her so happy. There was only one place where Rachel felt fully herself, and it wasn't here, with me.

"I want you to feel you can be yourself anywhere. Were you worried about bullying at school?"

Dearborn, the liberal school in the liberal city, has Pride celebrations and a director of inclusion. There are workshops and mission statements, but stories inevitably pop up bearing witness to darker undercurrents. #blackatdearborn, #gayatdearborn. Lately, #deadatdearborn.

Rachel turns to look at me, a girl, a young woman, hovering on the brink, desperate to take a step back and anxious to leap forward. "I wanted to do things in my own time. I thought I had that right."

It's sadder than sad to me that this most basic act, proclaiming who she is—something she was surely preparing for and practicing and fearing and excited about—is slipping out of her control.

"You do."

"You're telling me I don't, and Hannah doesn't."

"I wish it didn't have to be this way."

She won't get this moment back. It will forever be etched into the story she tells about coming out years from now. I wish I could promise her there will be opportunities to rewrite it, unshackled by circumstance, moments when she can fully own the choice and the process, but she wouldn't believe me.

She curls into the fetal position, clutching the pillow to her chest.

"Do you love Hannah?" I ask.

"I don't know. I thought maybe. I don't want to hurt her."

"She's hurting you."

"She's scared," Rachel insists.

Desire leads us to make excuses for anyone if it keeps us from losing them. Rachel may learn that when she's older, but most of us never do. I haven't, not really. I realized that the minute I saw Scott sitting across from me in the living room.

"I understand, but it's not fair to you."

"None of this is fair. What they do to Hannah isn't fair. Outing her isn't fair. Amanda dying isn't fair."

I curve around her, kissing the velvety hairline on the back of her neck.

"Sweetie, do you think Amanda knew about you and Hannah and was threatening to out her?" I ask carefully.

Rachel's body stiffens. "Why are you asking that?"

"You said Hannah would do anything to keep people from finding out."

It's hard for me to imagine that Hannah, so passive and anxious to be accepted, could do anything more than what Rachel claims, retreating ashamed, to cry alone in the woods. But it's impossible to discount the toll that all the years of casual cruelty and the threat of exposure may have exacted.

"I didn't say that. You did."

"That's not an answer."

"That's all the answer you're going to get."

*

The hot water of the shower pounds onto my back, my face.

As far away as Rachel is, she's closer than she was.

Maybe now there's a way back to each other. Tenuously, on different ground, but back.

I get out of the shower and wrap myself in a towel.

Somewhere nearby, Scott is in an Airbnb, waiting to hear Rachel's decision. Waiting, too, for more than that. A question he didn't ask, an answer I don't have.

I finish drying off and get into an oversized T-shirt.

Eliot sent a link to the Hudson Valley inn, and I click through the gallery, trying to picture us in the room with the four-poster bed and fireplace, at the candlelit restaurant overlooking a waterfall, but the images grow blurry around the edges. I post a heart emoji next to one of the screenshots he attached but don't write back.

I don't call Scott.

I need everything to stop while I try to get my bearings.

*

It's close to midnight when the phone rings. I reach across the bed to pick it up, prepared to tell Scott that Rachel hasn't decided what to do. That we need to give her time to get her bearings too.

"Abby, I know it's late," Hollis says, "but we need to talk."

Surprised, I sit up, pulling the sheets with me. "I don't think that's a good idea."

"I'm sure Kara told you about Daniel," she says. "He never should have involved Olivia, but he had nothing to do with Amanda's death. I hope one day Kara can forgive him, forgive both of us."

"You have to talk to her about that."

"I will, but that's not why I am calling."

"It's late, Hollis. I'm very tired. Whatever it is, can't it wait?"

"I don't think it can." She pauses. "I'm calling to warn you."

"Warn me about what?"

"Do you know why Eliot left Saint Stephen's?"

"He was going through a bad divorce and wanted a fresh start. What does that have to do with anything?"

"You're going to hear this anyway. I wanted you to hear it from me first. Other girls are going to come forward, former students of his. What happened with Amanda wasn't an isolated incident."

"I don't know what you're talking about, but I'm not going to listen to another word of this."

I hang up before she can reply.

*

The Chapmans will pay anyone and do anything. They'll plow over people. They'll ruin other people's lives if they have to.

I thought Hollis was different, but when it comes to our children, none of us is.

I pick up the phone from where I flung it on a pillow and call Eliot, but it goes directly to voicemail. I leave a message asking him to call me as soon as he wakes up.

He'll tell me how silly this is. How it's a desperate strategy doomed to fail. How there are no other girls, there never were. How he had nothing to do with Amanda. How could I believe such a thing?

I remember the night Eliot made me dinner and we talked about Daniel's paper. "There's something not quite right about him," Eliot had said.

There isn't, there wasn't.

I turn over, try to settle, but other images creep in unbidden.

The kids' papers he pushed out of view when we sat down to eat. The red notes scrawled on them. The volleyball game, Eliot's hands resting on Amanda's shoulders, the two of them talking intently, her smile.

I change positions, scrunch the pillows, tell myself not to let Hollis poison what I know to be true, but the red scrawls infiltrate my brain.

*

It's past two in the morning when I leave a message for Marci Carter.

"Marci, I'm not sure if you went through the box of Amanda's things the school sent over, but maybe you should. It's probably nothing, but maybe, look. Okay, good night."

I put the phone by my pillow.

Morning is still hours away.

Chapter 48

Hollis

Eighteen days after the murder
Tuesday, October 28

Waiting is a country of its own.

The apartment, in all its calculated neutrality, expands around me.

I shower, dress, dip in and out of rooms, but nothing holds my attention for longer than a minute.

Jordan has been in constant touch with every person in his favor bank for the past forty-eight hours. Miss Cleary swore to him that she did her part and was proud to do it. "I told them exactly what you said. Word for word."

And still, no news.

Jordan insisted we not give Daniel any information beyond assurance that Detective Bremmer will no longer be harassing him. As far as Daniel knows, we're buying time. That much, at least, is accurate.

"We're not doing anything wrong," Jordan admonishes me before leaving for work.

In my heart, I know that's true.

It just doesn't feel that way.

*

I don't call Abby. I don't call Kara. They don't call me.

They are waiting too.

*

The New York Times
Tragedy at New York's Dearborn Academy Leads to Investigation into the Dark Past of Elite New England Prep School
October 28
New York

The death of Amanda Carter, 16, a student at Dearborn Academy in New York City, has proved to be more than a tragedy for the family and friends of Ms. Carter. Originally thought to be an accident, Ms. Carter's death on a school-sponsored trip to the Forest Valley Camp has been classified as a murder by the Sullivan County Sheriff's Office.

In the course of reporting this story, The New York Times has viewed a confidential report detailing alleged abuses perpetrated by one of the chaperones on the trip, Mr. Eliot Handley, 43, while he was a teacher at St. Stephen's Preparatory School in Massachusetts. The elite prep school, founded in 1876, is known for educating the sons and daughters of the wealthy and socially connected for generations, including two United States presidents and four Supreme Court justices.

Three women, including two current and one previous student at St. Stephen's, have come forward to speak about past incidents allegedly involving

Mr. Handley. The young women, who were students of Mr. Handley over a period of seven years, have alleged that he acted inappropriately and pressured at least one of them into having sex with him. Anna Ericks, 21, claims to have had a consensual affair with Mr. Handley when she was a student at St. Stephen's. She was 17 at the time. Barbara K. (who asked not to be identified), 16, describes a pattern of grooming. "He started writing personal notes on my papers. I saw him as a mentor. He made me feel special." Barbara alleges that when she met Mr. Handley away from school grounds, he offered her alcohol and then tried to force himself on her sexually. "I managed to free myself and run, but I had bruises for days from where he grabbed me," she claims. When asked why she didn't report the incident, she said, "I was drunk at the time and didn't think anyone would believe me." She alleges that Mr. Handley provided her with alcohol on more than one occasion.

The New York Times has confirmed that two of the girls reached out contemporaneously to describe their experiences to friends. At least one incident was reported to the school's governing board, but the case was not pursued, and the local police were not informed of the complaints. None of the girls was aware of the previous reports, which were shielded by St. Stephen's confidentiality policy. "I'm sure there are more girls who were too intimidated to come forward," Ms. Ericks said.

Mr. Handley has not responded to numerous requests to comment on the allegations.

A spokesperson from Dearborn Academy, Ms. Charlotte Colson, stated Mr. Handley was given a stellar recommendation by St. Stephen's, and Dearborn was not told of previous complaints.

When they were made aware of the students' allegations against Mr. Handley, Ms. Carter's parents, Bill and Marci Carter, went through the contents of their daughter's locker that had been sent to them after her death. They found handwritten comments presumably from Mr. Handley on Ms. Carter's homework assignments that included an escalating sense of intimacy. A separate note, assumed to have been written in the days preceding the trip, includes a line drawing of the area where Ms. Carter's body was found.

"I wish we had looked sooner, but it was too painful to open the box," Mr. Carter stated. The contents have been turned over to the Sullivan County Sheriff's Office.

Toxicology reports indicate that both marijuana and alcohol were found in Ms. Carter's system. Ms. Rita Cleary, the lead chaperone of the class trip, has told this reporter that she witnessed Mr. Handley drinking with other chaperones on the night in question. She stated that she informed Dearborn's headmaster, Jerome Nederlander, about this previously, but no action was taken. Mr. Nederlander has not replied to requests for comment.

A lawyer for St. Stephen's issued the following statement: "Mr. Handley is no longer a teacher at St. Stephen's, and we cannot comment on specific allegations. We take all reports of misconduct seriously and strive to foster a community of respect. We are launching an investigation and will continue to look into all claims. We have set up a panel and have instituted a new anonymous board where students can feel free to speak in safety." Calls to trustees of St. Stephen's have gone unreturned. Mr. Carter will not comment on reports that he intends to file civil suits against Dearborn and St. Stephen's.

Sources within the Sheriff's Office, who requested anonymity because they are not authorized to speak, have said that a warrant to search Mr. Handley's apartment was subsequently issued. DNA from fabric threads found in shrubs near where Ms. Carter was found seem to be a match with Mr. Handley. Charges are expected to be filed shortly.

Jordan Chapman, a parent of one of the students on the trip and a recent addition to Dearborn's board of trustees, had this to say: "I am looking forward to bringing a fresh perspective to the hiring practices at Dearborn and will ensure the school engages in more scrupulous background checks of all employees in the future. It is unfortunate for all concerned that this information did not come to light sooner. We support every woman's right to come forward and speak her truth. To that end, my company plans to invest in an app, Jyst, that will give women a much-needed forum to post warnings and seek help about sexual misconduct. We are proud to be at the forefront of this renewed effort."

This is a developing story.

Jason Blakely

Chapter 49

Kara

I read the story twice, running my finger down the lines, going back, reading them again, as it slowly seeps in.

"How could no one have known about him?" I ask Peter.

"You mean Handley? People knew. People always know."

I shake my head, disgusted. You'd think they'd learn. You'd think they would know better by now. Or at least know enough to admit that it happened in the past. But they don't. I'm beginning to think they never will.

"Abby is going to be wrecked by this," I tell him.

"It appears he wrecked a lot of lives."

I rest my head on my knees and begin to cry, for Abby, for the girls at Saint Stephen's, for my own girls, for Hollis and everything I blamed her for. Most of all for Amanda, for Bill and Marci Carter, and all that could have been prevented.

"You didn't tell me that you took Chapman's investment," Peter remarks as he stands up to dress.

"That's because we didn't."

"Ballsy of him to take credit."

I glance at the iPad, then close the cover. I barely even noticed that line. "What happens now?" I ask.

"The investigators are probably still gathering evidence, but it sounds like they have enough to present their case to the DA and get a green light to press charges. I can tell you one thing, Eliot Handley will not be teaching at Dearborn today."

*

Olivia and Maya have never read a news story before breakfast in their lives, but by the time they come to the table, phones in hand, their early warning systems are on fire. They scroll madly, ignoring their cereal and toast.

Neither of us stops them. We're busy doing the same. The shock and anger are ricocheting across social media and texts, broken up only by those who claim they knew all along there was something fishy about Eliot Handley.

Olivia eventually looks up. "You owe me an apology. You were wrong about Daniel. You were wrong about everything."

"There's more than enough wrong to go around," Peter replies. "If you think this excuses your lying about that night, you're mistaken."

"Did you have any idea about Mr. Handley?" I ask. "Did anyone sense anything?"

"Everyone knew Amanda had a thing for him. We didn't know it was the other way around."

"Why didn't anyone say anything?"

Olivia shrugs. "No one thought it was a big deal. Mr. Fortini has been flirting with boys for years, and no one takes it seriously."

More talks will have to take place, with Olivia, with Maya, with all of them. More guardrails, more procedures, more consequences. For the teachers and the schools, for the whole system that remains, despite everything, stubbornly in place despite a few cosmetic concessions.

The girls go back to their phones.

"What do you think Dearborn is going to do?" I ask Peter while the girls get ready for school.

"I'm sure they've been hunkered down with their lawyers and PR team since dawn. I imagine they'll send out some sort of statement today." He rolls his eyes. "We're forming a committee; we are committed to total transparency and the well-being of our student body, blah, blah, blah."

"You know this could have happened anywhere, Peter."

"It can, and it does. I also know it will be mayhem at Dearborn yet again this morning."

"Can you take them this time?" I ask. "I need to go to Abby."

*

I press the buzzer of Abby's downstairs intercom for the fifth time, leaving my hand on the cold steel button, but there's no answer. When a FreshDirect deliveryman wheels his trolley out of the building, I slip in through the door.

"Go away," Abby grumbles when I ring her doorbell.

"Not a chance. I'm going to keep ringing until the neighbors call the police, so you might as well let me in."

She opens the door dressed in worn-out joggers and a T-shirt, her long hair pulled into a tangled knot, her eyes red and vacant.

"I can't do this now, Kara."

"You don't have to do anything. I only want to be here with you."

"So you can tell me what an idiot I am?"

"I don't think that."

"You should. I do."

I'm too tired to think much of anything. Coherence is still days away. I only know that Abby needs me. I need her too.

"Let's go inside."

She turns without speaking and pads to her bedroom, where she collapses on the unmade bed, curling into a tight ball. I kick my shoes off and lie beside her, our chests rising and falling in a steady rhythm.

When my arm begins to cramp, I roll onto my back, and she does the same, staring up at the ceiling.

"Can I get you anything? Tea?" I ask.

"Tequila?"

I smile. "Anything you want."

"What I want is for this not to be happening."

"I know."

"Hollis called and tried to tell me the other night," she says.

I pull away, confused. "Why didn't you tell me?"

"I didn't want to believe her. I thought she would do anything to get Daniel off."

"And now?"

"I still think that, but that doesn't make it untrue."

I lie back, trying to absorb Hollis's call and Abby's silence about it.

"Have you spoken to Eliot?" I ask.

"No. I left a message for him after Hollis called, but he never called back. Part of me still thinks it must be some terrible mistake, even though I know it isn't." Her eyes, though veined with red, remain dry, as if she is beyond crying. "How could I not have picked up on anything? What's wrong with me?" she asks plaintively.

I hand her a tissue from the night table, and she balls it up in her hand.

"Oh honey, there's nothing wrong with you. No one saw it."

"Those girls from Saint Stephen's did, and no one listened to them. I can't stop thinking about Bill and Marci. I should have done something. I knew he was writing notes on kids' papers."

"Teachers do that all the time. You're not responsible for this."

"It feels like I am. I was with him, Kara. I believed everything he told me." She rolls over, her back to me. "For the first time in so long, I thought I'd found someone I could love who could love me back. I've been wrong about everything. Rachel, Scott, everything."

"What do you mean?"

"Rachel told us she's gay. She and Hannah were together that night. That's why Hannah won't admit to being with her."

"Wow, I didn't see that coming."

"Neither did I."

"Look on the bright side," I say, trying to make her smile, "you were worried she had trouble forming relationships, and you were wrong about that too."

"If you plan on listing all of the things I was wrong about, you really should leave."

"Rachel may have been hiding who she loves, but my daughter was hiding she was cutting herself. If this is a 'bad mother of the year' contest, you've got competition."

The levity lasts less than a second.

"What did Rachel say about the news this morning?" I ask.

"She went on a tirade about how little the patriarchy has changed since #metoo."

"She's right. I thought our kids would grow up in a different world."

"Rachel doesn't know about my relationship with Eliot, so at least I was spared that."

"Are you going to tell her?"

"Not if I don't have to." She groans. "Her opinion of me is already underground. This would be the final nail in the coffin."

"What did you mean, you were wrong about Scott?"

"I thought he was deserting us, but he went to tell his children about Rachel. He's back, at least for a little while."

"That's a good thing, isn't it?"

I want that for her—she deserves it—but I'm way beyond making predictions.

"Nothing seems like a good thing right now, but yes, I suppose so. What am I going to do, Kara?"

"At some point in the not-too-distant future, you'll get up, take a shower, and get dressed. We'll take it from there."

"I was planning on staying in bed forever," she says.

"That's another direction."

She turns to look at me. "You don't blame me?"

"For what?"

"For being so blind."

"No, never."

I'd like to think I would have sensed something in Eliot, but I'll never know.

"Have you spoken to Hollis since she called the other night?" I ask.

"I'm too ashamed. I owe her an apology, but I can't bring myself to do it yet."

"I can't imagine what Dearborn is going to be like today. How are they going to contort themselves into making this a 'teachable moment'?"

"Whatever they do, I doubt Rachel will tell me."

"I can't count on Maya or Olivia either. I've come to the conclusion teenage girls are basically the Kremlin with better wardrobes."

We're staring up at the ceiling when the intercom goes off.

"Are you going to get that?" I ask.

"Absolutely not."

The buzzer goes off again.

"I'll handle it," I tell her and go to the front door.

"Who is it?" Abby calls out from the bedroom.

"Scott."

"Tell him to go away."

"I already let him in."

Chapter 50

Abby

I slip on a bathrobe and stumble, trancelike, into the living room where Scott is waiting. He takes a step forward to embrace me, but I evade him. I don't want the reproach skulking beneath his attempt at comfort. I feel enough of a fool without it.

"What are you doing here?" I ask.

I thought we'd agreed that he would wait for me to call.

"I came to see if you and Rachel are okay."

"She's at school."

"I know. Can I sit down?"

I motion to a chair, but he settles beside me on the couch. Our thighs are an inch apart. They would touch if either of us made the slightest shift.

"How is Rachel?"

"Relieved, confused, angry. I don't know."

"And you?"

"I had no idea, if that's what you're wondering."

"I would never think that."

"Why not? My lack of judgment when it comes to men has been firmly established."

The fury has to go somewhere. The only people in the room are me and Scott. It spears us both.

"Attacking me isn't going to help anything," he says, exasperated.

He's right, but the ire is so woven into our history it's hard to shed. It was the only survival technique I had to get through those early years. It's served its use though. Now the only thing it's accomplishing is preventing me from moving forward. Knowing that and acting on it are two very different things.

Scott waits until I mutter "Sorry" and then takes a deep breath.

"You have nothing to be ashamed of, Abby."

"We all do," I tell him. "It's no wonder our kids don't trust anyone or anything anymore."

"Sometimes we turn out to be wrong, but that doesn't mean the act of trusting is wrong."

"I trusted you," I tell him.

His face tightens with his irritation, his fingers clenched with determination not to rise to the bait.

I get up too quickly, and blood rushes to my head.

"Where are you going?" Scott asks.

"I want to show you something."

I find the drawing I did of him sleeping the morning before he left. Faint smudges of fingerprints from the night I pulled it from the closet mar the corners.

I smooth the edges and carry it back to the living room, placing it carefully on Scott's lap. "This is what trust looks like," I tell him.

It's impossible for me to look at the drawing and not see it through the lens of everything that came crashing down after.

He studies the charcoal rendition of the younger version of himself, his torso half hidden by the bedsheet. When he looks up, his eyes are moist. "You kept it all these years?"

"Yes."

"I knew you were doing this sketch. I woke up and saw you at work. I closed my eyes and pretended to be asleep so you could finish. I was waiting for you to show it to me, but you never did."

"You left," I remind him.

He looks back at the drawing. "It's also what love looks like," he says softly.

He's right, of course. The love I felt that morning is evident in every stroke. It's why I haven't looked at it in years. I take it from him and put it on the coffee table.

"Abby, we can't keep punishing each other forever."

"Well, we could," I reply wryly, meaning it, not meaning it.

"Is that really what you want?"

I shake my head. "No."

I want to let it go, to finally let it all go.

"Me either. Can I stay to see Rachel?" Scott asks.

"Not today, but soon."

*

Eliot Handley is arrested forty minutes after Rachel gets home from school.

Chapter 51

Hollis

Nineteen days after the murder
Wednesday, October 29

Within twenty-four hours of the arrest, news stories proliferate, tying what happened at Dearborn to the ever-growing chronicle of victimized students and recalcitrant administrations. There are carefully vetted nonapologies and earnest commitments to change. Think pieces are written, podcasts are given the green light.

More girls from Saint Stephen's come forward. A psychologist is brought into Dearborn to speak to the entire student body about setting healthy boundaries and the importance of coming forward in a discreet and orderly fashion. The children point fingers at the administration for willful blindness, at the police for assuming one of them could have had anything to do with what happened to Amanda. Dearborn points the finger at Saint Stephen's. The word *cover-up* is used more than once. The Carters are the only people who remain silent. They'll let their lawyers do the talking.

When Miss Cleary calls to ask if we would like to arrange a time for her to come over and help Daniel weather these troubling revelations, Jordan informs her that we will no longer be requiring her services. She has served her purpose. She tries repeatedly to make a case for staying involved, but he stands firm.

Daniel nods, relieved, when we tell him Miss Cleary won't be coming anymore.

"You'd think he'd show a little gratitude after all I did for him," Jordan snaps when Daniel brushes past him on the way to school.

I wait until they both leave, then hurry to dress.

*

Victoria Nadamy's assistant leads me into her office on the seventeenth floor of a nondescript office building in Tribeca. The grayed-out windows and absence of overt hustling are the polar opposite of Harriday's lair. The boutique firm of Nadamy and Greene is known for its cutthroat approach to family law and its unassailable discretion.

Ms. Nadamy, in a trim black pantsuit, large horn-rimmed glasses, and blond hair pulled into a low ponytail, stands to greet me.

"Good morning, Mrs. Chapman. It's nice to meet you in person."

Her handshake is firm, but her skin is soft, her nails the color of seashells.

"Divorce is never an easy decision," she begins as we sit down. "I encourage clients to be certain it's the right step before proceeding. Once started, it's rare that one can go back."

"I'm certain," I tell her.

"Good. I gather from our initial conversation that you have some specific concerns. Why don't we start there."

"As you know, I signed a prenuptial agreement before I got married," I say.

"Most men in your husband's position insist on it. Is it your goal to break that agreement?"

"No. I want to be sure that my husband, Jordan, doesn't break it."

"Do you have reason to believe he might try?"

"He managed to break the prenup with his first wife."

"I remember that case. It was unusual for a number of reasons. Infidelity does not generally invalidate the terms of a prenup unless it was specifically included as a condition. I'm surprised your husband got away with it. In most cases, these so-called lifestyle clauses are rejected by the courts, especially in New York state." Her deep-gray eyes are unwavering. "That said, I'm going to have to ask you some uncomfortable questions."

"Go on."

"Have you had any extramarital affairs?"

"No. I suspected my husband had relationships with other women, but I never had proof. I've recently learned my son witnessed him having sex with the mother of one of his classmates."

"I'm sorry. That must be painful for all concerned. Unfortunately, while I imagine that would have emotional repercussions, it's not necessarily a legal matter."

"There are other things Jordan has done that he wouldn't want to have come to light. I've been keeping careful records."

Ms. Nadamy nods. "Threats to reputation can be a useful form of leverage. Are you looking to renegotiate the financial terms of your prenup?"

"I want assurance that my son, Daniel, will be taken care of."

"Under New York law, child custody and support cannot be mandated in a prenup. Why would you think Mr. Chapman wouldn't want to support his son?"

"I don't know what he would or wouldn't do."

"People do unpredictable things in divorces," Ms. Nadamy agrees. "Still, there's no excuse for using a child's well-being, financial or otherwise, as a means of revenge." She glances at her notes. "Do you believe your husband was forthcoming about his holdings at the time of the prenup?"

"I have my doubts."

"And were you forthcoming?"

I hesitate. "I was honest about my finances."

She considers this but doesn't delve further. "Does Mr. Chapman know you're contemplating taking action?"

"Not yet."

"Excellent. Stealth is one of our most effective weapons. The first thing I'd like you to do is establish your own bank account and credit cards."

"I've already done that." For years, I've been skimming money from the sums allocated for my mother's care, my clothing, and household expenses, and stashing it away, insurance for an unpredictable future.

"The next step is to make copies of any joint financial records, deeds, and bank statements that you can access and upload them to our encrypted online vault. After I go over those documents, we can decide when and how to strike, but speed is of the essence."

"Jordan left this morning for a business trip to Seattle, and I'll see what I can do." I pause. "You do understand who my husband is and the type of resources he has at his disposal?"

"I've dealt with many Jordan Chapmans," Ms. Nadamy assures me. "I promise you I'll protect your interests and those of your son. Any agreement we reach will be airtight."

Nothing is ever airtight with Jordan.

*

The taxi crawls slowly uptown through streets clogged with congestion.

I've imagined this moment for so long, and for so long fear held me back.

I hoped when I married Jordan that his genes, bred over centuries for solidity, would outweigh the madness in mine. I stayed with him despite everything because I thought his money and connections would protect Daniel if circumstances went the other way. Both have proven true in ways I couldn't imagine.

I never considered that the price would be losing my son's respect.

When Daniel gets home from school, I wait while he makes a peanut butter sandwich before knocking on his door.

"Can we talk for a minute?"

He pushes aside the plate, strewn with crusts, before reluctantly agreeing.

He's been watching me hopefully, then warily, and finally with abject disappointment, since we sat on the bench in Bryant Park and he told me about Jordan and Teddy Finster's mother. Whatever explosion he expected it to set off between his father and me has not occurred.

"How was school today?" I ask as I sit down on his bed.

There's not a child, certainly not a seventeen-year-old, who welcomes that question. They know it's a shell game. Nevertheless, he attempts to answer.

"Weird. It's like everyone is surprised but not surprised."

"By Mr. Handley?"

"By him, the administration, everything."

"Aren't you relieved that your part in this is over?"

"Yeah, but I know Dad had a hand in it. I don't know exactly what he did, but he did something."

"You have every right to be angry with your father for what happened last year, but whatever you think of his methods, at least this time he helped stop a man who was taking advantage of young women. Isn't that at least good?"

"It may be good, but that doesn't make it right."

"I know." I take a breath. "Daniel, what I wanted to tell you is that I'm leaving him."

"Because of what I told you?" he asks warily. He doesn't trust me. Not yet. Maybe not ever again.

"Because of many things."

"Does Dad know the truth about your mother?"

"Not yet. I need you to leave the timing of that up to me."

Before I went to see Nadamy, I reached an agreement with Adam. I'll support an appeal to have our mother's mandatory stay changed to a voluntary one. As long as she agrees to the treatment plan the hospital decrees, she'll be able to check herself out. I'll continue to cover all expenses. In exchange, Adam promised to wait until that plays out before following through on any of his threats. It is, at best, a shaky truce.

Daniel nods but shows little emotion. He picks up a snippet of bread crust, rolls it between his fingers, and puts it back on the plate. Forgiveness, if it's to come, is still off on the horizon.

"I'm going to go out for a run," he says, getting up.

"One more thing," I tell him as he reaches for his sneakers. "I've arranged for you to have a visitor's pass at Harkendale next weekend to meet your grandmother."

*

Daniel is out the door ten minutes later.

Standing alone in the hallway, I'm suddenly rocked by the realization of all that I've set in motion and all that might follow. I go into my bedroom, strip off the suit I wore to meet Nadamy, and step into the shower. I turn the hot water up as high as I can stand it and let it pound against my face, my shoulders, my back, scrubbing until my skin is inflamed.

I'm still drying off when I hear knocking on the front door that quickly escalates into loud banging. I quickly tie my robe and go to let Daniel in, determined not to reprimand him for forgetting his keys yet again.

But it's not Daniel waiting for me.

Chapter 52

Hollis

Miss Cleary, her face flushed, eyes blazing, shoves the door open with the heel of her hand.

"Where is he?" she demands, spittle clustered in the corners of her mouth.

Her usual hesitancy has evaporated, revealing a naked rawness.

"I'm sorry," I say, confused, tightening the belt of my robe. "Daniel isn't home. I thought my husband told you we won't be needing tutoring anymore."

She makes no show of hearing me. "Where is he?" she repeats harshly. "Where is your husband?"

"Jordan?" I ask, baffled.

"Yes, *Jordan*," she sneers.

"He's not here. Why do you . . ."

She pushes past me before I can finish speaking and storms into the living room, as if expecting to find him hiding behind the furniture.

I have no idea what she wants or why she's here, but I recognize the rage boiling up within, threatening to explode. I've witnessed the way it can transform someone you thought you knew into someone you don't know at all. Someone dangerous and unpredictable. I do what I learned to do long ago: go still.

"If there's been a misunderstanding," I say carefully, "we'll continue to pay you through the semester."

"You think this is about money?" She swivels around, infuriated. "If your husband assumes this is over, he is very, very wrong," she spits out.

"I'm sorry, I really don't know what you and Jordan discussed, but if you explain it to me, I'm sure we can figure something out."

I still believe I can defuse the situation. As long as I remain calm.

"After all I've done for him, for all of you, for *Daniel*, he thinks he can dismiss me?" she retorts. "That's not how this is going to work."

"It's nothing personal," I assure her. "We simply don't feel Daniel needs tutoring anymore."

Rather than soothing her, everything I say enrages her further.

"I don't care about goddamned tutoring. Don't pretend you don't know that your husband got me fired from Dearborn today."

I blink, bewildered. "There must be some mistake. Why on earth would Jordan do that?"

Miss Cleary burns with indignation. "I've given everything to Dearborn. My time, my soul. People like you flit in and out of fundraisers and committees as if that makes a difference, but I'm the one maintaining standards. You think I don't know they call me Miss Clearly Not? You think I don't hear all the snide comments? Just because I'm trying to teach your children right from wrong when none of you can be bothered?"

"We're grateful for all you've done for Daniel. I'm sorry if we didn't make that clear."

"You have no idea what I've done. Why don't you ask your husband? He can tell you all about it."

My muscles grow taut. Jordan rarely tells me what he does behind closed doors. Early in our marriage, I resented that, but I came to see the value in ignorance, deniability. That might have been a mistake. "What do you mean?"

She takes a step closer. I can feel her breath, the heat of it. "I held up my end of the deal. I did everything your husband asked me to. I told the detective and the reporter exactly what he said, word for word, about the chaperones' drinking. Who do you think gave me the money to go up to Saint Stephen's and convince those girls to talk?" The torrent of resentment crashes through the shell of propriety that, through sheer will, she's held in place for so long. "Don't you get it? I'm the reason your son isn't rotting in jail."

My legs begin to crumble as a cold sweat trickles down my back. I grasp the back of a chair to steady myself.

All the strings Jordan pulled, all his machinations. I didn't ask for details. I try to block out her words, but they slither through my defenses, insinuating themselves into my consciousness. Is she saying it was Daniel after all? Daniel who killed Amanda? Daniel who Jordan, despite everything, was trying to protect?

I force the thought out of my head. The woman is deluded, mad.

Whatever her agenda is, whatever she thinks she's doing here, she's mistaken.

She has to be.

"You have to leave. Now," I tell her.

Miss Cleary laughs bitterly. "Did you really think I was going to disappear while you get on with your pampered little lives?" she rants. "I'm not the idiot you all take me for, Mrs. Chapman. I've kept a record of every penny you've given me. Every phone call with your husband. Every step I took—*we* took—to keep your son safe and make sure someone else paid for what happened to Amanda."

I shake my head. None of this can be true.

"I don't believe you," I insist. "I don't believe anything you're saying."

"Fine. You want proof?" She reaches into her bag and pulls out a worn brown leather planner. "It's all here, Mrs. Chapman. *Hollis.* Every conversation. Every penny. You think you and your husband are the only people who know how to protect themselves?"

She opens the planner to show dated handwritten entries, not close enough for me to read but close enough for me to see they are notations of calls, of money changing hands.

"What do you want from us?" I plead.

"All your husband has to do is get me reinstated at Dearborn, and this goes away."

She waves the planner in my face, taunting me with it. Inside is the evidence she needs to destroy us. Before I know what I'm doing, I lunge for it. We're caught in a frantic swirl of limbs as she fights me off when, over her shoulder, I see Daniel slipping through the front door.

"What the fuck?" he exclaims, coming up behind us.

I freeze, the planner still in Miss Cleary's hands.

"It's all here," she says to Daniel. "Everything your father did to keep you out of trouble. Every lie he had me tell."

His eyes narrow, and he turns to me. "I don't know what she's talking about. I didn't need him to do anything for me."

"That's not what your father believed," Miss Cleary retorts. "Why do you think Eliot Handley is in jail?"

"Because he killed Amanda," Daniel says flatly.

"No," she replies harshly. "Because your father and I made sure he was put away."

Daniel stares at her, motionless, and then suddenly grabs her from behind, snatching the planner from her grasp. She tries to stave him off, but he's too big, too strong. With one shove, he pushes her down onto the couch, kneeling over her to keep her from escaping.

"Take it," he says, thrusting the planner at me while he pins her down.

I sink into the chair, the closed planner in my lap. I don't want to open it. I don't want to know.

"Whatever this is, we can get rid of it," I tell Daniel.

"Go on. Open it," he demands.

I take a deep breath and turn to the first page. The entry is dated October 11, the night they got back from Forest Valley. I read it to myself, silently mouthing the words, before slowly saying them out loud, trying to make sense of them.

"It happened so fast, in a flash, but she left me no choice. If she hadn't been there, none of this would have happened. People get what they deserve in the end. Besides, no one was innocent last night. Why should I take the blame?"

I put my forefinger on the page and look at Miss Cleary, studying me intently, waiting.

"It was you? You killed Amanda?"

Her eyes bore into me. There is no regret in her expression. No remorse.

"Don't you see?" she exclaims, straining against Daniel's hold. "I knew Eliot was planning on meeting her up on that mountain. I heard them talking about it. I couldn't let him get away with that. All I was going to do was take my phone and get proof so everyone would know who he really is. And I was right, she *was* waiting for him. I never meant to—"

"To what?" Daniel interrupts angrily. "To kill her?"

"It was an accident," Miss Cleary protests, the words racing out, falling on top of each other. "I never meant to hurt her, but you know what Amanda was like. She was such a goddammed little snot. I was angry, okay, yes, I admit that. But she started coming at me and . . ." Her voice trails off, evaporates.

"The police said Amanda was struck with the rock from behind," I remind her.

"It was so dark," she mumbles, all the fight seeping out of her. "Maybe she turned around, I don't know. I only wanted to make her stop talking, stop saying those horrible things. I had to make her stop," she repeats.

"So Eliot Handley was never there?" I ask.

"No, but he was planning to be. That's what matters."

Daniel, still pressed against her, begins to loosen his grip. He looks over at me as we both struggle to make sense of the kaleidoscope of truth and lies.

"Did Jordan know what really happened?" I ask finally.

Miss Cleary shakes her head. "No. He assumed Daniel had something to do with it. He didn't care who took the fall as long as it wasn't his son. Eliot made it easy. I sent him up to look for Amanda as soon as I got back to the lodge, and then I called the grounds crew. I figured they would find them together, and if not, at least they'd find evidence he'd been nearby," she says, matter-of-factly. She looks at us as if she expects admiration for how canny she was, how underestimated she's been. "Eliot Handley deserves to be in jail. Look what he did to all those girls in the past. Don't you think he would do that again? It's better for everyone this way. I'm saving them."

"You're saving yourself," I tell her.

Miss Cleary grows preternaturally calm. Her voice, when she speaks, has sunk an octave.

"What do you think will happen to your husband if his role in this comes out?" she threatens.

"Exactly what he deserves," I reply.

I stand up on wobbly legs to get my phone.

Miss Cleary listens as I call the police and give them our address.

Her body is completely still.

Her face is completely blank.

*

Daniel is still holding her down on the couch when two uniformed officers arrive ten minutes later.

"We'll take it from here," they tell him.

We watch, stunned, as they lead Miss Cleary away.

Chapter 53

Kara

Twenty days after the murder
Thursday, October 30

I believe what Hollis told me when she called last night, as crazy as it sounds. The shock still strangling her voice as she repeated the details of what happened over and over, as if saying them enough times would cement them into reality.

And Abby's simple text: It wasn't Eliot.

But still, there are gaps. There's been no official verification, no announcement or email from the school.

Doubt is a hard habit to break.

*

The Google alert Peter set up pings at 6:17 a.m.

I roll onto my side, watching as he reaches for his phone to read the story in *The New York Times*. And then I do the same.

> Teacher Freed in Student's Death as Colleague Confesses

October 30
New York

A Manhattan teacher jailed in connection with a student's death during a school trip has been released after a colleague confessed to the killing, authorities said Wednesday night.

Eliot Handley, an English teacher at Dearborn Academy, a private school on the Upper East Side, had been arrested following the death of Amanda Carter, 16, whose body was found during a junior class trip to Forest Valley Camp in Sullivan County earlier this month.

Mr. Handley's arrest was based on several factors, according to Sullivan County Sheriff Jim McMurtry: his proximity to the victim near the time of death, DNA traces on fabric near the scene, prior allegations of sexual misconduct, and correspondence with Ms. Carter that investigators said suggested inappropriate behavior.

However, investigators now say those conclusions were premature.

Rita Cleary, a Dearborn teacher and lead chaperone on the trip, was taken into custody following a confrontation with a Dearborn parent. She confessed to Amanda's death during subsequent questioning. Ms. Cleary told investigators she overheard Amanda making plans to meet Mr. Handley after curfew and went to the meeting spot intending to document what she suspected was an inappropriate relationship.

Finding Ms. Carter alone, Ms. Cleary confronted her. During what police described as a "heated conversation," Ms. Carter reportedly admitted she was waiting for Mr. Handley. Ms. Cleary then struck Ms. Carter with a rock, according to her confession, and disposed of it in a nearby lake.

Upon returning to the lodge, Ms. Cleary told Mr. Handley that Ms. Carter and five other students were missing. Believing Ms. Carter was still alive, Mr. Handley searched the area. Fibers from his jacket were later found near the body.

"Mr. Handley's actions that night, once viewed as suspicious, now appear to have been those of someone trying to help," Sheriff McMurtry said.

According to one official briefed on the case, Ms. Cleary "has not expressed clear remorse" but indicated she thought she was protecting others. She claims she believed Amanda Carter was still alive when she left her, but there is no evidence that Ms. Cleary checked the student's condition or summoned help until she was forced to.

The Sullivan County District Attorney's Office has not announced what charges it will pursue. Sheriff McMurtry indicated that the initial detective on the case, Ned Bremmer, has been placed on probation. Dearborn Academy has not commented on Ms. Cleary's arrest or Mr. Handley's release.

Ms. Carter's family, through their attorney, declined to comment.

Jason Blakely

*

For a long while, neither of us says anything. There will be time to parse the ramifications, how they all could have been so wrong, how blame and guilt taint everyone—the school, the staff, the police, us. But not yet.

"Okay," I tell Peter quietly.

He turns to face me. "Okay, what?"

"Okay, yes. It's time for us to leave here."

"Are you sure?"

I take a deep breath. "Yes."

I know moving away won't solve everything. There will be a new home to be found, new therapists for Olivia, wounds to heal with Maya. But it's the first step to breaking through the tangle to see who we once were and who we can be again as a family. The first step to choosing us.

Peter leans over to kiss me softly on the temple.

His place.

Chapter 54

Abby

Twenty-two days after the murder
Saturday, November 1

Eliot left three voice messages and four texts.

I haven't answered any of them.

I'm not ready. I may never be.

Every time I try to reconstruct my perception of him, of who I was with him, it disintegrates.

He didn't use these exact words, but the subtext of each of his messages was *I told you it wasn't me.*

But he didn't tell me everything.

*

On Saturday afternoon when Rachel tells me she's going to Hannah's to study for a World History test, I don't ask if anyone else will be there or when she'll be back. I smile and tell her, "That's good."

She stops before she gets to the door. "Are you sure, Mom? It's your birthday. I can stay home." She is inching her way back to me.

"We'll celebrate at dinner tomorrow with your father."

It will be the first time the three of us have a meal together.

"I have plans for today," I assure her.

*

I've never believed that closure is anything more than a placebo that somehow infiltrated the collective mind. It's why I never contacted Scott over all those years. Yet here I am.

Eliot is huddled under the arch in Washington Square Park as I cross the street.

He takes a step forward to hug me as I approach, but I stay out of reach.

"I've missed you," he says. His eyes are flickery, nervous.

He leans closer, waiting for me to tell him that I missed him too.

I have a sudden urge to push him away, hard. To hurt him for what he did. For not being who I thought he was. For all of it.

"This was a mistake," I tell him, turning to leave. "I shouldn't have come."

"Stop, Abby. Please." He reaches out to touch my arm, but I shrug him off. "I only want to talk. You owe me that much."

"I don't owe you anything."

"Do you have any idea what it's like to be falsely accused? To see my name bandied about in the press, to be trolled on social media and have my career destroyed? But the worst part was knowing you didn't believe me."

"You were coming on to Amanda. You abused girls in the past. Are you going to tell me none of that was true?"

"I never abused anyone. I might have made some errors in judgment, but whatever happened was always consensual."

"There's no such thing as consensual when they're teenagers and you're their teacher."

"That's debatable. Don't you think teenage girls have agency?"

"It's absolutely not debatable. Were you planning on meeting Amanda that night?"

"What I planned or didn't plan is irrelevant. The only thing that matters is that I didn't go. Do you want to know why? Because of you. You made me want to be better."

"Don't put any of this on me. Were you leading on Rita Cleary too?"

"Of course not. I was nice to her and took her seriously when no one else did. Don't you think she knew what you and the kids all thought of her, the way people made fun of her behind her back? I was the only person who didn't treat her as if she were absurd. Whatever fantasies that set off in her warped mind had nothing to do with me. I'm not saying I haven't made mistakes, but that's not one of them."

His breath forms a faint white spiral in the first chill of fall. He waits until it dissipates before speaking again.

"Do you remember the night we first met? I told you I believe people have the capacity to change. Can't you at least admit the possibility of that?"

"You told me a lot of things that night. Was any of it real?"

"What do you mean?"

"Do you even have an ex-wife?"

"Of course I do."

"Don't say 'of course.' Nothing is 'of course.' Your divorce obviously wasn't the reason you left Saint Stephen's."

"What I felt for you, *feel* for you, has always been real. You asked me once for a second chance, and I gave it to you. Can't you give me the same grace?"

I search his face—obstinate, frustrated—for anything I recognize, and shake my head.

"None of it was real."

Chapter 55

ABBY

It takes a minute for my eyes to adjust to the amber light inside the Carlyle Hotel's Bemelmans Bar. It's been eighteen years since I was here with Scott the night he tried to tell me it was over, but the chocolate leather banquettes and painted murals haven't changed.

I spot Kara and Hollis sitting in a corner booth, chilled martinis before them.

I've spoken to each of them individually, but this is the first chance the three of us have had to get together.

"What was so important to make you late for your own birthday toast?" Kara asks as I sit down.

"I'll need more than one drink to answer that."

"That can be arranged." Hollis smiles and motions for a waiter. She seems lighter somehow, the surface cracks fainter.

The first sip of the bone-dry vodka martini shimmies down my throat. The second wraps around my brain, managing to both sharpen and dim it as I look about the room where so much began and so much ended. My gaze stops at the banquette where I sat with Scott, drunkenly pressing him for the promise of a future together.

"Why did you choose this place to meet?" I ask Kara. "You know what it meant to me."

"Because it's time for you to recode it."

"With everything that's happened, I think that's the least of our issues."

"We have to start somewhere," she says.

Hollis looks at me questioningly.

"I'll explain later," I tell her. "But first, how are you? How's Daniel?"

There are so many questions, it's hard to know where to begin. I choose the one that's been rattling through my brain, one that only Hollis can answer. Why *her* house? Why *that* night?

Hollis puts her glass carefully down, staring into the clear liquid before she speaks. "We hired Miss Cleary as a tutor for Daniel at the beginning of the year. We didn't tell anyone because we knew it was against Dearborn's rules. It was Jordan's idea, really, just in case."

"In case of what?" Kara asks.

"Daniel has had problems in the past," she admits. "Jordan wanted someone from Dearborn on his payroll to smooth things over if there was trouble again. After Amanda died, he assumed Daniel was involved." She pauses, looks at both of us. "He paid Miss Cleary to make sure Bremmer looked in another direction. I'm sure there were threats involved." She shakes her head. "She was smarter than any of us thought. She was writing entries in a planner she knew would incriminate him."

"Did Jordan tell Miss Cleary to turn on Eliot?" I ask warily.

"He didn't care who it was as long as it wasn't Daniel, but all the evidence led to Eliot. After he was arrested, we all believed he was guilty," she reminds us. "Jordan assumed it was over, but he needed to get Miss Cleary out of the way to make sure no one learned about his role. He went to Dearborn's board and got her fired. They didn't ask questions. They were more than happy to have another scapegoat."

We both stare at her, speechless.

Hollis leans forward, looking from Kara to me. "I hope you believe I didn't know about any of this until Miss Cleary came over the other night," she says. "I'm not sure if it makes a difference, but I'd already decided to leave Jordan."

"Does he know that?" Kara asks.

"He does now. I was worried about it becoming a very ugly divorce, but Jordan's involvement with Miss Cleary gives me the leverage I need." She smiles wryly. "It's funny, he used to bring me here when we were first dating. He thought it would impress me."

"Did it?"

"Yes, but not for the reasons he thought. I loved it because it seemed so solid. At the time, stability was the most seductive thing in the world to me." She runs her fingers around the rim of her martini glass. "My mother was in and out of institutions for most of my childhood. I was desperate for a more secure life. It was the only way I could have had a child."

"You gave that to Daniel," I tell her.

"Maybe. I never told Daniel about my mother until now. I didn't want him to grow up with the same cloud of fear that hung over me. I never stopped to think about the cost."

"How did he take it?"

"He's angry. It's ironic, I stayed with Jordan because I thought it was best for Daniel, and the only thing it accomplished was him losing respect for me. I hope one day he'll understand. Right now, he wants to get to know my family. I'm not sure it will give him the answers he's searching for about who he is or who I am, but I have to let him go." She sighs. "If you can't forgive me or Jordan for any of it, I understand."

"You're not the one who needs forgiveness," Kara tells her.

Relief washes across Hollis's face, and she turns to me. "All right, so tell me why you need to recode the Carlyle."

"Rachel's father, Scott, is a man I once loved." A simple statement of facts it's taken me a lifetime to say. "He and I were here once, a long time ago."

"Is he in your life now?"

"I don't know what it means, but yes. It's going to take me a long time to trust anyone again. And it's going to take Rachel even longer to trust me. But she deserves to have a relationship with her father no matter what happens between the two of us."

"Do you still love him?" Hollis asks.

"I'm not sure first love ever completely goes away. It's imprinted so deeply in your blood. It's too soon for me to know if being with Scott is a second chance at real happiness or nostalgia for something we lost long ago."

"Give it a chance, Abby," Kara says gently.

"I will," I tell her. "We both will."

That much, at least, I do know.

Kara nods, pleased. "When I first moved to New York, I wondered if I'd ever be able to afford to come to a place like this. It symbolized everything it meant to succeed in this city. I wanted so much to feel like I could belong here."

"And now?" Hollis asks.

"Now I know for sure I will never belong in rooms like this."

Hollis begins to protest when Kara stops her. "No, the point is, I don't care anymore. It's a relief. This isn't my room." She plays with the edges of her napkin. "Peter and I decided to leave the city at the end of the school year."

"Is it definite?" I ask.

"Yes. I'm not giving up on what brought me here or what we started. I'm just leaving Manhattan. What happened at Dearborn was the last straw for Peter. For all of us, really."

"Where are you going?" Hollis asks.

"Peter's job is in the city, so someplace close."

"You're going to take Olivia out of Dearborn before senior year? Don't you think that will look strange on college applications?"

"It's a chance we have to take. Olivia isn't thrilled, but even she realizes something has to change. We promised she'd be near enough to see

Daniel on weekends, and we'll get her the help she needs. It will be good for Maya too. She can start over, without living in her sister's shadow."

"What about Jyst?" Hollis asks.

"We'll still work on it when we figure out how to get funding." Kara turns to me. "I finally told Peter about the money I took out of our accounts."

"Was he okay with that?"

"I wouldn't say he was exactly 'okay,' but we've stopped keeping score."

"I want to talk to you about that," Hollis says. "I didn't know Jordan was going to tell that reporter he was involved with Jyst, but he couldn't care less about it. He only said it because he thought it would make him look good, but I believe in it. I'd like to invest if you're open to it."

"You don't have to do that."

"It's not a favor. It's a sound business decision. It's been a while, but I do have a background in finance, and I plan on getting a very generous settlement from Jordan," she says, smiling.

Kara and I exchange looks and smile too. "That would be amazing."

We clink glasses carefully, the vodka threatening to overflow the edges.

The second round of drinks is almost gone when Kara turns to me. "Are you ready to tell us why you were late?"

"No, but I'll tell you anyway. I went to meet Eliot."

"Are you crazy? Why would you do that?"

"I thought it would help me understand how I could have been so wrong about him."

"You weren't completely wrong," Kara says.

"Wrong enough."

Eliot's face, reddening in the cold air, telling me he wanted to *be* better, *do* better. Because of me. Somehow, I believe that's true. But it doesn't matter.

"I thought I might be able to forgive him if he showed any regret for what he did in the past, but he doesn't seem to understand it, much less regret it," I say.

"Did he suspect Miss Cleary?" Hollis asks.

"He says not, but he didn't seem that surprised."

"How is that possible?" Kara exclaims. "She was so holier-than-thou with all her rules and her bullshit, but she killed a girl, for God's sake."

"Maybe his compass is so off he's beyond being shocked." I turn to Kara. "Did you ask Peter what he thinks will happen to Miss Cleary?"

"It wasn't premeditated, so she'll probably be charged with voluntary manslaughter. Peter said she could get up to twenty years, but her lawyers will try to bargain that down. They'll claim she was provoked and reacted in the heat of the moment."

"How is that an excuse?" I ask, shaking my head in disbelief.

"It's not an excuse, it's the law." Kara sighs. "What about Eliot? Is he going to stay in New York?"

"I didn't ask. If nothing else, his teaching career is thankfully over. Maybe he'll go back to writing and do an exposé about what happened. 'Sex, lies, and videotape, prep school edition.'"

"I think the Carters have been through enough," Hollis says.

This will never be over for them. They will relive that night forever, step by step, trying to stop what happened, but the ending will always be the same.

*

It's early evening when we stand outside the Carlyle, tipsy in the best possible way.

"Thank you," I say, hugging them both. "This may not be the fortieth birthday I had planned, but it's definitely the one I needed."

"Do you want us to get you an Uber?" Hollis asks.

"I think I'll walk."

I kiss them both goodbye and head downtown, passing places I went with Scott, places I wandered aimlessly when I was pregnant and alone and had no idea what my life would be, places I found friends and almost lost them. All these cities, all these selves, a prism of who I was, who I thought would be, and who I am now. I'm still uncertain what the future holds. Now, though, I have roots. Whatever happens, Rachel and I will be all right.

I'm halfway downtown when I climb into the bowels of the subway to go home.

Epilogue

The first light snow is falling on the morning of December 18 as parents and students file into Dearborn's two-story auditorium for the annual candle-lighting ceremony to celebrate the last day of the fall term. Every seat is taken as choral music wafts through the stately room, waiting for students from the upper school to walk down the center aisle in pairs. Every year, one student from each grade is chosen to light the candles on the stage, forming a pyramid of lights that flicker brightly in the darkened hall.

This year, the stage remains empty while the students cluster outside the auditorium in groups. The music fades, and the new acting headmistress, Ms. Henrietta Perkins, walks solemnly to the stage. Though the parent body has been informed that Headmaster Nederlander chose to retire early, this is the first time they've seen his temporary replacement.

Ms. Perkins speaks in a soft voice that nevertheless carries through the room. "I want to welcome you to Dearborn's Solstice Festival," she begins. "I've thought long and hard about the word 'festival' and what it means, particularly this year. It seemed at first unfitting, almost disrespectful. But after reflection, I found myself thinking of it in a different way. The winter solstice is historically the shortest day of the year. In many cultures, the period that follows is considered one of rebirth. As we dedicate this year's candle-lighting ceremony to the memory of Amanda Carter, I ask you to take a moment of silence and pray in whatever way feels appropriate for her family, that they may find peace in the coming year, and for the rebirth of our mission to better serve the lives of our young people." She doesn't mention that Bill and Marci Carter are suing Dearborn along with Rita Cleary.

Abby and Hollis, sitting next to each other, bow their heads. Scott, sitting on Abby's other side, does the same, their fingers intertwined. Three rows behind them, Kara's eyes fill with bittersweet tears as she takes Peter's hand, knowing this will be their last solstice celebration at Dearborn.

*

Outside the auditorium's door, the students wait to file in.

Standing midway through the crowd, Olivia brushes against Daniel, thinking about the night she found him alone by the lake when they spread their jackets on the mud and made love for the first time.

When he held her afterward, she knew she would do *anything* for him.

Daniel, feeling Olivia take his hand, opens his eyes enough to smile at her. She wants things from him he's not sure he can give to her or to anyone. The anger that filled him for so long isn't gone, but now that his father has moved out, it's gradually receding. He doesn't know yet what will take its place.

A few feet behind them, Rachel stands with Hannah. She hasn't forgiven Hannah for lying about that night, denying not only where they were but also what they felt, but she will give her time. She would tell her that confidence only comes when you stop trying to be someone else, but Hannah will have to learn that on her own.

When the moment of silence is over, the auditorium doors open. The students' faces are solemn as they walk in twos down the aisle. As Rachel walks with Hannah, she searches for her parents, a word she never thought would have any relevance to her. She doesn't understand what it means, but the fact that it exists is enough. Olivia and Daniel look straight ahead, as if they're alone in the room.

No one has been chosen to light the candles this year. The acting headmistress does it on her own.

*

The snow has thickened into fat white flakes as parents, teachers, and students leave the auditorium and gather on the street. For years, Kara and Abby took the kids out for hot fudge sundaes after the festival while restaurants near the school filled with families celebrating the season. Today, though, their children have plans of their own. Abby, Scott, Kara, Peter, and Hollis stand together talking quietly as the snow continues to fall in slow motion before finally separating and heading out into their own corners of the city.

Acknowledgments

Writing may be a solitary endeavor, but it's also a team sport—and I'm lucky to have the best team imaginable.

My heartfelt thanks go to the incredible team at Thomas & Mercer, led by Jessica Tribble Wells, whose insight, enthusiasm, and unwavering belief in this book have meant the world to me. I'm especially grateful to Angela James, Miranda Gardner, Cortni Merritt, and Will Fairless, for their brilliant editorial stewardship. Thank you to Val Frankel for her steadfast support and advice. Special thanks to Greer Hendricks for her lasting friendship and generous advice from plot points to hair tricks. Judith Newman and Penelope Green are not only terrific writers but also the smartest (and wittiest) sounding boards anyone could hope for. To my friend and cofounder, Nadina Guglielmetti, thank you for your savvy and all the fun we've had along the way.

At the heart of this novel—and the lives of so many women—are friendship and motherhood. Both have been central to my life. To Lynn Schnurnberger, Rebecca Sanhueza, Karen Fausch, Denise Langer, Judy Glantzman, and Eve Bercovici, the brilliant women in my book club, and so many more who have supported me through life's ups and downs, thank you for keeping me (semi) sane.

Like many people, women in particular (yes, this is a generalization), I took time off from writing to concentrate on caretaking. I offer this book in loving memory of Andrew David Listfield and Helen Listfield. For others going through similar situations, I see you.

Being a mother has been the greatest joy of my life. Infinity love goes to my daughter, Sasha, who really wasn't that bad of a teenager. Her dedication to protecting First Amendment rights for all writers, her kindness, generosity, and adventurous spirit inspire me every day.

About the Author

Photo © 2025 Lindsey Bell

Emily Listfield is the author of seven novels, including a *New York Times* Notable Book of the Year. Her books have been published in numerous foreign countries. She is the former editor-in-chief of *Fitness* magazine and executive editor of *Parade's HealthyStyle*, and her writing appears frequently in *Elle*, *Harper's BAZAAR*, *Allure*, *The New York Times*, and many other national publications. Listfield has served as a panelist at SXSW, has worked across media platforms, and was the cofounder of Jyst, a crowd-sourced relationship advice app for women. She lives in New York City.